THE HAUNTING ON WEST 10TH STREET

HELEN PHIFER

Storm

PUBLISHING

To request permissions, contact the publisher at rights@stormpublishing.co

Ebook ISBN: 978-1-80508-103-6
Paperback ISBN: 978-1-80508-104-3

Cover design: Blacksheep
Cover images: Getty Images

Published by Storm Publishing.
For further information, visit:
www.stormpublishing.co

ALSO BY HELEN PHIFER

Annie Graham Series

The Ghost House

The Secrets of the Shadows

The Forgotten Cottage

The Lake House

The Girls in the Woods

The Face Behind the Mask

The Good Sisters

Lake View House

Detective Lucy Harwin Series

Dark House

Dying Breath

Last Light

Beth Adams Series

The Girl in the Grave

The Girls in the Lake

Detective Morgan Brookes

One Left Alive

The Killer's Girl

The Hiding Place

First Girl to Die

This book is dedicated to the late Gail O'Neill and her husband, Paul O'Neill, the kindest, most supportive friends a writer could ever hope for.

PROLOGUE

Homicide Detective Maria Miller stared at the television screen as the camera panned around the crowds of spectators; thousands of them all crammed into the Rockefeller Plaza underneath the huge Christmas tree. Sam passed two cardboard coffee cups over to her.

"Have a good one Maria."

"You too Sam, thanks," Maria called back as she juggled the scalding cups of coffee along with the heavy door of Sam's Deli on Waverly Place.

Frankie Conroy, her partner, was watching her with a grin on his face. Maria reached the car and he reached across to open the door for her. As she got in, the aroma of the fresh coffee and a hint of perfume filled the front of the Toyota Prius.

"Do you miss working the streets on days like this?"

He turned to stare at her. "Let me see, it's cold and there are probably around thirty thousand people currently in midtown. Every single one of them trying to get a glimpse of the tree-lighting ceremony. We would be stood there for a full shift, smiling and talking to tourists—and you miss standing around for hours."

"You know what I mean. It's always such a good atmosphere. Sting and Mary J Blige are singing tonight. I like them both."

"You'd be lucky if you got to hear them; you never get close to the plaza unless you've been ass-kissing all year. No thank you, give me my warm car, hot coffee and a homicide any day of the week."

"You're so full of crap. I bet you'd be there if Frank Sinatra was playing."

He shrugged. "I wouldn't be there even if old Frank had come back for one night only to croon to the crowds and flick the switch on that tree."

Maria rolled her eyes, took a sip from the cardboard coffee cup and sighed. "You can keep your Starbucks, this is the real deal."

Both of their cell phones rang in unison.

"Hell no, tis the season to be jolly. What's wrong with people? Where's their Christmas spirit?"

Maria smiled. "It's probably in the same place as yours."

She answered the call. "Yep, we are. What address?"

Tucking her cell under her chin, she pulled a pen from her top pocket and wrote the address on the back of her hand. "Right, on our way."

"Homicide West 10th Street. Officers on scene, suspect at large."

"Be nice for once if we weren't the ones catching all the calls."

"Quit complaining, we get paid, don't we? Did you not just wish for a homicide? You need to watch your mouth Frankie, the universe is always listening."

Frankie parked as close to the police circus as he could. The usually quiet tree-lined street was lit up with flashing red and blue lights. Maria looked around. The street was deserted apart from the police cars and an ambulance. She took a large gulp of the coffee knowing that it would be cold by the time she got back into the car.

Frankie did the same. "Just as well we haven't eaten yet."

She nodded, put the cup in the holder and got out of the car. She looked around the street. All of them were nice properties. But this one had a marked difference to the others: its steps went down to the front entrance, not up, and that struck Maria as unusual.

Tugging her ID out of her pocket she flashed it at the officer standing in front of the door to the large brownstone. The officer stepped aside to let her in and as she crossed the threshold she felt as if she was walking into the depths of hell. As quickly as the thought entered her mind, it was gone. Maria Miller was tough; she lived on her own and didn't believe in ghosts or demons. What she believed in was that there were good and bad people in the world. Unfortunately for her and Frankie, they rarely got to see the good. Their work was dealing with murdering scumbags who didn't care about anyone except themselves. Even so, as she stepped into the entrance of the once grand house, which had been turned into apartments, she felt a cold chill run down her spine. It was so violent, her whole body shuddered.

"You, okay?" Frankie whispered in her ear, his hand touching the small of her back. A look of concern etched across his face.

She nodded. Two paramedics came down the dark oak stairwell carrying their heavy bags.

"Evening Maria, Frankie. There's nothing we can do for the patient. God bless their soul." The paramedic crossed himself.

"How bad is it, Don?"

He made a swiping gesture with his hand across his neck and Maria grimaced.

"We better suit up now," Maria said. "I was kind of hoping it was a mistake. That it was just a serious assault."

"You and your wishful thinking, kid. I suppose we better had." Frankie sighed, passing her a plastic packet.

They both pulled on the paper suit, nitrile gloves, shoe covers and a mask and went upstairs. Maria quickly surveyed the first two floors they came to, casting her eye around and finding nothing out of the ordinary, pointed up. Frankie held out a hand gesturing for her to go first; they climbed on in silence.

An officer was stood at the foot of the next staircase, his face whiter than the paper suit Maria was dressed in. "Next floor. I hope you have a steel stomach because this isn't pretty."

A gut lined with steel was a requirement for her job. She didn't ask him what had happened, preferring to take in the scene herself without any preconceptions. The stairs up to this floor had been brightly lit, the hallways of the first two floors warm. She stared up at the uncarpeted, almost black wooden steps which led up to the attic, a terrible sense of dread filling the pit of her stomach as she sensed a definite shift in the atmosphere. It wasn't as well maintained as the rest of the house. Frankie grabbed her arm and she turned to look at him. His bright blue gloved fingers began to play out rock, paper, scissors. She formed a fist as he opened his fingers, and he groaned.

"You won, it's your call."

"I'll go first." She tugged up the face mask around her neck, covering her nose and mouth, and inhaled deeply, ready to hold her breath. Even though every nerve ending in her body was screaming at her to get out of here she forced herself to carry on.

The wooden stairs creaked and groaned as Maria walked up, staying close to the wall in case the killer had grabbed the handrail. As she reached the top, a whiff of the all-too familiar tangy, coppery smell threatened to overpower her. She crossed the small landing toward the open apartment door and stood at the threshold, staring at the sight which faced her. Blood, splattered all over the painted, antique white walls and beige carpets of what was otherwise a light, airy open-plan living space.

That was one of the reasons she preferred to go first. Once she'd seen what was waiting for her, she could cope. Her mind would switch to cop mode and she'd be fine. She always was.

It was a nice apartment—would have been a nice apartment. Maria tilted her head and stared at the kitchen, trying to figure out what it was that was on the worktop.

"Jesus Christ where's the head? Where are the arms and legs?" Frankie muttered behind her.

In that moment, she realized she was staring at a naked torso drenched in blood, with torn bits of muscle, tendons and bones protruding from where the limbs should have been. She stepped closer, her mind trying to process the scene and what had happened. The most beautiful, intricate tattoo of roses and vines ran from where the thigh should have been up the side of the torso and snaked across from one side of the body to the other, ending between the two breasts.

Frankie spoke. "Nice tattoo."

It *was* a nice tattoo; a quality piece of art done by someone who was very talented. This wasn't your average drunken girl's night out, "let's get matching tattoos done" down a back street in Hell's Kitchen.

Maria tore her eyes away from the bloody torso and looked around. She approached the huge fridge, opened the blood-smeared door and let out a shriek. She barely managed to move back in time as the missing limbs fell out, narrowly avoiding being covered in blood and gore. Frankie grabbed her arm, dragging her back.

"Where's her head?" Maria whispered, her eyes wide in horror at the assortment of appendages that had fallen to the floor next to her feet.

ONE

THREE YEARS LATER

Frankie drummed his fingers on the steering wheel as he stared at the run-down building that had once been the City Hotel but was now abandoned and condemned. Maria, who was trying to decide how many grey hairs had sprouted in her bangs since the last time she'd had it colored, turned to stare at him.

"Give it a rest. I'm bored out of my tree as well."

He looked at her and scowled. "Two days we've been hanging around here and for what?"

"You know what. The perp is hiding out in there. You know it, I know it. He has to come out at some point."

"You think so? What if he doesn't need to? What if he's got lots of supplies and is holed up in there for a month?"

"If he doesn't put in an appearance by the end of—" She stopped mid-sentence and elbowed him. A man wearing a navy hooded sweatshirt with NYPD blazoned across the front, and a matching NYPD baseball cap, appeared at a third story window and stepped out onto the fire escape. With aviator shades covering his eyes, he stood on the top rung of the rusted, metal ladders and surveyed the street. Seemingly happy, he climbed down the steps and began to walk toward Seventh Avenue.

"Well I'll be damned." He stared down at the black-and-white photograph of Jackson Quinn, the man they'd been waiting for and who was wanted for the murder of his wife and attempted murder of her lover.

Maria didn't gloat, she just gave him a knowing look. "Follow him as best as you can; when it gets too busy I'll jump out and follow on foot. As soon as I'm sure it's him, we'll go for it."

The man was walking briskly toward Seventh Avenue and she wanted him apprehended whilst they were still on Barrow Street. A taxi pulled in front of their car, narrowly missing them. Frankie instinctively honked the horn and their guy turned around. He stared at Maria, then turned and began to run.

"Crap, he's onto us."

Frankie swerved to the sidewalk and they both jumped out. Maria felt a surge of dread as the newly opened Manhattan Media Corporation loomed into view. The vast glass-fronted office block was owned by Harrison Williams, who ran the mass media enterprise. The only reason Maria knew this was because she'd recently skimmed over an article about him in the *New York Times*.

Jackson Quinn glanced behind him, then darted through the revolving door of the tower into the huge glass, marble and oak entrance.

Unluckily for the receptionist, as she walked out from behind the reception desk Jackson skidded to a halt, pulled the .38 revolver from his waistband and grabbed onto the reception-ist, pointing the gun at her head. She let out a deafening scream as Maria came through the doors, closely followed by Frankie, both of their weapons drawn.

"Drop your gun, Jackson, come on. Nobody needs to get hurt here, just put the gun down and we can sort this out."

Frankie carried on talking whilst Maria moved to where she could get a clear shot.

"Fuck you. Drop your gun."

"You know I can't do that whilst you're pointing a gun at the lady's head. Come on, man, you know you don't want this."

The woman whimpered as Quinn tightened his grip on her. Frankie whispered to Maria. "Are you thinking what I'm thinking?"

Maria didn't take her eyes away from Jackson but nodded her head. In the perfect situation, she would aim for his chest and shoot to kill. She wasn't fond of using her weapon to kill unless it was a matter of life or death, which this situation was—especially for the petrified woman Jackson was holding hostage. Without a clear shot of his head, Maria glanced down at his legs, aimed and fired twice. Frankie lunged for the woman and dragged her away as Jackson let out a loud howl and fell to the floor.

"That bitch shot me... she shot me! Get me a medic!"

Maria didn't waste any time and in a matter of seconds had kicked his gun away from him and cuffed his wrists.

"Sorry Jackson, does it hurt real bad?"

"You bitch."

Maria smiled at him. "Really? Jackson Quinn, I'm arresting you on suspicion of homicide. You have the right to remain silent. Anything you say can and will be used against you in a court of law. You have the right to have an attorney present during questioning. If you cannot afford an attorney, one will be appointed for you."

Sirens filled the street outside, swiftly followed by paramedics and officers streaming through the doors. She stepped aside to let the paramedics work on Jackson; he was bleeding like a pig all over the new white, pristine, marble floor.

A tall blond-haired man in a pair of Nike shorts and a tank

top came running toward her. "That was outstanding, thank you, officer. I don't know what to say. You saved her life."

He held his hand out and Maria shook it, wondering if he was the security guard and had nipped to the gym on his lunch break.

"Just doing my job, thanks."

She turned and walked back to Frankie who was talking to two uniforms. He looked at Maria and grinned. "Nice shooting, shame about all the paperwork but at least they're both alive. Are you okay?"

She rolled her eyes at him. "Gee thanks, Frankie, nice of you to ask."

"Come on Miss Smarty-Pants, let's go back to the station. Quicker we fill out the forms, the quicker we can call it a day."

TWO

The brownstone situated along West 10th Street was Emilia Carter's favorite place. She laughed as she helped roll out the dough for the fresh bread for breakfast in the morning. She was never happier than helping Missy down in the kitchen. She loved being in the city, away from her suffocating mother and odd brother. Everyone stayed in the sprawling mansion on Staten Island from June to September; everyone except her father who used the town house as a base for when he had business to attend to in the city. Her mother stayed at the Staten Island home full stop, refusing to come into the city, much to Emilia's relief.

Tomorrow was a big day for Emilia. She was meeting Mae for lunch and it still made her stomach swirl thinking about it. She was still not sure what to call her, though *her father's lover* was probably the most accurate description.

Emilia and Mae had met under the most peculiar circumstances a week ago. Emilia had been downstairs before bed, helping Missy again, and had paused when she'd heard the laughter and music coming from the parlour. She'd looked at Missy, who shook her head.

"It's nothing to do with us miss Emilia. Maybe you should stay down here. It might be best you don't go up there."

"Why? Do you know something that I don't?"

Missy shook her head.

Emilia washed her hands in the sink, drying them on the warm dishcloth off the stove door handle, and went upstairs to investigate. She didn't know who was more shocked—her or her father—as she pushed open the heavy oak doors and found him with a woman who was most certainly not her mother perched across his knees. The woman's arms were wrapped around his neck, their lips about to touch. Emilia screamed, and they pulled apart. She turned and ran for the stairs, mortified, her father running behind her. He'd reached out and grabbed her arm, tugging her back.

"Emilia, I'm sorry. I know it's wrong, but she's my best friend. I need you to listen to me. Your mother knows all about Mae and me. She doesn't care—in fact she doesn't care too much about anything. I don't know if you've noticed, but she barely speaks more than two words to me. She makes me sleep in a separate room... But I love her, despite how this all looks. She isn't a well woman, you know yourself how she suffers with her nerves."

Emilia didn't know what to say to him. She loved him dearly. Despite their differences, she also loved her mother, who was an outspoken woman and not the most affectionate of people. Suddenly, she realized that her parents were adults and probably deserved to lead their own lives—lives which had nothing to do with their grown-up children. Emilia looked at her father for the first time as a man and not her protector.

"I'm sorry, it was just a shock. It's none of my business... I'm going to bed now."

"Why don't you come and say hello to Mae. She's an actress. She's starring in a play at The Belasco. We could go and watch it if you like. I know how much you love the theatre."

Emilia was intrigued; she did love the theatre. Hesitantly, she followed him, all the time wondering if she was betraying her mother by agreeing to speak to the woman who made her father happy when she couldn't.

When Emilia walked into the parlour; the beautiful woman with bleached blond hair and ruby red lips was stood staring out of the huge bay window, onto the leafy, tree-lined street, her back toward them. As she turned around, Emilia realized that she wasn't that much older than herself. Emilia crossed the room toward her and was shocked to see Mae draw back into herself and flinch. Emilia was horrified: the woman thought she was going to hit her. Holding out her hand, she smiled, and the woman's shoulders dropped as she smiled back at her. The woman grasped Emilia's hand and shook it, her ruby red nails, which matched her lips, contrasting against her pale skin. Emilia marvelled at how silky soft her hand was.

"Hello, you must be Emilia, I'm Mae Evans. I've heard so much about you."

She smiled at her, wondering exactly what her father could have told her that was interesting enough to have held a conversation. Compared to the beautiful creature standing in front of her, Emilia lived a very sheltered life.

"I wish I could say the same about you, Mae, but it's still a pleasure to meet you."

Mae laughed and her whole face lit up. Her green eyes sparkled and Emilia couldn't help but join in: Mae had the most infectious laugh she'd ever heard. Behind them, she heard her father let out a huge sigh.

"Phew. Boy... I had visions of you wanting to claw my eyeballs out of their sockets. I'm so glad you're not the angry type. You're very much like Clarke, he has a great sense of humour."

Emilia turned to her father. "Yes, he does, on occasion. If

you'll excuse me, I'm going to bed now. This whole thing— Well... it's all a bit strange."

"Of course, it is, isn't it? Would you like to meet me sometime for lunch? I know a great place near the theatre. It serves up the best clam chowder in midtown."

Emilia flinched; she couldn't think of anything worse to eat for lunch. Mae began to laugh.

"Sorry, I couldn't resist. It serves the best pizza. Honey, I couldn't eat clam chowder if James Stewart served it up."

Emilia wanted to dislike Mae, but she couldn't. "I'll have a think about it if you don't mind. I'm not really sure how I feel about this, if I'm being honest."

"I'm sorry, I'm being forward. Of course you can... it is a bit of a mess. If you decide you want to meet me, just let Clarke know. I'm available all week before the show starts. I'll pick you up at twelve and we can go shopping afterwards. I need some new shoes. Is that okay with you, Clarke?"

"Emilia can do whatever she wishes, as long as you look after her."

Emilia frowned at him. "I'm twenty-two, I think I'm good to go for pizza and shopping, thanks."

He held his hands up as a peace gesture. "Yes, you are."

"Goodnight, Mae, Pops." She left them to it, confused and wondering how she had just become friends with her father's lover.

THREE

PRESENT DAY

Maria sighed as she signed her name on the last of the forms. She heard some clapping and looked up to see Frankie heading toward her with a huge bouquet of flowers. She wondered if he'd gone mad—she knew he had a bit of a thing for her. A couple of times when they'd been to the Fat Black Pussycat after work and had too many beers, he'd stare at her or grab her hand too many times. She always managed to brush it off, as she really liked him, despite the fact that he was ten years older than her and married. She'd told him another time another place and who knew. Thankfully, when he was sober he never did anything of the sort—except now.

What the hell was this all about? He stood in front of her with a huge smile on his face and held the flowers toward her. A voice shouted: "Get down on one knee Frankie boy," to a round of applause.

"What are you doing, Frankie?"

He laughed. "Nothing to do with me, I'm a married man." Maria stood up to see if there was a card. There wasn't. She looked at the flowers. They were beautiful, expensive; all white roses, lilies and the most beautiful, scented tiny white flowers that she'd never seen before. Her first instinct was to bin them, amid the raucous laughter of her mainly male co-workers.

She took them from Frankie, inhaled and gave the rest of department the finger. They would look gorgeous on her coffee table, matching the newly painted walls of her apartment perfectly. For once she did something that surprised everyone and put them on her desk. Realizing that she wasn't taking any crap, they all began to carry on with what they were doing.

Frankie perched on the corner of her desk. "So, what do you say we go to the Pussycat for a cocktail or two? Celebrate not getting ourselves and anyone else killed."

"I don't know, I have a headache."

"I only asked if you wanted a cocktail, not sex."

She glared at him. "Sometimes you amaze me, Frankie. You're such a pig I don't know how Christy puts up with you."

"Guess you're not in the cocktail mood."

"Take me and my flowers home, I'll think about it on the way." She winked at him.

Frankie pulled up outside the apartment building where Maria lived on Sullivan Street. Its flaking paint and boarded-up first floor windows had seen better days, so had the back rub shop a couple of doors down.

"This place is a shithole, when are you going to move? I worry about you living here."

"Beauty is in the eye of the beholder. Yes, it looks like a slum, but the majority of rentals are nice people. I feel safe here; I know all my neighbors. There are no scumbags, and we look out for each other. Plus, I have Miss Lily's across the road for my morning pastries. What more could a girl ask for?"

"It's not like you're destitute though, is it? You can afford a better place than this."

"I'm saving up for my dream apartment, and whilst I'm

saving this does the job, so stop disrespecting my home. In case you haven't noticed, you're not my pops."

She got out of the car, leaning across the back seat to get the flowers.

"Who do you think sent those?" Frankie asked.

"No idea—and I don't really care."

"So do you want to go to the Pussycat?"

She shook her head. "I'll give it a miss tonight, thanks. I'm going to have a long soak in the bath and an early night. Hey, you should send Christy flowers sometime. Ladies like flowers you know, just saying."

"She'd complain I wasted too much money; wouldn't appreciate them... I'll see you tomorrow."

Maria shook her head and slammed the car door shut. Turning, she walked up the steps to the front doors. He was right, this place looked almost as desolate as the City Hotel they'd been parked outside earlier. One day she would move into a huge apartment with views of Central Park, but for now this was good enough.

She heard the familiar sound as her elderly neighbor came out of the elevator and shuffled toward the entrance, her strings of pearls jangling.

"Good evening, Miss Green, how are you today?"

The woman looked up, squinting in the poorly lit entrance. She always dressed impeccably. If Maria wasn't wrong, she was wearing a vintage Chanel suit and pumps. What she'd give to go through her wardrobe. It was full of beautiful, vintage designer clothes. Miss Green had told her she'd been a stylist for Vogue back in the day.

"Ah Maria, good evening. I'm alive thank you, which is always a good thing. Look at you with a bunch of flowers as big as your arms can carry. Who you been keeping from me?"

Maria giggled. "No one—I don't know who they're from, but they were so beautiful I decided to keep them."

"Wise choice honey. You have a secret admirer. How exciting."

"Or the florist got the wrong person."

"Tut, tut, don't be so negative. I'm off to the store, do you need anything? Have you eaten today?"

"I'm good thank you, I'm going to make a huge bowl of chilli and have a glass or two of wine."

"Good, you need it. You work too hard. Goodnight, Maria."

"Night, Miss Green."

Maria called the elevator and was relieved when the groaning doors opened immediately. She was tired, hot and would have cried if she'd had to walk up eight floors.

FOUR

PRESENT DAY

He walked along the tree-lined sidewalk, shrugging his backpack higher onto his shoulders and keeping as close to the houses as he could. It had been three years since he'd last visited this particular brownstone. He had tried to find out if he could rent the empty, top floor apartment. He'd like to live there legally, only the rental company had told him it wasn't safe. It needed major remodelling to make it liveable, so they'd taken his name and cell number in case it became available. It hadn't mattered really, he'd gotten access to it once before, so he could do it again.

His battered VW van was parked a couple of blocks away with his worldly belongings inside; once he got inside, he would move it nearer. He reached the brownstone, which was situated on the corner. The main entrance was situated on West 10th Street, while the fire escapes could be accessed around the side on Washington Street. If there was no one around, he could climb up to the fire escape and get to the top floor. He'd already been last night and prised the board from the window, placing it against the empty frame from the inside so it still looked secure. There were no buildings which looked onto this part of the street, luckily for him. The bus stop opposite was a bit of a problem, but he'd just need to be cautious and avoid rush hour.

He turned the corner into Washington Street, which was deserted, and climbed up. This was where being taller than most of your high school friends finally paid off. He pulled himself up effortlessly onto the fire escape, and scanned the street to make sure no one was watching. That was the beauty of being a New Yorker: nine times out of ten nobody gave a crap what you were doing. Everyone was too involved in their own world to give you much attention.

He climbed the metal rungs of the ladder quickly, his stomach a mess of knots. He'd dreamed about this for three, long years. The last time he'd been here, he'd been scared and immature and left in a rush, regretting it ever since. But there was something very special about the apartment. He'd had the same dream about it almost every week since that night. Ever since he let the voices in, he'd heard them calling to him every night when he closed his eyes. Ever since he'd come here, it felt as if a part of him had been left behind and in its place he'd taken away the darkness that lurked deep inside of the room.

He reached the attic window and pushed the board open wide enough so he could clamber inside. Taking off his backpack, he unzipped the side pocket and took the small but powerful flashlight out. Pushing the board back across the window and making sure there were no gaps, he turned around.

He blinked a couple of times, letting his eyes adjust to the shadows of the apartment. Then he turned on the flashlight and shone it around; it was just as he remembered. The furniture was covered in sheets, and he hoped it was the same sofa that he'd sat on with her. He lifted a corner of the dusty sheet. The cracked, brown leather sofa made him smile. He'd spent a magical couple of weeks sleeping on it. He dropped the sheet back down and mesmerised, walked across to the breakfast bar, shining the light on it. He traced his gloved finger though the thick film of dust.

He closed his eyes, picturing every last detail of that night. This apartment was the only place he'd ever stayed in that truly felt like home. Moving away from the open plan kitchen-lounge he walked toward the bedroom door. Wrapping his fingers around the brass knob, he marvelled at how cool it was despite the humid temperature outside. Turning it slowly, he pushed the door open, remembering that if you opened it too fast it creaked loudly. He didn't want whoever lived in the flat below realizing there was someone upstairs.

He stepped into the large, airy bedroom. It had no window, but a huge skylight above the queen-sized bed. He smiled to see the bed was still there. Walking across, he dragged the dust sheet off. There were no covers, and he could see the huge, dark brown stain on the left-hand side of the mattress. They hadn't taken it away. He was shocked to see it still there. There had been a lot of blood. As he stepped closer, he could see where the CSIs had cut pieces of fabric from it to take for forensic sampling. Whoever they were, they hadn't been clever enough to catch him, so they weren't that good. He was supposed to have killed again soon after, but hadn't been able to—partly from guilt, partly because it had been out of his control.

He shook the dust sheet several times and lay it down across the mattress. He couldn't wait to lie on it—although there was something he had to do first. Going back into the lounge, he picked up his bag, tugging the zipper open. The glass jar inside was heavy and his shoulders ached from the weight of carrying it around the streets on his back. He smiled at the perfectly preserved head inside it. He'd finally been able to bring her home after all this time. She was still beautiful.

Carrying the jar across to the kitchen, he opened the pantry cupboard which had once been full of every imaginable pasta and rice you could buy from Walmart. He placed the jar on the middle shelf and stepped back; he'd had to keep her hidden for so long. Now, it was nice to have her in a place he could have easy access to. They were going to be very happy here, as they had been before until the time had come to end it.

He'd done well and managed to ignore the noises that had begun in his head. At first it was like white noise, a static buzzing around his ears. He'd gone to the doctor who'd examined his ears and given him some drops, which hadn't worked. It was always far worse at night. He'd lie there in bed with his hands over his ears trying to block the noise out. Then one night he'd realized that no matter how hard he tried, it wouldn't go away because it was coming from inside of his head. A few nights later, the noise had turned into whispers, words spoken in an exotic language he didn't understand. It wasn't just one voice either; there were several of them, and he felt as if they were having a conversation about him. He'd been scared back then... Hell! He'd even been terrified until one of the voices realized he was listening to it and began to whisper to him. Then it all made sense. The others faded away and he didn't hear them as much. This voice was stronger than the others; it told him things he didn't always want to hear, and yet it also told him many things that he longed for. He'd been so alone for such a long time. The voice had become like a friend—even if it did tell him to do things that he didn't want to do.

FIVE

Frankie drove home thinking about Maria; he liked her far more than he should. She was his friend and he was married. It wasn't that he didn't love Christy—he had once upon a time—it was more that she'd fallen out of love with him. The last time he'd had too much to drink and made a stupid pass at Maria, she'd made it quite clear where he stood with her and that was okay. He respected her for being straight with him; it still hurt though. In fact, she'd told him to grow a set of balls and do something to sort his shitty sex life out and to work on his marriage.

As he drove past the old church on the corner of Sullivan, he noticed the metal sign swinging in the breeze: Marty's Dancing School. When he met Christy, she was a dancer at Radio City Music Hall. He used to go dancing with her once a week even though he had two left feet. Once they were married and working long hours to pay the bills, the dancing went out of the window. He wondered if he should take her dancing, although it had been so long he'd be rusty. Maybe if he had some dancing lessons and surprised her with a fancy date at one of the charity balls they held at The Plaza, she might start seeing him how she used to.

He stopped off at the grocery store and picked up a bunch of pink roses, and instead of the usual six pack, he spent ten minutes looking at the wine before picking up a bottle of chardonnay, hoping Christy would like it or that would be twenty bucks down the drain. He knew Maria would approve: she always had a bottle or two in her fridge. He paid and got back in his car, determined to try and rekindle the fire that had long ago been extinguished.

Frankie lived just a few blocks away from Maria on Hudson Street. His apartment was bigger, with a Starbucks and Pret a Manger on the ground floor. No massage parlours, no boarded-up windows, and the rent was a lot more. Christy liked it and that was all that counted. They could have downsized; they didn't need a three-bed apartment. The kids they'd longed for had never appeared, but she wouldn't hear of it. She wanted to live in a spacious apartment, so they did.

As he got into the elevator, he held the wine and the flowers feeling stupid. What if she wasn't in? She got angry with him when he was late home, and sometimes went out to meet her girlfriends for cocktails. The elevator doors opened and he grinned to see his younger brother Adam standing on the other side.

"Hey man, what you doing? You leaving already?"

Adam laughed. "Yeah, well I wasn't going to wait around all night for you. Besides, Christy is in a shitty mood, so I figured I'd leave her to it."

Frankie frowned. When wasn't Christy in a shitty mood?

"Are you coming back in for a beer?"

Adam shook his head and pointed at the wine and flowers. "Good luck, I don't want to spoil your surprise. I'll catch up with you at the weekend."

They swapped places and Adam pressed the ground floor

button. Frankie nodded a goodbye then walked down the corridor toward his apartment. He opened the door and sniffed the air, which smelt of vanilla and cinnamon. "Sorry I'm late, honey..." He could hear the taps running and walked down to the bathroom. Christy was in her dressing gown, her face freshly cleansed.

"Nice of you to come home."

He handed the bunch of roses to her and for the first time, she smiled.

"Sorry, you know how crazy work can be."

"A phone call would be nice, now and again." He had phoned her and left a message: she hadn't picked it up.

He was too tired to fight, which was what she was edging for, so he counted to five and waved the bottle at her. "Would you like a glass of wine?"

She nodded, her lips curving into a small smile.

"I'll go pour us a glass."

He left her in the bathroom, making his way to the kitchen. There was already a lipstick-stained wine glass on the coffee table in the living room, along with an empty beer bottle. At least she'd offered Adam a drink.

Frankie sighed. He had no idea why she was so angry with him all the time. She knew what his job was like, the long hours. She didn't complain when she went to spend his paycheck at the end of the month, did she? He picked up the wine glass and put it into the dishwasher, then dropped the bottle in the trash. Taking two clean glasses from the cupboard he opened the wine, filled them and took a huge gulp of the wine. It wasn't the best thing he'd tasted, but he'd had worse. Then he downed the rest of the glass, poured himself a refill and carried the wine through to Christy, who was already in the bath.

"So, what kind of a day have you had?"

She rolled her eyes at him. "Well, obviously not as busy as

you. Life is pretty boring when you just have an ordinary nine-to-five job."

He nodded solemnly and left her to it. She was still looking for an argument, and he didn't have the energy. For once, it would have been nice to come home to something to eat. Instead, he had to make do with going through the fridge and cupboards to see what he could throw together. At least he could tell Maria he'd tried to be nice to his wife.

SIX

GREENWICH VILLAGE, 1952

Emilia checked her reflection one last time. Her long, black hair was the opposite of Mae's shoulder-length, platinum blond curls. She pouted her peach-colored lips at the mirror. The lipstick had been a birthday present from her brother last year, but she'd been too shy to wear it. If they were going for lunch and shopping, she couldn't look drab; the last thing she wanted was to look like a wallflower compared to the exotic Mae.

Her stomach was full of butterflies. She was excited to be doing something so different from the usual baking, reading and wishing her life was better, more exciting than it was. At the same time, she also knew that she shouldn't be so happy to be friends with the girl who was her father's lover. It was wrong, and she was as guilty for betraying her mother as much as he was. But she lived in the most amazing city in the world and hadn't really had the chance to explore it. This was something she was determined to put right and having Mae to help show her the sights was just wonderful.

Her brother had arrived that morning. She'd seen him to say hello, and he'd disappeared with barely a word to the attic, which he'd taken over as his living quarters. He was always so quiet—and he stared, a lot. She didn't like it and had caught him on several occasions watching her with an expression on his face that she found quite disconcerting. He was strange, but she left him alone to get on with it.

He never used to be this way. When they were younger, they'd spend hours chasing each other on the beach, fishing and crabbing. They'd play games that consisted of hiding around the huge beachfront house they lived in. But as he'd turned into an angry, surly teenager, he'd practically stopped speaking to her and spent much of his time on his own reading. Otherwise, she had no idea what he did up in the attic. Every time she saw him, he had an old leather-bound book tucked under his arm. He didn't go anywhere without it.

She heard the beep of the cab outside and grabbed her purse off the dresser. She ran to the front door and opened it, looking up to see Mae leaning out of the cab window waving frantically at her. Emilia waved back and ran up the stone steps, pulling open the cab door. Mae smiled at her. She didn't have quite so much make-up on today as the first time they'd met. Her lips were a pale pink this morning and were just as beautiful. Emilia didn't think she'd ever really taken notice of another woman's mouth before, but Mae's was captivating.

She sniffed the air. It smelled exotic and sultry. It made her think of freedom.

Mae giggled. "Chanel No 5, I never leave home without it. Do you like it?"

"I do." Emilia blushed.

"Good, in that case we can call into Saks and pick some up for you. Whilst we're there we can find you a red lipstick. Every girl needs a red lipstick, and my neighbor Betty works in the beauty department; she'll find you the perfect shade. You wouldn't believe how many red lipsticks there are to choose from," Mae chattered on.

As the cab drove along Fifth Avenue, Emilia had to pinch

herself. She'd only ever been along here once before. The thought of going into Saks and buying beauty products made her fizz with excitement—she'd never done anything like it. Her mother had always frowned upon the women who made up their faces. What would she say if she went home smelling like some exotic creature with ruby red lips and eyelashes as black as coal? Suddenly she didn't care one little bit. She was an adult now; she would do what the heck she pleased.

The cab pulled up outside Saks and Emilia got out while Mae was busy paying the driver and giggling at something he said. A warm arm pushed underneath hers and she was tugged in the direction of the huge, brass, doors. A doorman pulled the door open for them.

"Well look at you Miss Mae, as pretty as ever. How are you this fine day?"

"Thank you, Fred, you look real swell yourself. I'm good, how are you?"

He grinned and tipped his hat to them both.

"All the better for seeing you Miss Mae, have a grand day."

Emilia smiled and thanked the man as she stepped into the brightly lit store and gasped as her eyes took in the room. It was bigger than she ever could have imagined, filled with elegantly decorated counters and the intoxicating smell of different perfumes lingering in the air.

She leaned in close to Mae and whispered. "How do you find what you need?"

Mae laughed. "Trust me honey, five minutes in here and you'll know where you want to be."

Two hours later they were walking out of the store, Mae with her huge shopping bags over one arm. Emilia had one small bag clutched between her fingers; inside was a bottle of Chanel No 5 perfume, a red lipstick, face powder and some eye make-up.

She stole a glance at her reflection in the shop window and did a double take. Betty had made up her face perfectly. This was certainly not the face of the woman who had walked into the store.

Mae hadn't stopped chattering the whole time and Emilia had loved it—and Mae. All her reservations about her were gone. She loved how talking to her new friend was so easy— she just wished that Mae wasn't her father's lover.

Mae hailed another cab, and they climbed in as she gave directions to the diner. Emilia was glad: her stomach had begun to growl in the most unladylike manner. She'd been too nervous to eat breakfast earlier and the louder her stomach protested, the more she regretted it. As they walked into the diner, she inhaled the smell of pizza dough, garlic and herbs.

"Smells good, doesn't it? I told you I knew the perfect spot for lunch. You might not be able to move much after one of Toni's pizzas though but trust me, it's worth it."

They took a seat in a booth which looked out onto 42nd Street. People were hurrying by on their way to work, shopping, sightseeing. Mae was chattering to the waitress, who was listening intently to what she was telling her. Emilia felt a little intrusive; just as Mae was friends with Betty, she must have been friends with this gum-chewing, young woman. She heard her name mentioned and realized that she was staring at the pair of them.

"What's up, Em, cat got your tongue?"

"Sorry, I was daydreaming..." No one called her Em, yet it sounded so right coming from Mae.

The waitress winked at her. "Now that I am an expert at, I daydream all the time. I'm still waiting for my big acting break. One day I'll be just as famous as Mae and it will be my name on that billboard across the way."

Mae giggled. "Shush Susie, I'm not famous. This is Clarke's daughter by the way, she's my new gal pal."

Susie scrutinised her and Emilia felt the blush rise up from her neck.

"Nice to meet you Em, say hi to your pa for me."

As Mae gave their order, Emilia pondered how on earth Susie knew her father, but she was too afraid to ask. It seemed everyone knew him better than she did.

SEVEN

PRESENT DAY

He squatted on the floor, unzipped his bag, then pulled out the antique board that was allegedly made from wood taken from an actual coffin. He'd stolen it from the weird, little occult museum on East 9th Street.

He'd used Ouija boards a few times before to impress the other kids at school, and at first it had been a big joke. But then things started to happen. He realized the planchette really was moving itself. After that first time, he'd thrown the board straight in a dumpster but it had been the start of his insomnia. It was hard to sleep when you were scared to close your eyes and you knew something had attached itself to you. He could feel it, following him, watching him, but never saying or doing anything. It was like a dark shadow, always there.

Then he'd found another board in the cupboard of the attic three years ago and after a few drinks had tried again. How he wished he hadn't. It led him to find the antique Ouija board in the museum, setting in motion things that could not be changed. He knew that now, and he had no other option than to continue what he'd started. It was all a matter of how far you were willing to go with it. And this time, he wanted to go all the way.

No, he didn't want to summon his Aunt Patsy, who'd died of a heart attack two years ago. Why would he? She'd been a mean old bitch when she was alive—being dead wouldn't have improved her. No, he wanted more. Knowing his luck, his aunt would probably put in an appearance, but she'd soon leave once he summoned who he really wanted.

He'd thought long and hard about whether he should even attempt to do this. It was dangerous. He didn't doubt that, but the voice had told him of all the things he could have, things that were there for the taking. The power and the energy that only the darkest of demons could give to him. He was more than willing to trade his soul if it meant he got what he wanted so very much.

Placing the board on the kitchen counter—where he'd left his first offering on that fateful day—he ran his fingers over the cool marble. How easy the blood had pooled on it. How easy it had cleaned off. It had been three years and he wondered if it had been too long. He'd never expected to have a mental episode after it. The police had picked him up days later and, unable to talk much sense, he'd been given a psychiatric evaluation and thrown in Greystone Park Psychiatric Hospital. He'd been amazed the cops had never matched any of the evidence to him. Luckily or unluckily for him, the guys who'd caught up with him hadn't wanted too much paperwork so they'd driven him straight to the hospital where he'd been kept indefinitely until he proved he was as normal as he could be.

At first, he'd been angry about it, and then he realized it was to his advantage. He had somewhere warm and dry to sleep; he got fed, meds and counselling. There was no trace of him to link him back to the murder this way, yet if he'd been left outside to his own devices he'd have been compelled to kill again. At least this way the heat had completely died down. The Torso Killer had gone to ground as far as they knew. He imagined they were hoping he was dead.

The apartment had been sealed up, ready and waiting for him. Whoever the current owner was must have been superstitious: they were losing out on rental in a prime area of Manhattan. He'd smiled as he'd listened to the realtor trying to rent him something else, too afraid to admit the real reason the apartment wasn't for rent. They might not have known about the murders in 1952 that took place inside it, but he did, thanks to the Ouija board. All things considered, it was perfect. If he was quiet and didn't alert the neighbors whenever he visited, he should be able to come and go as he pleased.

He stroked the small heart shaped wooden planchette and rested it at a distance from the board. He wasn't ready to place it on the board; it wasn't time. He'd learned it was never a good idea to leave them laid out together when not being used. He'd seen it with his own eyes once when he'd left it on the board and walked away. The planchette had begun to move all on its own. When he was ready to begin his reign of terror, he didn't want to summon anyone other than the dark force with which he now so familiar.

Pulling the book of Dark Magic from his bag, he placed it next to the board; now, all he needed was candles, lots of them, but would get them later from his van. He didn't bother flicking on the lights, despite the fact it was gloomy and hard to see. He wouldn't risk any observant neighbors noticing and ringing the cops. Just in case, he took the rug and, rolling it up, lay it across the bottom of the door. That should block out any light from his flashlight or candles.

The walls in the lounge had been painted over since his last visit, giving him a blank canvas to start again. In the 1950s when the first murder occurred, the cops had broken down the door and found the entire apartment's walls covered in pentagrams, drawings of winged, horned beasts, and line upon line of Latin. He doubted any of the original drawings still existed, but he would peel back any layers of wallpaper and check under the carpets, just in case.

Three sacrifices were needed before the incantation and summoning could begin. He just hoped that the huge gaps between the murders wouldn't make a difference. Decades had passed since the first sacrifice took place and it had been several years since he had made the second killing. As soon as a third and final victim was found, he could complete what was started so many years before. And finally, the power he'd been promised would be his to claim.

EIGHT

Maria decided to walk to the station. It was one of those cooler, fresh mornings that she loved. Summer in the city could be unbearable—she was definitely more of a winter gal. She tugged on her Nikes and slung her purse over her shoulder. She was on a health kick. No more burgers, pizzas or burritos, but lattes she couldn't live without. As she turned to check everything was switched off, she spotted the flowers and once more asked herself where they'd come from.

She exited the building and ran down the apartment block steps, noticing a limousine with blacked out windows parked opposite. A brand-new Mercedes. The only person around here that used limousines was Miss Green. The rear door opened and a man stepped out, smiling right at her. In that moment, it dawned on Maria: he was the security guard she'd met at Harrison Media. She smiled at him, then carried on walking not wanting to get involved in an awkward introduction or conversation about the shooting. She didn't get far before a hand tugged at her arm, taking her by surprise. She moved fast, throwing it off, and spun around. He was standing directly behind her grinning.

"That's a bit rude. I send you flowers for saving my receptionist's life then come to visit, and you turn your back on me.
You could at least say hello."

Maria looked at him; he was older than she'd guessed yesterday. His eyes were a little crinkly around the edges and his
blond hair was peppered with silver strands.

"Excuse me? What do you think you're doing? And how the
hell do you know where I live?"

"I know everything."

"Well, how about I take you to this little precinct I know,
we can have coffee and you can explain yourself better." She
was standing with her arms folded, glaring directly into his
eyes.

He laughed. "Well, that's a first. You buy a girl some flowers
and come to ask her out to dinner. A simple yes or no would
suffice."

"Look mister, I don't know you. Thank you for the lovely
flowers, but I don't care too much that you've gone to the
trouble to find out where I live. They have laws against that
kind of behavior you know?"

"Who do you think I am?"

"I have no idea, possibly the world's worst security guard
judging by yesterday's showdown. Shouldn't you have been
doing your job instead of messing around on a treadmill?"

He let out a loud laugh. "I like you, Maria, you're funny. I'm
sorry, but you have this all wrong. Please let me introduce
myself properly. Harrison Williams." He held out his hand for
her to shake and she gripped it as hard as she could.

Holy crap, I hope he's not friends with the Commander.

"Maria Miller."

"Yes, I know. I wanted to thank you properly for yesterday.
I'm not a stalker, I own a media company. I have people on my
payroll who know things and if they don't know, then they sure
as hell find them out."

She stared at him, not sure whether to arrest his sorry ass or be flattered.

"Why don't you let me give you a lift to work, if that's where you're heading? We can talk in the car, and you can decide whether or not to come out for dinner this evening."

"I'm fine thanks, I like to walk. On my own. It helps me to clear my head before the start of a shift."

His smile disappeared. She imagined he wasn't used to people saying no to him. Well, he would have to learn. She didn't care about his business or how much money he had.

"What about dinner?"

"I'm sorry, I have no idea what time I'll be finished, and I've already made plans to go out for a drink with a friend."

He smiled. "Tomorrow?"

"It was nice meeting you, Mr Williams. Have a nice day."

With that she turned and began to take the biggest strides she could to get as far away from him as possible. Her cheeks were burning; she'd never been hit on so openly in all her life. It was crazy—of course she wasn't going to agree to get in a car with a man she didn't know. Did he not realize she was a homicide detective? How many bodies had she attended of women and men on first dates or picked up in a bar by total strangers. Hell no; it wasn't happening. Her life might not be amazing at the moment, but it didn't mean she wanted it to end.

Shaking her head, she carried on walking, trying to get rid of the image of Harrison Williams floating around in there. Whether she wanted to admit it or not, he was attractive, but so was Frankie—that didn't mean she threw herself at him whenever she could. She really hoped today was going to be better than yesterday. Her definition of a good day was very different to most peoples'. No homicides and not having to shoot someone. She wasn't asking for much.

NINE

Frankie was in a rush for work, having got stuck in a jam on Sixth, and was now driving like a maniac to make it to the precinct before Sergeant Addison realized he was late again. By the time he got parked and ran into the department Maria was already there, coffee in hand, scrolling through the list of jobs that had come in overnight.

Fortunately, he made it to his desk without being caught.

"Nice of you to join us, Frankie."

"Traffic."

"Why don't you just walk, or get the subway?"

He frowned at her. "I'm too lazy to walk and I'm not being crushed against some hairy, sweaty, guy for ten minutes."

She laughed, but not for long as she heard Addison bellow.

"Miller, Conroy. My office now."

Maria looked at Frankie, and he shrugged. At least it wasn't just him getting called. They stood up and walked the short distance to Sergeant Addison's corner office. Ever the gentleman, Frankie let Maria go in first, because then she'd be the one in the sergeant's line of fire—metaphorically, and literally. Addison was an okay boss, but when he was angry or excited, spittle flew from his lips—and far. Frankie noticed Maria trying to keep a safe distance. When she looked over her shoulder and glared at Frankie, he gave her a wink.

"Take a seat."

They both sat down, relieved that Addison was neither angry nor excited. He had a file spread out across his desk. Maria glanced at the technicolor photographs, then glanced at Frankie. They both recognized the crime scene, the torso and limbs from that night, three years ago. It had caused them so many sleepless nights, but the trail had gone cold and they had never come across a viable suspect. Whoever had killed the woman had dropped off the face of the earth.

"We've had a call from a student asking all sorts of questions about this case, she wanted to know if we were aware that in the fifties, a semi-famous actress was found murdered in the same way, in the same apartment. Her limbs were hacked from her body and her head was missing. According to this student it was never found."

"How did we not know this?"

"How were we supposed to know? It's not like it was a few months ago, I mean that's seventy years ago." He was trying to count on his fingers.

Addison shrugged. "I'm not saying you should have known, hell I had no idea about it and I'm older than the pair of you. I want you to go back over everything you have. Work the case again. I've pulled you off the active on-call duties to work it for the next ten days and see what you can come up with."

Maria picked up and clutched the photograph of the entrance to the apartment. Every cop had a case they didn't solve; a killer they couldn't catch. This one had been the one that gave her nightmares. She'd told Frankie how she would wake up in the early hours in a cold sweat, her hands checking to make sure her head was still attached to her body.

"Who is this student?" Frankie asked. "How the hell do

they know about the other murder—could they be a suspect chief, because it's a bit wacko if you ask me?"

Addison's cheeks began to turn crimson. "It's my daughter. She's studying for a degree in criminology. She told me she started looking into it when it first happened but then lost interest when no killer was caught. She's just begun writing about unsolved crime for her dissertation and chose this one from a few years ago. She was researching the street, happened to stumble upon the original story and asked me about it. Had to say I didn't know. I haven't got the time to look into it and, let's be honest, the Lieutenant would think I'd lost it if I told him why."

Frankie was staring at the photograph of the limbless body. "Christ, I was hoping I'd never have to look at this ever again. It gave me nightmares for months."

"Wouldn't you be better asking the cold case review team to take a look?"

Addison shrugged. "I can't, you know how much use Peters is. He'll laugh his ass off at me when I tell him it's my daughter who found a possible link. I want you two to at least make a start on it. If you can pull something together that could link any of it, I'll pass it on to them to take over."

Frankie knew what an asshole Peters was and as much as he didn't want to have to pour through the files again, he did like the thought of giving it one last shot to find the killer. Whoever it was deserved to be locked up. In fact, they deserved much worse than that. To know that whoever it was had been brought to justice might just help them both sleep a bit better at night. It wasn't as bad now as it had been three years ago, but he still had nights where he tossed and turned, wondering where the victim's head was.

"Yes sir, we'll make a start on it right now. Won't we, Frankie?" Frankie didn't look as convinced as she sounded, but he replied in the affirmative too.

Addison scooped up the photographs and put them back into the file. "These are copies. I xeroxed everything from the original file." He pulled open his top drawer and pulled out another file and passed it across to Maria. "And those are copies of everything Gina found in the archives concerning the murder back in 52."

He wrote a cell number across the front of the file, holding it toward her. "You need anything else, that's Gina's number. Give her a call."

Maria took the second file. "Thanks."

"Oh and can the pair of you keep this to yourselves, I don't want the rest of the department thinking I'm going soft in my old age."

They both nodded, stood up and walked out of his office, neither of them saying a word until they reached their desks.

Maria looked at Frankie. "Coffee?"

"Of course, you know me baby. I'm anyone's for a cup of Sam's delicious, caffeine-infused drinks."

TEN

Frankie found a parking bay a block down from Sam's Deli and Maria high-fived him. If they were leaving the car, it had to be in a proper bay. Traffic cops were prone to tow anything they could get their hands on. Maria grabbed the two files, ready to find a quiet booth, order breakfast and see what they could come up with.

For the first time in months, she felt glad to be doing something different, and to be able to delve even deeper into their cold case. She'd been devastated that they never recovered the poor girl's head. Or caught the sick creep who took it away in the first place. As much as it was going to reopen a can of worms inside her own head, she was grateful to be given a second chance.

She pushed open the heavy door to Sam's, which was full of wise New Yorkers eating breakfast and ordering coffee to go. She spied an empty booth at the back near to the bathrooms and made her way toward it. Frankie stopped to chat with a couple of beat cops who were on their way out and she didn't recognize, which meant she didn't need to bother with the small talk. Shuffling into the booth, she lay the files down on the table, knowing she wouldn't open them until Marge had taken their order. It wasn't fair to subject nice, normal people to the horrors that they had to deal with.

She picked up the menu and began reading, her stomach groaning in appreciation. Despite the fact that she'd eaten a bowl of granola, she was still tempted to have one of Sam's huge breakfast bagels stuffed with bacon, eggs, mushrooms, tomatoes and topped with Swiss cheese. Frankie finally sat down opposite her.

"I wasn't hungry until I stepped in here. Why does it smell so damn good?"

"Have you eaten?"

He stuck his tongue out at her. "Have you?"

"Yes, some granola."

"I told you, eating that bird food isn't enough. I've had some coffee."

"And the rest?"

"A couple of eggs—what are you, my mother?"

She shook her head, and before they could get into an argument, Marge appeared like a vision from God.

"You two love birds at it again? What can I get you?"

Maria rhymed off her order. Frankie screwed up his eyes. "I'll have the same please, Marge, and two of Sam's lattes please."

Marge wrote down their order, tucking the pencil back behind her ear. She scooped up the menus and pointed to the files. "You got something juicy going on in there?"

"It's horrific Marge, enough to put you off your food."

"That good? Why don't you two get a change of department, work something nice? It can't be good for your brain seeing the crap you two look at every day." She tapped the side of her head with her pointed, bright red fingernail.

"Someone has to catch them and we're quite good at it."

Frankie snorted and Marge smiled at him. "Grow up Frankie."

She walked away leaving Maria giggling. When she composed herself, she wagged her finger at him. "Yes, grow up Frankie."

Frankie rolled his eyes. "So, this is a turn up for the books; if we play it right, we won't have to deal with any crappy homicides this side of Christmas."

"This isn't some kind of working holiday, it's serious. We have to start from the beginning; go over everything, pull the evidence and crime scene logs."

"I know that, I'm just saying it's nice. Who'd have thought old Addison would be such a pushover for his kid? I'm shocked, I had him pegged as an asshole."

"You peg everyone as an asshole."

"Not you."

"Good, glad to hear it."

Maria opened the folder from Gina and looked at the assortment of black-and-white photocopied articles. There was a grainy black-and-white photograph of the outside of the brownstone, and the caption underneath read, *Family Home turned Slaughterhouse*. She shivered. The house looked in a much better state than it did now. She began to read the article, only to be disturbed by Marge carrying a tray with their drinks. She gathered the pieces of paper up and closed the file, not wanting to upset her, and thanked the older woman who had been serving people here forever.

ELEVEN

GREENWICH VILLAGE, 1952

Emilia pushed her plate away; she couldn't eat any more if she tried. Mae did the same and rubbed her stomach.

"I hope my costume still fastens tonight. Beatrice will go crazy if it doesn't zip up." She began to laugh, and Emilia joined in.

"What play are you in and who is Beatrice?"

"Beatrice is the wardrobe mistress. It's a musical called *Fanny* about a woman whose childhood love leaves her to go away to sea. After he leaves, she discovers she's pregnant and has to marry an older man. I'm not actually the lead, I'm in the chorus. I'm the lead's understudy and stand-in. If she's ill or can't perform then I step in, but don't tell Clarke that. He came to see it the night I was standing in and was so besotted, I didn't have the heart to tell him the truth."

"Oh, I won't. I'm sure that being the lead's understudy is just as important."

For the first time Mae's cheeks flushed red. "Thanks Em, I know you must think I'm a terrible person. Carrying on with your pa and lying to him, but I'm not. I like him and I know that

I shouldn't, but he's kind and funny. In a way, I wish he wasn't married to your mom— then I wouldn't feel so bad about it all."

Emilia wasn't sure what to say. She had a sense of duty toward her mother, despite the fact they weren't close and never had been—her brother had always been her mother's favorite by far. Yet she didn't know this girl well enough to condone her relationship with her father. She didn't even know her father well enough, and she'd known him all her life. But she wanted him to be happy; and she really liked Mae. Unable to put how she felt into words, she found herself shrugging.

"Sorry Em, this is heavy stuff to lay on you the second time I've met you. I just feel as if I can talk to you way more than anyone else. I've been friends with Betty since high school and we've never felt this close. I shouldn't put you in this position—I hope you're not angry with me?"

"Of course not, Mae, I like you too. I just don't know what to say. It's difficult."

Mae held her hand up for the cheque and Em began to pull some dollars out of her purse.

"No way kid, this one's on me. I dragged you shopping and to eat enough pizza to feed a small country. It's the least I can do."

She pulled the money—plus enough for a generous tip— from her purse and left it on top of the bill. Standing up, she let out a groan and held her hand out to help Emilia up. Both girls were smiling at each other. They were friends who shared a secret that made both their lives difficult, but Emilia didn't care. She'd had more fun the last three hours than she'd had in five years. This was how it was supposed to be: shopping, seeing the sights and eating dinner with your girlfriends. Not being shut away in a mausoleum on Staten Island with only your mother and brother for company.

They carried their bags outside into the chilly, autumn air.

Emilia felt Mae's warm arm slip through hers and she smiled. It felt right. That they should be walking arm in arm—or was that reserved for lovers? For a fleeting moment, she imagined what it would be like to kiss Mae... and then it was gone.

"Should I hail a cab?"

"Thank you, but no. I need to walk a little, I'm so stuffed. If you need to go and get ready point me in the right direction, I'm sure I'll find my way home."

Mae shook her head. "I don't think so. I'm not leaving you to navigate the city on your own. Clarke would kill me. We'll walk together. I'll catch a cab back to the theatre."

Emilia felt the tight breath she'd been holding release. She would have walked on her own, and she'd have been terrified, but it wouldn't have stopped her. Stubbornness was a Carter family trait.

They headed away from the crowds of people and back down toward the village. As they reached West 10th Street, she saw Mrs. Smith who lived across the street and waved. She liked the older woman. She was always smiling and so friendly. Mrs. Smith waved back at her then disappeared through her front door.

James watched his sister and her new exotic friend walk toward the house from the attic window. They both looked pretty; his sister looked different. He wasn't sure what made her look so attractive; maybe it was having a friend and a smile on her face. It made a change to see her smiling and not with her nose stuck in a book.

He laughed to himself and turned around to look at the old, cracked, leather book which was open on his bed. It was a bad book, he knew that, and he knew that the best thing to do would be to take it and throw it in the river. Ever since he'd discovered it tucked away on the bottom shelf at the back of the library whilst staying in Staten Island, he had done nothing but think evil thoughts. It was as if it controlled his mind and he knew that was ridiculous—or was it?

He'd always had an interest in witchcraft and the occult, but when he'd asked his mom who the book belonged to, she'd told him to throw it away. His grampa had been fascinated with the occult and she thought she'd disposed of all of his old books. James had lied and told her he had put it out in the trash. Instead, he'd hidden it in his case and told her he was off to the city to see his pa and Emilia, which had been a complete lie. He rarely spoke to his sister; these days he found it hard to converse with girls, even her. He got tongue tied and his cheeks would burn. He was desperate to know if the strange creatures that were so carefully illustrated on the pages of the book existed. He kind of believed that they did, but he needed proof. He was going to start working on the ritual to see if he could summon the demon like the book promised.

He didn't need money; his pa had plenty of that. What he did want was the power that the dark forces promised. Then the girls he so desperately wanted would be attracted to him and maybe even he'd be able to hold a conversation with them without the usual shame that crept over him. It said in the book that human sacrifices were needed: three of them. He didn't have a problem with this—in fact he already had them lined up thanks to his sister's new friend.

Emilia had always looked down her nose at him so he had no issues killing her. Then there was Mae and Missy, their housekeeper. Together, they would be perfect. His problem would be killing them and doing what he had to before his pa found out. It was ambitious, and it didn't come without risk. His pa wouldn't be too pleased to find his daughter, lover and house-keeper's decapitated and dismembered bodies. But it wouldn't matter so long as he didn't find out until James had summoned his demon. Once he had, he would have enough power to take on an entire army. Then his angry parents would be of no consequence whatsoever.

TWELVE

PRESENT DAY

Maria was engrossed. Looking into the cold case again was a welcome change, and she was going to start with visiting the brownstone on West 10th St to speak to the old lady who lived below the attic—if she was still there. Maria hoped she hadn't died. She remembered the woman telling her that she'd lived in the same apartment most of her life.

Frankie dropped her off outside the station. She was glad to be free of him for a while; he had a dental appointment, conveniently giving her some time with her own thoughts—and the opportunity to call on the elderly lady without overwhelming her.

Maria jumped out of the car, the case folder tucked under her arm. She wanted to make copies of it, so she'd have a file to work on from home. Frankie would scold her if he knew, but this was more her thing. There had been two occasions where she'd almost transferred to the Cold Case Department. The only thing that had stopped her had been Frankie; they made a good team. That and the fact that Lieutenant Peters was a pain in the ass.

She ran up to the department and duplicated everything,

before making her way to the address. It wasn't as if she needed Frankie to babysit her; she could do this on her own. She was a big girl now. But as she found a gap big enough to park in, she wondered if she should have waited for him. The village was a thriving part of New York and Maria loved its crooked tree lined streets, the quaint shops and the laid-back feel to the area well known for its bohemian feel thanks to the number of artists who flocked here.

She got out of the car and crossed the road, walking back down toward the brownstone. It stood out amongst the others on the street, and she wondered if that was because she knew of its disturbing history—or was it simply because it was so badly neglected. The brownstones in the village were worth a lot of money, so why had the owners chosen to leave this one to decay? As she reached the stone steps leading down to the front door, she stopped and stayed rooted, her hands on her hips. Was it her or did it give off bad vibes? Almost like it was its own living, breathing entity.

She had no idea how long she'd been staring at the building when a car horn beeped behind her, making her jump. She looked around, disorientated for a moment. At the same time, the front door was pushed open with a loud groan and a dreadlocked man came running up the steps, an invisible cloak of cannabis shrouding him. Maria stepped to one side to let him pass and he looked her up and down. She shook her head in response—she wasn't interested in him—and he nodded back. He knew she was a cop. He could probably smell it on her like she could smell the recreational drugs on him. He lifted his headphones onto his ears and began to walk away but she reached out and touched his arm.

He turned, glaring at her. "What you want? I'm minding my own business."

"Hey, sorry. Yes, you are, I wanted to ask you about the apartments."

"You don't want to live here. It's not good for someone like you." He said and walked away.

What did he mean—or know? She jogged to catch up and asked, "Why do you say that?"

"It's the kind of place you only live if there's nowhere else. That's all."

"Have you lived here long?"

The look in his eyes told her she was annoying him big time. He put his hands on his hips and she took a step back. "Ten years. Now you gonna let me get on my way?"

"Yes, sorry. Thanks."

He turned, striding away from her as fast as he could. Left with no choice but to settle for the cryptic insight he'd given her, she walked down the steps, pressing several buzzers in the hope that someone would let her in. The door clicked and she pushed it open, peering in. As she stepped inside, the memories of that night three years ago flooded her mind. She felt her body shudder, not sure if it was a replay from the past or the fact that this place truly freaked her out. Until now she'd forgotten how she'd felt when she'd first entered the house. It was creepy as hell, there was no doubt about it.

A faint smell of cannabis tainted the air, mixed with fried onions. They were masking an underlying odour of something damp and rotten; she wouldn't have been surprised if the whole block was full of dry rot. There was something very wrong with this place. It unsettled her. It was so quiet it was eerie—it was hard to believe it homed at least ten residents.

She began to climb the stairs. As she reached the third floor, she stared at the apartment and willed the woman would still be there. Before she could knock on the heavy, black oak door it opened a crack.

"Yes?"

Maria pulled out her badge and held it up. "Good afternoon, ma'am, NYPD Homicide. Could I speak to you about the murder three years ago?"

A thin hand reached through the gap in the door and took the badge out of her hand. After a few seconds, the door opened and a frailer looking version of the woman Maria had interviewed that night stared at her.

"I remember you."

Maria smiled. "I remember you too. Could I come inside for a few minutes?"

The woman stepped back, allowing her inside. It was gloomy in the hallway and the first thing Maria noticed was the number of crucifixes hanging on the wall and above each doorway. The woman led her into a spacious living room, where a huge crucifix hung above the fireplace; the crucifix was so grand that it wouldn't have looked out of place in Saint Patrick's Cathedral. Maria tried not to take too much notice of it; religion was a sticky subject for her. The woman pointed to a chair, and she sat down, relieved it wasn't facing the enormous cross.

"So, what do you want? I spoke to you when it happened. You never caught him."

There was no arguing with the woman in front of her; it was all too true. She didn't catch him.

"I'm afraid we didn't, you're right. Sometimes they get away despite us doing our best to find them, but I never stopped thinking about it."

"Sometimes, they have a little help."

Maria frowned, not sure what she meant. "Have you lived here long, Mrs—?"

The woman began to laugh. "Miss Carter, you can call me Emilia. Yes, the house belonged to my parents. I've lived here all my life and that's a very long time."

"How long?"

"I moved in here permanently when I was twenty-two."

Maria tried to work out how old Emilia was, failing miserably.

"Sixty-five years to be exact. I've been here since I was twenty-two and never left."

"Wow, that's a lot of rent."

"I don't pay rent, like I said this house belongs to me."

Maria was shocked: the woman had never mentioned it when she'd spoken to her three years ago.

"So, you remember the murder in the fifties?"

The woman's already watery, dark brown eyes blinked several times.

"Yes, I do, as if it was yesterday."

There was a loud dragging noise on the ceiling above them and Emilia looked up, horrified. "No one lives up there. It's empty; it has been since the night of the murder."

"Someone must have broken in?"

"No... No one lives there; no one wants to live there. It's haunted." She stated the fact as if she was telling Maria it was cold outside or rain had been forecast.

"I don't understand. Has anyone been in and checked there isn't anyone squatting up there?"

Emilia nodded. "More times than you can ever imagine. It's always the same. Scratching, dragging, knocks, bangs. The footsteps are the worst. Heavy, clattering footsteps, but not the kind that you or I would make. Oh no, these sound like hooves, stomping on the wooden floorboards and always at the same time. Three am is when it likes to get busy."

Maria could feel the hairs on the back of her neck begin to prickle, a feeling of unease spreading over her. Did the woman in front of her have some kind of dementia?

"Right now, you're considering if I'm a crazy old bat aren't you? Trust me honey, I'm not, I've lived with it all my life. I knew it was a mistake renting the attic apartment out, but the realtors who handle the rentals insisted. They had someone come in and paint all the walls white, sand the floors, clean the windows. It looked good enough, I even went up there to take a peek. I hadn't been up there for over fifty years. I couldn't go inside because no matter what they did to it, I'd never get that image out of my head."

"What image was that?"

A loud scratching on the ceiling directly above where they were sitting made even Maria jump from her chair.

The woman crossed herself and shook her head. "I don't talk about it and neither should you. I need you to leave now, I don't want to upset it any further. You don't have to live here, I do—and I do what I can to leave it be and not cause any trouble."

She stood up and led Maria to the front door.

"Thank you," Maria said, and passed her a card. "If you do decide you want to talk, call me. That's my cell. Any time. Oh, one last thing, who's the guy with the dreadlocks?"

"Mikey." The woman took the card from her, slamming her apartment door shut.

Maria couldn't ignore the fact that she'd clearly heard someone moving around in the empty apartment above them. She had to check it out, whether the old lady wanted her to or not; it was her duty. Turning to make sure she wasn't being watched by Emilia, she began to walk up the next flight of steps. She shivered as she felt a chill across her skin, goose bumps breaking out all over her arms. That lady had unnerved her more than she'd ever care to admit.

As she reached the small landing, she paused remembering that night three years ago and how dark it had been back then. It was even gloomier now; even if it was empty it wouldn't cost much to run a single bulb to illuminate the place. A faint whiff of sulphur and rotten eggs hit her nostrils. Maybe there was a gas leak.

For the second time in less than an hour, she wished she'd

waited for Frankie to come back from the dentist before coming here. She stood staring at the door, an image of the bloodied torso she had come face to face with flashing across her mind. She had to force herself to move forward, dragging her legs which had turned into lead weights. When she was as close to the door as she could be, she placed her ear against the wood to listen.

The foreboding sense of dread which shrouded her entire body made her knees go weak. Her gut instinct told her to get the hell out of there; her stubborn cop mind chose to ignore it. She squeezed her eyes shut, concentrating. The image of a huge, cloven-hoofed beast filled it. She had a vision of it standing on the other side of the door, imitating her and waiting for her to make her next move.

The smell of rotten eggs emanated through the cracks around the door and she began to wonder if there was another body in there. She couldn't enter without a warrant, but more to the point, she wasn't sure she was brave enough to go in with no back up. Her gut felt like lead, she straightened up and stepped away from the door. If she was going in it was with a couple of officers. *And a priest,* a voice whispered in her ear.

She turned away, walking briskly to the stairs. Then, as she hurried back down the staircase, she heard a faint scratching. Like razor-sharp talons being dragged across wood. Maria didn't stop; she was well and truly getting out of there. How the hell Emilia had lived in that house for sixty-five years without losing her mind was a miracle. As she reached the ground level the guy with the dreadlocks, Mikey, was opening one of the apartment doors. He took one look at her pale face and wide eyes, then shook his head.

"I told you this place was full of bad shit."

Maria nodded, forcing herself to walk out of the door when what she really wanted to do was run as fast as she could and never look back.

THIRTEEN

Just as Maria pulled up back at the station, Frankie arrived with a fat lip.

"Do you want to tell me why you look so terrified?"

Maria cursed his perceptiveness. "Do I?"

He nodded.

"I went to pay the old lady a visit at the house." It was pointless lying to him because he'd never shut up.

"You need to give me more than that. What old lady? Which house?"

"The house on West 10th Street."

She held her breath, waiting for a lecture about going out alone, being careless. It didn't come; instead, he put his hand on her arm.

"What happened?"

She looked around to make sure there was no one in hearing distance.

"I don't know exactly, but that house is creepy. I went there to talk to the woman in the apartment below the attic."

"I remember her, she was a grouchy old bird and wasn't very helpful."

"She wasn't, but not only does she remember the first murder, she owns the damn building and was there when it happened."

"Well, maybe we should bring her in for questioning. There can't be that many people alive who remember what happened the first time around and have been there for a second murder."

Maria was shocked; it hadn't even crossed her mind that the frail woman could be the one responsible for the horrific murders.

"Are you for real? She's almost ninety and that's a hell of a long gap between murders if she is a killer."

"Age is just a number. She might be fitter than the pair of us. It's not unheard of."

"Nah, it's not her. You didn't see the look of fear on her face."

"Why was she scared?"

"You promise you won't laugh?"

He rolled his eyes.

"There was this dragging and scratching sound on the ceiling above from the empty apartment. It really made the hairs on the back of my neck prickle."

"It's an old house, Maria, it probably has rats the size of alley cats. If the attic doesn't get used for years on end, they'll be running riot up there."

Maria thought about it. This could be very true. Hell, it probably was very true, but her stomach was still rolling around like a lead ball and that normally meant her gut was telling her something. And in this case, it didn't believe that what she'd heard was a rat.

She wasn't about to let this on to Frankie—he'd only march her right back there to check it out. She didn't want to set foot inside that house again unless she had to. "I guess you're right."

"Of course I'm right, baby. I always am."

She stepped forward and slapped his arm. "Christ, you're so

full of shit." But she couldn't help laughing and instantly felt better. She'd spooked herself, and that crazy old woman and all her crucifixes hadn't helped. They walked up the station steps and along the corridor to their unit, which was busy with detectives who looked to be working for a change, went to their desks and sat down. Neither of them spoke; they didn't want the others to know what they were working on.

After an hour Maria looked up to see Frankie standing up, tugging on his coat.

"Come on, I've had enough of this place. My mouth is aching. Let's go to the Cat and talk in there. Maybe we should see if we can get Gina to meet us and we can hear everything she has to say."

Maria wanted to go and get a cold beer. Maybe even a cocktail or two—and it would be good to meet the girl who had thought the case was important enough to drag it all up and get them reassigned to it.

The Cat's regular crowd of patrons were propped up at the bar. Inhaling the aroma of hamburger and fried onions, Maria hadn't realized she was hungry until her stomach let out a loud growl. She walked to the bar, signalling for Frankie to take a seat as he spoke to Gina on the phone. He stuck his thumb up at her so she ordered two bottles of Bud and a cheeseburger with fries, onion rings and almost everything else she could think of.

He finished his call as she placed a beer in front of him. "My mouth is still swollen, forgive me if I drool."

She laughed. "Well, there's something you don't hear every day. So, what did she say?"

"I haven't lost my charm, she'll be here in thirty minutes."

"Good, that means I'll have enough time to eat my burger before she comes and puts me off it."

Frankie groaned. "I want food, but I can't chew yet."

"You can have some of mine. Your mouth should be working properly by the time they bring it out."

They sat in silence, sipping their beers as they waited for Gina to arrive. The bartender, who neither of them had seen before, brought Maria's food over and Frankie stared, his mouth open wide.

Maria grabbed a couple of French fries and pushed them into her mouth. "What you staring at?"

"I can't believe you're eating without me."

"Get over it. Here." She pushed the plate toward him, and he picked up the biggest onion ring on the plate.

"Hi, are you Frankie?"

Maria looked from the young woman to her partner next to and couldn't help letting out a chuckle. His already swollen face was bulging at the sides, making him look like a hamster stocking up for hibernation. He nodded and mumbled 'Mhmm,' pointing at Maria.

"You must be Gina, I'm his partner, Maria. Pleased to meet you." She held out her hand and the woman shook it.

"I've heard a lot about you."

"I hope it isn't all bad, your dad doesn't always see the best in me," Maria replied, winking.

The girl threw her head back and began to laugh, a big, hearty, laugh which instantly made Maria like her. When she'd composed herself, she spoke. "He doesn't always see the best in anyone. But he's not that bad—he could be worse, I suppose. At least he's taken me seriously. That surprised me. I thought he'd tell me to stop interfering when I showed him the clippings."

"He did. So seriously that he's given me and hamster boy here a few weeks to reopen the case."

The girl sat down next to Frankie, and Maria, ravenous, picked up her burger and took a huge bite.

"So, I've heard the condensed version from your old man, now we'd like to hear the full length one." Frankie said, raising his beer.

Maria held up her hands. "Please let me finish my food

before the gory details come out. And where're your manners? Go and get Gina a drink."

FOURTEEN

He opened his eyes and had no idea where he was. It was dark and he could feel a firm mattress beneath him. The beads of sweat on his forehead and his pounding heart brought back the memories of the nightmare he'd struggled to wake from. He'd been in a cave, far below the ground, where a fire was burning so hot, he had felt the heat from the flames scorching his skin. The cave had been full of dark, wispy shadows that moved and changed shape. He saw the outline of his mother and walked toward it only for it to dissipate. Just like she had been when she was alive – never there for him, not interested in his life, not interested in him. Why would she be there for him now she was dead? There was an old, cracked wooden door in the cave and he had stumbled toward it, needing to get out of the suffocating darkness. Then the noise came, a scratching behind him. Loud, claw-like, dragging sounds against the rock face of the cave. He'd felt true terror at what was making the sound. It had scared him so much that the fear woke him up with a jolt.

He sat up and remembered where he was. He was in the apartment. Asleep on the bed where he'd last slept with the beautiful girl, Anya. He remembered tracing the outline of her beautiful tattoo from her hip to her breasts before he'd killed her. He hoped Anya wasn't still trapped in here, her soul unable to leave because of what he'd done to her.

The apartment had been used for satanic rituals and murders. No-one wanted to live in here because of the bad atmosphere and the dream had reinforced how evil this place was.

In a rare moment of lucidity, he knew he should leave and get as far away from here as possible. He'd managed to survive three years without being caught for Anya's murder. A sharp pang of guilt stabbed him through his heart. This had been her apartment that she'd rented under a false name for a cheap rate. She'd told him she was using a fake ID because of her Russian connections. She'd brought him back here and they'd spent twenty-four hours making love and drinking vodka—and she'd told him about the voices she heard in here. Whispers that she couldn't understand and, at first, he'd thought she'd been crazy.

But two days later when she'd gone to work and he'd been here alone, he'd heard them. Faint at first, hard to understand, they were in a language that he'd never heard before. Once he'd realized he could hear the whispering, it got louder, as if it knew it had his attention. He'd heard his name called several times and at one point had thought Anya had returned. Realizing that she hadn't, he then proceeded to search the entire apartment only to find nothing. He was alone; just him and the voices.

It had been none of his business, he knew that now. He should have walked away and none of this would have happened. He would still have a job, an apartment. Anya would still be alive. He wouldn't be back here where it had all begun so long ago. It was like a sickness, this obsession to come back here. The atmosphere up here was heavy; it felt as if he was cloaked in darkness. This apartment had been all he'd thought about whilst in the psych ward.

When the police had picked him up, he'd had no ID on him

and gave them false details so they wouldn't be able to trace him to here or to Anya. He'd never been in trouble before, never had his prints taken; the officers thought he was unstable, and all they'd wanted was to get him off their hands so they could finish their shift. Even though he knew it was wrong, he had desperately wanted to be back here. Now that he was, he knew it wasn't going to end well. There would be more deaths. There had to be—it had been written in blood. Whatever it was that had been summoned many years ago was still here. Lurking in the shadows, waiting to be called forward into the light to take over. As scared as he was, he couldn't stop. It knew his name; it knew every part of him and wouldn't let him go. He was a pawn in this game between good and evil, fighting on the side of the darkness that he knew would consume him and there wasn't anything he could do to stop it.

He dragged himself off the bed, his head groggy. It felt as if he had a hangover from hell. He laughed. It was a pretty apt description. As he walked into the living area he heard the whispering, then slapped at his ears with the palms of his hands as if it would clear the voices. It didn't, as he already knew it wouldn't, and they purred in the background.

The odor was strong: as if someone had been striking hundreds of matches. He went to check and see if the candles were lit. The wicks were untouched but something had been in here whilst he was sleeping. A cold shiver ran down the full length of his spine as he wondered whether he would be able to control it when the time came. If it was coming and going as it pleased already, did it really need him at all?

FIFTEEN

Gina sat back and took a large gulp of the bottle of Bud she'd been nursing in her left hand. Maria did the same.

"Let me get this straight, you think the house has some kind of curse on it?" Frankie asked.

She shrugged. "I don't know if I believe that it's cursed, but there's something wrong with it. There have been two murders in the same attic apartment. Both women had their limbs cut off and their heads removed. Not to mention the number of suicides and deaths by natural causes in the rest of the building."

Frankie let Maria speak. "How many other deaths?"

"Seven, well... nine with the murders. There were two tenants who died from cardiac arrests out in the hallway, not even in their apartments. Then there have been five suicides, two hangings, one woman gassed herself by putting her head into the oven and two more women died from prescription drug overdose. You have to admit, that's a lot of deaths for one house."

"You get that with rentals. Were they around the same time period?"

"I know, and no, there seems to have been one every ten years or so give and take, but they've all been women. Don't you think it's strange?"

"Yes, I do. It's not that I don't believe you, it's just I'm a trained detective who relies on cold hard evidence. I'm not very good when it comes to something that's not black and white."

Frankie joined in. "It's true, she isn't."

"Well, what are we going to do about it? I can't leave it as it is—there has to be some connection between the murders."

"There are seventy years between the murders, who would even remember the first?" Maria was trying to keep calm, but she felt unsettled. Wound up.

Frankie was staring at Maria as he spoke. "What about the old lady you spoke to who owns the building? You said yourself that she knew all about the first one. We need to go back and interview her again, she must know something. I can't believe that she doesn't."

Maria glared at Frankie, realizing why she was so angry with Gina. It was fear. The house on West 10th Street made her blood run cold and lodged a fear deep down inside of her heart. She wasn't going back—and she would have to if they wanted to interview the old lady again.

Gina finished her beer and stood up. "Sorry, I know I've gone on and got all defensive. I can't help it. I feel as if we have to find out what happened. Why do the women who live in that house die there? It's as if it's gotten under my skin. It's all I think about, and I feel like it's my duty to put their souls to rest because they're not at peace. I think that whoever has died in that house is stuck there. It's a purgatory they can't move on from to the light, and are stuck in the dark..."

She glanced at Frankie who was sitting there with his mouth open. Maria smiled at her. "It's not often Frankie is left speechless. It was nice to meet you, we'll see what we can find out and be in touch. Is that okay with you?"

"Yes, I guess it is. Thank you both. Hey, please don't tell my dad any of this. If he thinks I'm getting too involved he'll send me to go stay with my grandma for the rest of year even though I'm old enough to do what the hell I want."

She grabbed her purse and strode toward the exit, not looking back.

Maria stared after her, and then turned to Frankie. "Well, what do you make of her?"

"I want to say that she's nuts."

"But you can't, can you, because you think she's on to something."

"Yeah, I think so."

"I do too. I'm telling you now, I really don't want to go back to that house."

"Then what are we going to do? We have to question the old lady who owns the building, you know that, Maria. She's the only link we have and she's lived there for decades. We go together, in the daylight. Neither of us are to go there alone and not after dark."

She stood up. "I need to go home, I'm tired."

"Hey, I need to ask you a favour?"

"What?"

"Will you come dancing with me tomorrow night?"

Maria frowned at him. "Ask Christy."

"It's for Christy, you told me to put some spark back in my marriage. Well, I figured if I learned how to dance for real, I could take her to one of the fancy Christmas balls at The Plaza. Surprise her. What do you say? It's good exercise. You'll be able to burn off that burger and fries you just swallowed whole."

"Do you have a death wish, Frankie?"

He held his hands up.

"If I need to burn the burger off, I'll go for a run, but since this is the first half decent, romantic idea you've ever had, I'll go with you. On one condition."

He grinned. "What?"

 "You don't crush my feet."

He pretended to look hurt.

"I'm going home Frankie, you should do the same. You better get some beauty sleep."

SIXTEEN

GREENWICH VILLAGE, 1952

Emilia had never been so excited to go to the theatre, and it helped that Mae was taking the lead tonight. Who would have thought she'd have such a beautiful and talented friend?

Her brother James had come down from his room in the attic looking frightful, an unhealthy pallor cloaking his face.

"Are you ill James? Do you need a doctor?"

He glared at her. "No, do you?"

"What do you mean by that remark, why would I need a doctor? It's not me who looks like a patient from a tuberculosis hospital."

Realizing how harsh that was, she spoke in a much softer tone. "Why don't you come with me to the theatre and watch Mae? I've seen the way you watch her, you like her. It would do you good to get out of that attic and get some fresh air into your lungs."

He carried on glaring at her. "Does it not strike you as strange how you have suddenly become such good friends with the whore who is sleeping with our father? His place is by Mother's side, not shacked up with a cheap hooker who sleeps with him for his money."

Emilia crossed the room, raised her hand and slapped him hard across the face, leaving an angry red handprint etched into his skin.

"Why do you have to be so mean? You're just like Mom. No wonder Pop would rather spend time with Mae. Go back to your creepy attic where you belong, you don't have a decent bone in your body."

"You'll be sorry, just wait and see." He stormed out of the room down to the kitchen and Emilia wondered what had just happened. She had never struck anyone before and was considering if she should apologize to him when the loud honk of the cab's horn sounded outside. Instead, she went to the front door and ran up the steps to the sidewalk and the waiting car.

She had been given a seat in her father's friend Mr Lawson's private box to watch the show. Seeing Mae on the stage from her own private box would surely calm her down. Then, by the time she came home, she could go and apologize to her brother. The thing was she didn't know if she even wanted to. James had always been jealous of her—and now it seemed he was jealous of Mae.

She got into the cab and pushed all thoughts of her strange brother out of her mind. If he was that bothered about Mom, he could go back and be with her. Emilia couldn't understand why he'd come into the city anyway. It wasn't as if he had any business or friends to catch up with. He'd always been such a loner —and judging by the way he was carrying on, he always would be.

* * *

James heard the heavy oak door slam and ran to the window to watch. His sister was getting far too big for her breeches, but not for long. He would be putting an end to that very soon. How dare she think she could strike him across the face and not pay a penalty? This Mae was having a bad influence on her and the sooner he killed her the better. Mom would thank him for it when she knew what had been going on. She would be more than a little upset to discover her husband was sleeping around so openly. Maybe he should kill him too, take all three of them out in one go. But he only needed three bodies and it might throw things out of order if he killed his father too. Three was the magic number. Three was the devil's way of throwing his scorn on the holy trinity. By killing his father, assuming he could even overpower him, it might ruin what he was trying to do and it would all have been for nothing.

He went back upstairs to his attic room, for he had many things to prepare. He took the Ouija board from under his bed and put it on the table. He took the planchette out of the drawer, his hand trembling as he lifted it to his eye and checked whether it was watching him. Slowly moving around the room while staring through the small wooden planchette, his mouth felt dry. This time there was nothing there. No dark, smoky shadows lingering in the corners. No strange-looking creatures, which considering the anger and hatred that was bubbling inside of him, he found surprising.

He swung around to the sound of a long, drawn-out scratching sound behind him. With the planchette still held up to his face, he stumbled backwards. A huge, black, beast was standing in front of him. His blood turned to iced water in his veins as his heart pumped it around his body faster, turning him into a shivering wreck. The thing had its back to him and for that he was grateful. He wasn't prepared for this yet.

He stepped backwards away from it. Banging into the small table behind him, he dropped the planchette. Frantically searching the floor, he panicked. Without it, he couldn't see the beast, didn't know where it was. As he scrabbled on the floor to grab the planchette, he felt hot, rotten breath on his face.

Looking up, there was nothing in front of him, yet he knew different. He could smell it, inches from him.

James had never felt terror so extreme in his life. He wasn't ready. When he wanted it to appear, it would be on his terms; he would be in control. The whole point of this was that the creature would be grateful to him for summoning it from the depths of hell and it would want to do whatever he told it to appease him. It wasn't here on its terms.

Every hair on his arms stood on edge as the sharp pain of gut-wrenching dread made him double over. The air was charged with static electricity and for a moment he thought this was it. Was his life about to end? All his planning would be wiped out with one swift blow from the demon standing in front of him.

He closed his eyes, forcing his dry mouth to open as he whispered.

"Beast, be gone. You will not return until I summon you. You are not to come and go as you please. By the power vested in me as the one who will bring you back, I command you to leave. Your time is almost here; we have to be ready, or the ritual won't be a success and you will be forever stuck half in this world and half in the dark."

The room felt lighter, the smell gone, and his heart began to slow down. Opening his eyes, he lifted the planchette to use as his mirror to the other world. This time he saw nothing through it; no dark shadows and no terrifying beast. For now, it was safe, and the space was his once more.

He needed to toughen up if he wanted to do this. How could he command a demon from the depths of hell if he couldn't raise his voice above a whisper?

* * *

Emilia gave a standing ovation. She thought Mae had been amazing. She had turned into someone else on the stage, even more captivating than her usual glamourous self.

Making her way from the private box, Emilia was met at the side of the stage by a young boy of no more than fourteen. He looked at her and grinned.

"You must be Mae's friend, she sent me to find you."

He held out his hand and she grasped hold of it, shaking it.

"I'm Billy, you can call me Bill. I work here every night. I'm going to be on that stage soon."

"Well hello Bill, I'm Emilia. I can't wait to see you up there."

He laughed. "Come on, she's waiting for you. She told me not to talk too much."

He turned and Emilia followed him to the far end of the first floor and a door which led to a stairwell. He ran down to a door with a gold star bearing her name, *Mae*. Emilia tried to imagine how marvellous it would feel to be like her friend: full of confidence and beautiful. Lifting her hand to knock, she paused as a sense of terrible foreboding fell over her like a black shadow. It clung to her making her feel sick and dizzy. Her knuckles grazed the wood as she fell against it; her legs felt as if they didn't belong to her. The door opened, and she fell into Mae's arms. She let out a scream as Mae caught her and then the room went black.

SEVENTEEN

PRESENT DAY

Miss Green was shuffling to the elevator when Maria pushed her way through the glass doors of the lobby. Maria caught up with her and did a double take.

"Miss Green, what's the matter?" She'd never seen the old lady with no make-up or jewellery on, ever.

Her neighbor didn't look at Maria. "Today isn't a good day."

Maria felt her heart tear in two. In all the years she'd known her, whenever she'd asked her how she was she always replied, *Today is a good day*.

Maria gently entwined her arm through the old woman's and pressed the call button. "Come on, why I don't I make us a nice pot of tea and you can tell me what's wrong?"

Miss Green nodded, still not looking at her, and for the first time in forever it struck Maria just how old and frail she was. There was so much running through her head. She was afraid to find out what was wrong in case it was something that no amount of tea could help.

The rickety elevator finally came to a stop on the ground floor, the doors rattled open, and they both stepped inside. Maria pushed the button for their floor, and as it ascended,

Maria could feel the burger she'd eaten earlier moving around in her stomach. She waited for the elevator to judder to a halt and took hold of Miss Green's elbow and led her down to her apartment, where she took the old lady's keys, opened the door for her and followed her in. Maria pointed to the armchair and went to the kitchen counter to switch the kettle on.

"You're a good girl, far too good to be living on your own. You deserve a nice man or woman—whatever you prefer to keep you warm in bed each night."

Maria laughed. "I do. We both do. Although there's a lot to be said for being single. I like being able to eat what I want and watch crappy cable shows all day in my sweats."

Miss Green looked up, her watery eyes fixed on Maria. "I do too, but when you get to my age it gets lonely. It's all very well pretending you're happy doing your own thing, but wouldn't you like to have someone waiting for you when you got in from work? You work so hard, doing a terrible job. I can't begin to imagine the horrors of what you must face every day. You are very brave and deserve to be taken care of—why don't you find yourself a rich boyfriend. There's no shame in being a kept woman if it's mutually acceptable and makes you happy."

Maria laughed and carried two mugs of tea over to the coffee table, then she went back and grabbed the half-eaten packet of Oreos from the cupboard and put them on a plate. When Miss Green picked one up and started nibbling on it, Maria smiled; she really was a woman after her own heart.

"Thank you, dear, I've just realized how hungry I am."

"You're welcome. Can I fix you a sandwich?"

"These are just fine, I'm partial to a chocolate cookie."

They sat there in silence, both sipping their tea, Maria waiting for the opportunity to ask what was wrong. She didn't have to wait long.

"I bet you think I'm crazy, look at the state of me. I didn't even put my lipstick on before I left the house."

"You look fabulous with or without it."

The woman's cheeks turned pink, and she laughed.

"You're a sweetheart. I was about to put my make-up on when the letter came, out of the blue; just like that, it was pushed under the door. So, it must have been hand delivered. I knew it must be something bad and I should have thrown it in the trash like my brain was telling me to. I didn't. My inquisitive nature got the better of me and now look what a sorry state I'm in."

Maria sipped her tea, waiting for her to continue. Miss Green pulled a letter out of her purse and passed it to her. She read the single sentence, again and again. Trying to understand what it might mean and couldn't. The words filled her mind.

It's come back.

Maria held it out toward Miss Green who shook her head.

"Please would you be a sweetheart and get rid of it for me, I can't bear to think about it."

"What does it mean? Who sent it?"

The old woman stared at her. "It means that someone has been dabbling in black magic, messing with things they have no concept of. When I finally fled that house I'd lived in for years, I hoped I'd never have to go back. I saw things with my own two eyes that I never knew existed. Things that I never want to see again. Something that I swore I would never talk about ever again."

The hairs on the back of Maria's neck were standing on end and she felt as if a dark cloud had descended over her. She'd spent most of her life oblivious to anything remotely paranormal and now twice in one day, she was discussing it like it was nothing new. She looked around the apartment, surprised to see how dark and gloomy it was in here despite the lights being on.

"You can tell me. It might make you feel better to get it off your chest."

"I wouldn't drag you into this, you're much safer kept out of it."

"I'm a cop, it's my job. I chase the bad guys and the killers every day. Hell, I shoot them if I have to, and I don't think twice about it because they're *bad* guys. Please let me help you Miss Green, I want to help."

A single tear fell from the corner of her eye, and she shook her head. "You are a good girl, Maria, God knows this, and He will look after you. Don't ever doubt that." She pushed herself up from the table. "Come on, off you go. You have your own life to live and I'm just being a silly, morbid, old fool. I'll have a large brandy and go to bed. Tomorrow is another day. I'll forget about that stupid note and make sure I put my lipstick on."

She winked at Maria who smiled and stood up. "Well, I'm only across the hall if you need to talk to me, even if it's in the middle of the night. You just call or give me a knock."

"Thank you, I will."

"Promise?"

"I'll be fine. Thank you for taking the time to listen to a crazy, old bat like me ramble on. I swear, even though it sounds it, I'm not senile just yet."

Maria bent and kissed her cheek. "I know you're not and I'm serious about you calling me." She walked toward the front door, sensing that Miss Green needed to be on her own.

Maria shut the door behind her and waited to hear the dead bolt turn before heading into her own apartment. She kicked off her shoes and turned on all the lights. If she hadn't been creeped out enough before, she was now. Not bothering to turn the TV on she switched the radio on instead and began to check each room. She felt as if she was being watched. Changing into her pyjamas and pouring herself a large glass of wine, she picked up a notebook from the table. Then sitting crossed-legged on the sofa, she began to write down a list of everything weird that had happened to her today. She felt compelled to keep a record of it because she'd never experienced anything remotely similar and worried that her mind would try to block it out and make her forget something that could be important to the case.

The lively chatter on the radio interspersed with a selection of pop songs took away some of her unease. The wine helped as well, as she wrote down what had happened at the house on West 10th followed the bizarre conversation with Miss Green. She questioned whether there was some connection. But how could there be? She hadn't told anyone except Frankie about the house. It was all just some weird coincidence, nothing more.

She sipped the wine, questioning her beliefs in the paranormal. It wasn't something that she'd ever had to think about before. She didn't believe in stuff like that, being a black and white, say-what-you-see kind of girl.

Yeah, but what about saying how you feel, Maria? You know there was something up in that attic apartment. You felt it, you heard it, Christ, you smelled it. Are you going to deny how scared you were? Maybe Miss Green and that house aren't connected; maybe you're the connection? Her entire body shuddered at the thought. She needed to take her mind off it, needed to relax, or she was never going to sleep.

She thought about the girl who was the reason she was involved in this. If they could finally trace who did the tattoo, they might be able to identify her. Three years ago they had tried, but it had come to nothing. She picked up the phone and waited to see if Frankie would answer but it went through to voicemail. She then picked up her iPad and began to search tattoo shops specializing in floral work, writing down the names of the ones that looked a possibility judging by the photos on the website. By the time she was done, she was beginning to fade. Downing the rest of the wine, she grabbed the throw off the back of the sofa and lay down, an overwhelming feeling of exhaustion making her yawn. Wrapping herself in it, she closed her eyes and hoped that sleep would come fast. The sound of the radio and the dim lights she'd left on illuminated her flat, enough to make her feel safe.

EIGHTEEN

The hammering on Maria's apartment door was so loud she jumped off the couch, confused. Her heart racing, she felt fearful of what could be wrong. She ran to the door, her first thought being her neighbor, and peered through the peephole to see Frankie standing there. His shirt buttons undone, sleeves rolled up and his eyes glassy. Relieved it wasn't Miss Green, she began to slide back the assortment of bolts and chains, opening the door. She looked at the clock on the wall realizing it was almost two am.

"What the hell, Frankie? You scared the living crap out of me."

He grinned. "You rang me and then I couldn't get hold of you. I was worried. Sorry about scaring you. I also need somewhere to stay, I'm locked out."

She stepped back to let him in, and he stumbled past her, the sour smell of bourbon turning her stomach.

"Where have you been? When I left you a couple of hours ago you were on your way home to Christy to be a better husband? How did you get in this state?"

He laughed. "She ripped my head off as soon as I walked

through the door. She's a monster, Maria. I just couldn't face her anymore; left and went back to the Cat." He collapsed onto the sofa.

Maria let out a sigh and turning around, began to fill the percolator to brew a pot of fresh coffee.

"I need to pee." She turned to see him stumbling along to the bathroom. He was going to need an IV of black coffee pumped straight into his veins to sober him up. Remembering that he hadn't eaten, she began to make him a sandwich. He needed carbs in his stomach.

The noise of the percolator disguised his return and she screeched to see him standing behind her. "What the hell, Frankie!"

"I'm not that ugly."

She smiled. "You're not ugly at all."

"Then why doesn't Christy ever want me?"

He reached out a hand and touched her cheek. "You're beautiful, Maria, I love you."

For a moment she was tempted to kiss him; he was very attractive, and she liked him a lot—more than she should. She came to her senses and pushed his hand away. "Yeah, you've got beer goggles on. Tell me that when you're sober."

He lowered his hand, the moment gone, and smiled at her, but the smile didn't reach his eyes like it normally did. It was the saddest smile she'd ever seen—and it broke her heart a little.

She passed him the sandwich. "Eat this, or you're gonna be barfing all day."

"Thanks. Sorry for waking you up."

She carried two mugs over, placing his on the coffee table. Nursing hers, she sat back down on the armchair. He stuck his thumb up at her as he tried to eat his sandwich without making too much mess. She sipped at her coffee, trying not to watch him, wondering if she would be able to get back to sleep. She wasn't angry with him; in fact, she was glad of the company.

He'd woken her from a dream; she'd been terrified, about to go back into the house on West 10th.

Frankie finished his sandwich and Maria passed him the mug.

"Good job we're not on an early shift tomorrow."

"Old Addison has done us a favour. No fresh meat for a while."

But Maria had a gnawing feeling that this was just the start, and they were about to get involved in something she'd never dreamed about even in her darkest nightmares.

Frankie finished his coffee and kicked his shoes off. "Can I sleep on here?"

"Of course. I'm going to bed. Take your pants off or they'll be creased to shit—and don't tell me you're not wearing boxers because, if you aren't, leave the damn things on."

He let out a loud laugh. "I'm wearing underwear."

"Good to hear, get some sleep."

He saluted her, his eyes closing before he'd even laid down. She shook her head and left him to it, going to her bedroom. She closed the door to the sound of his gentle snoring, wondering if she should text Christy and let her know he was okay. She decided against it. Frankie was a hard-working, decent man and Christy did treat him like crap. He was too good for her. Maybe she needed to realize that and stop taking him for granted. Christy didn't know how lucky she was to have a husband who loved her so much.

Being single had never really bothered Maria, but she didn't know if it was the events of the last few days, or the wine, but she couldn't help wondering how nice it would be to have someone to snuggle up to and take her out on dates. She climbed into her bed, this time turning out the light. She felt safer knowing Frankie was asleep on her couch, even if he was in a drunken stupor.

. . .

Maria reached out to press snooze as her alarm went off what felt like only minutes later. Her eyes didn't want to open. No wonder, when she remembered her late-night visit. Forcing herself to get out of bed, she walked out of the bedroom to the smell of bacon crisping on the griddle. She took one look at Frankie, who apart from having dark circles under his eyes and a pair of crumpled pants looked better than she did, and no sign of a hangover.

"Morning. Sorry about last night, Maria. Was I a complete asshole?"

"No, not at all." She wasn't sure whether she was mad or envious of him; if she'd drank that amount of bourbon, she'd be in bed for a week feeling sorry for herself.

"I shouldn't have come here, but thank you for letting me in. I appreciate it."

He passed her a plate of food which she took from him.

"Thank you. Are you not feeling like crap?"

"Well, apart from a headache and my mouth feeling like it's been licking the men's locker room floor at the station, no. I'm good."

"Jeez, if I'd consumed that much I'd be dying. So, have you spoken to Christy?"

"Not yet, I'm going to go home and apologize. Then ask her what the hell is wrong with her."

"Don't get angry with her, keep calm. And if you two aren't getting on you know you can sleep on the couch here, don't you?"

He smiled. "Thanks Maria, I don't know what I'd do without you."

"If you're going to cook me breakfast every day it's to my advantage. I'm being completely selfish."

He crossed the room and bending down, kissed her on the cheek. "I'll see you later. I need a shower, some pain killers and a couple of hours in my own bed. We can decide what we're going to do later."

He let himself out and she wished that Addison had never given them the cold case to work. No matter what, she just could not shake the bad feeling that was hanging over her.

NINETEEN

Maria knocked on Miss Green's door, waiting to hear the familiar shuffling of her feet along the hallway. When she finally heard the old lady after a couple of knocks, Maria released the breath she'd been holding.

"Who is it?"

"Maria, just checking you're okay."

"I am thank you, I look a frightful state so I'm not going to open the door and scare you."

Maria chuckled. "You couldn't look a state if you tried. I'm going out now. Do you need anything?"

"No thank you, I'll see you later, honey."

"Bye."

Glad her neighbor hadn't given herself a coronary in the middle of the night, she left to go to the New York Public Library on Fifth Avenue. A man was sat on the bottom steps of her apartment building, talking on his cell. It wasn't exactly sit-on-your-ass-on-a-marble-step kind of weather.

He stood up as she passed him. "Maria."

She turned to him and shook her head as it dawned on her. "Tell me, Mr Williams, a busy man such as yourself must have better things to do than hang around outside my apartment block?"

She stared at him, her arms crossed waiting for his answer.

"I haven't been here long and to be honest with you, not today: it's my day off."

She scanned the road for his fancy town car. There wasn't one. He wasn't dressed in a suit either today and was more casual in a pair of sweats and sneakers.

He smiled at her. "Look, all I want is to buy you a coffee, maybe get to know each other a little. You never know, when you have a conversation with me you might not think I'm such an asshole."

"I never said you were. I said there were laws against this kind of behavior; it's called stalking in case you're not familiar with it."

He held his hands up. "Sorry, I guess I am a little weird. I sincerely wanted to thank you. I like you and I'm not used to not getting what I want. So, I am an asshole, but I'm also extremely grateful for what you did the other day. You'll be pleased to know I've hired another security guard. You don't expect that sort of stuff to happen. I get the message, hopefully I'll see you around. Bye, Maria."

He turned and began walking away, and instead of doing what her head was telling her, she followed her heart and ran after him.

"I'm going to the public library to do some research. You can buy me a coffee in there if you want." She looked down at his feet and laughed to see his shiny, new Nikes. "You came prepared today?"

His cheeks turned pink. "I did."

"Come on then, you can break your sneakers in."

They walked toward Washington Square Park. Even though it was winter, it was still busy. Maria liked Central Park, but she loved the atmosphere here. There were always the same faces mingled in with the tourists, and some of the buskers were talented. In fact, on many a warm summers night, she'd sit here with a cool drink and a book in her hand, people watching and listening to performers who were worthy of Broadway. She paused to listen to Marvin playing the piano that he wheeled there himself whenever the mood took him. His bright blond spiky hair always perfect, he nodded at her, and she mouthed, *Morning*. She pulled a ten dollar note from her pocket and felt Harrison's hand on hers.

"Let me."

She watched as he pulled two fifties out of his pocket and pushed them into the cap on the top of the piano. Marvin's eyes widened and Maria winked at him as he carried on playing and she still put her ten dollar note in. He blew her a kiss and she laughed, then waved and carried on walking.

"That was very kind of you."

"You're not angry?"

"No, if you can afford it then it's nice. So long as you're not just showing off for my benefit. And besides, Marvin deserves it. He lets Sam—one of the homeless veterans who sleeps in the park—sing along next to him when he's in the mood to. Then he gives Sam some of the money people have given them. He's one of the good guys."

"He's talented as well."

"He is, extremely. I've never heard anyone play a rickety old piano like Marvin. Sometimes he moves me to tears with his music."

They carried on walking up Fifth toward the library. It was a fair distance and she wondered if Harrison was regretting his decision to accompany her. She stole a glance at him; he looked happy enough.

"So why aren't you at work today? Is it your rest day?"

"I wish. Frankie, my partner, turned up drunk in the early

hours and slept on my sofa. He's gone home to make it up to his wife and sort himself out, so we're working a late shift."

Maria wondered if she should have told him about Frankie's business, but if Harrison wanted to be friends with her, then Frankie was a big part of her life. He needed to know this, not find out later on.

"Frankie is lucky to have you, I take it you're good friends?"

She didn't detect any jealousy or anger in his voice, which was good. He seemed genuinely interested.

"Yes, we are. In our field, you have to be able to trust your partner; your life depends on it. He's like an older brother and my best friend rolled into one."

"That's good to know. I like him already. You have a dangerous job, Maria. What made you decide to become a cop?"

He took her by surprise with his answer about Frankie. She'd thought there might be some Alpha male thing going on, even though she belonged to no one but herself. Although her loyalty would always be to Frankie, she found herself warming to the man next to her. She didn't know Harrison Williams any better than she knew Marvin the busker but he was surprising her—and in a pleasant way.

"I like helping people. I don't like seeing nice people having their lives ripped apart for someone else's pleasure. It pays well, and my customer service skills leave a lot to be desired."

He let out a loud laugh. "You're also very honest, I like that." He stared up Fifth as they walked against the crowd of tourists heading down toward the Empire State Building. Maria smiled.

"You don't walk much, do you?" She didn't intend it as a criticism; she just knew he'd have a suite of luxury cars and driver at his disposal. In contrast, Maria walked everywhere because it was cheaper, and she hated driving in the madness of the city. The never-ending symphony of car horns drove her insane. But if she could afford her own driver, then she probably wouldn't be walking either.

"Not really. I play squash, I swim, I'm not into the whole gym culture although there's a pretty decent one at the office. At least that's what the staff say, I don't really go in there."

The beautiful building of the New York Public Library came into view, and she thought she heard Harrison sigh with relief. They went up the stone steps and joined the queue to get inside. When it was their turn, she smiled at the security guard, who stepped forward and hugged her.

"Maria, where have you been?"

She laughed. "Working."

"You tell them not to work you too hard, takings are down over at the café."

"Abe, you are far too cheeky for your own good." He winked at her, and she carried on walking through. Harrison following her to the small café tucked beneath the grand staircase. He was looking around, his mouth open.

"It's beautiful in here, I had no idea."

"Please don't tell me that you live in this city and have never visited."

He shook his head, and she rolled her eyes at him. "What about the Empire State and Rockefeller?"

She watched as his cheeks began to burn for the second time. "I've been to functions in the Rainbow Room and the NBC studios, had meetings in the Empire..."

She tutted. "You live in this amazing city, with some of the most wonderful buildings and landmarks in the world, and you've never visited them, been to the top of them to take in the views?"

"I don't do tourist stuff." His voice was defensive, and she began to laugh.

"I'm not criticizing you. I just can't believe you've never

been. I love the Top of the Rock, it's my favorite view of the city, plus, you can see the Empire from there."

"You surprise me, Maria, I thought as a tough New York City cop the last thing you'd want to do is to visit the tourist attractions."

"Yeah, well, I think it's important to love where you live. I love New York, I love the buildings, the architecture and the history. I feel as if I'm pretty blessed to be here."

"I've never thought of it like that."

"But you like the library and that's probably full of more tourists than New Yorkers."

"Yes, it's stunning. I had no idea."

She turned so he couldn't see the smile on her face and went to order. The woman behind the small kiosk greeted Maria with the same amount of cheer that the security guard had shown her. She returned with two large coffees and placed one in front of him.

"I took a guess and got you an Americano." She couldn't stop the laughter which erupted from her mouth. "Sorry, it's not funny. I just have you down as an Americano kind of guy."

He began to laugh. "So, what were you coming here for?"

"I need to do some research on a property."

"Can't you do that at work? Surely you have all sorts of information there you can't get in here."

"Not this type of research. I actually come here because I have a thing for libraries; I find them soothing, relaxing. The whole atmosphere is one of tranquillity—plus, I love reading. I spent hours in here as a kid; it was warm and safer than being outside on the streets. What is this anyway? All we've done is talk about me. Are you a stalker?"

"No, I'm not, I'm just not used to doing the talking, especially about myself. I guess you could say I'm a bit of a spoiled brat. I always get what I want."

"And what is it that you want, Mr Williams?"

He took a sip of his coffee, then looked her in the eye. "You Maria, only I wasn't expecting it to be so difficult."

Maria stared at his face, trying to read whether he was being serious or was just not used to getting what he wanted. "Are you saying that you thought I'd be easy and throw myself at you because you're the big 'I Am'?"

He squirmed and she realized that was exactly what he'd thought.

"Well, now you know that I'm not that kind of girl, to be honest I never have been. Your money or status doesn't interest me. I've dealt with millionaires who have battered their wives and lovers to within an inch of their lives. I don't care if you're homeless or on the *Forbes* Rich List, if you treat me with respect, I'll be respectful back. You need to know that you can't buy me. I'm not for sale and never will be. If I like someone, I'll be their friend. That's it."

He stared at her completely in awe. "So, if I offered you a chauffeur-driven car and a penthouse apartment in The Waldorf when the renovations are done, you'd turn it down?"

"Don't get me wrong, I'd be crazy not to be tempted. Hell, The Waldorf is my favorite of all the hotels, and it broke my heart that they've shut it down. But it would be a definite no."

He grinned at her. "So, if I wanted to take you out for a date, where would we go?"

"That would be telling, you'll have to work it out for yourself."

"So, can I take you out on a date?"

"Why? I'm not in your league, I never will be. There must be a queue of society girls with good manners all lined up to be the next Mrs. Williams."

It was his turn to laugh. "Yep, there probably is. I'm not after a Mrs. Williams though, I want a woman I can take on dates, have fun, and enjoy my life with. I just want to have someone to talk to if I've had a shitty day without worrying they'll sell my story to the *New York Times* before sunrise."

"I can understand that; I suppose being rich can be a right pain in the ass at times."

"More than you know. So, what do you say, Maria, if I can come up with a date you'll enjoy, will you accompany me? No strings attached, just a fun evening."

"If it's not something horrific—don't bother flying me to the opera in San Francisco, I hate opera. But yes, I suppose I would."

He looked at her blankly.

"*Pretty Woman*. Richard Gere flies Julia Roberts to the opera. You never seen it?" He shook his head and she laughed. "Forget it, just a joke."

He finished his coffee and stood up. "I have to go, I'm already late for an appointment. May I have your number so I can call you with the details?"

She pulled a notepad and pen from her purse, ripped a sheet of paper out and wrote her details down. "Nothing too fancy; I don't like fancy food. And I thought it was your day off?"

"Leave it with me, I like a challenge and it is sort of, but I still have stuff to do. Take care, Maria, and thanks for the coffee."

"You're welcome."

He turned and walked toward the exit, leaving her watching him. A glimmer of excitement tingled as the butterflies in her stomach got the better of her. It would be nice to have a no-strings-attached relationship, she could go with that. It would do her good to have a bit of fun after work, someone to talk to without having to marry them and be stuck with them for the rest of her life. Frankie would no doubt disagree, but he had his own crappy marriage to sort out. She couldn't wait forever for him to decide to divorce Christy, although after last night it looked as if the cracks were getting too much for him. She loved him, but it would be too much effort juggling work and a relationship for them both. One of them would have to move departments and it wouldn't be her. For now, she would let Harrison Williams take her out for some fun and see where it went from there.

Standing up, she made her way to the Rose Main Reading Room. The light streamed in through the windows making the beautiful chandeliers sparkle. Maria had stared at them numerous times in her teenage years whilst sitting at one of the long, wooden tables with a pile of books. Nowhere made her feel the way this library did. It felt like home, like her security blanket. When she was lost, she would gravitate here knowing that she would be safe nestled amongst the shelves lined with books, under a ceiling covered in pink, fluffy clouds and celestial cherubs watching over her. She made her way to the desk and asked the librarian for books on the history of Greenwich Village, particularly the 1950s, then waited patiently to be pointed in the right direction.

TWENTY

Maria ran her finger along the lines of the leather-bound antique book. It was exactly what she'd hoped for: a history of Greenwich Village in the 1950s. There was a chapter about the house and the murder, which she read, horrified. The wealthy family who owned it had lived a nice, happy life until the day it was all turned upside down.

Gina was right; the newspaper articles and the book confirmed that the murders were very similar to their cold case from three years ago. Both women had had their heads and limbs removed. It made Maria feel sick just thinking about the level of violence used by the killers. This was next level stuff—and she'd attended some horrific murders since she'd first become a cop.

She picked up the other book she had spotted on the shelves when searching for information on the occult and devil worship. As she turned the first page, a cool chill settled across her shoulders. Flicking through the book, she could not shake the feeling of something dark hanging over her. Slamming the pages shut, she pushed it as far away from her as possible and picked up the history book instead, trying to focus her mind on the murders.

Either they had a geriatric serial killer on their hands or a copycat. But if it was the latter, how would they have found out about the murder in the fifties? Unless they were a bit of a history buff or had been told about it by a relative. Once more, the feeling of being watched made the skin on the back of her neck crawl and she lifted her head to see if anyone was blatantly staring. The room was relatively empty, which was a first in all the times she had been there. A couple of students were both working on laptops at the far end, headphones pushed into their ears. An older woman was sat a few rows in front of Maria, but none of them were looking in her direction.

Maria turned to take in the magnificent room and see if there was anyone trying to hide that might be watching her. There wasn't, and yet nevertheless, a coldness enveloped her from behind as if some invisible person was giving her an icy embrace.

Closing the book, she pushed her chair back, scraping it along the tiled floor. She jumped up. Her chest felt as if there was a pair of huge arms pressing against it, suffocating her. For a moment she thought she was about to have a heart attack and die. It was hard to breathe, the cold band was pressing so tight against her lungs, squeezing hard. She did the only thing she could think of and began to pray. If she was going to die on her own, here, she wanted God to acknowledge it. She hadn't been to church for years, not since her dad had died way too young. She'd been angry with God about taking him from her. Even so, he wouldn't abandon her, would he?

Finally, the woman in front of her turned around to stare at Maria with the blackest eyes she'd ever seen. Their eyes locked, Maria unable to speak, pleading with God to help her while the woman stared straight back at her as if she was looking into the depths of her soul. The shrill ringing of her cell phone snapped

Maria's attention away, and she felt a surge of relief as she gasped and took in a huge mouthful of air. Her oxygen-deprived lungs were on fire. Grabbing her purse, she pulled out her cell and began to walk toward the exit. She had to get out of here, away from the suffocating atmosphere and the woman with the black eyes that looked like chasms big enough to suck her soul right out of her body.

Shaking, Maria reached the stairs and ran down them, pushing her way through the entrance to the library, which was now full and out of the exit. Abe was nowhere to be seen, not that she'd tell him what had just happened; she didn't know herself. She was either having some kind of medical episode or she had experienced her second strange encounter in as many days.

Outside, she felt the warmth of the sun on her face. Standing to one side for a moment beside the huge marble lions, Patience and Fortitude, she placed her hand on the lion closest to her and took in deep breaths of air whilst rubbing her other hand across her chest. It felt sore: the pressure on it had been so great, it was as if it she was being crushed. Maria decided it might be time to pay a visit to church; it wouldn't hurt to catch the early evening mass at St. Joseph's. The feeling of being watched wasn't as intense now she was out in the fresh air—if you could call the traffic fumes that. But she couldn't shake it off completely and she didn't like it one bit.

She began the walk back down Fifth to head back to her apartment, again feeling that knot of fear in her heart that she had inadvertently stumbled upon something that she didn't understand, nor did she want to. Supernatural, paranormal, psychic, whatever you wanted to call it, she had never been remotely interested in anything of the sort. Yet how else did you explain what had happened to her? It was crazy and she would be the first to laugh and twirl her finger at the side of her head if Frankie began to tell her this kind of crap. Maybe she was ill.

She could have some disease that was fucking with her mind. Before she even considered telling Frankie, she was going to go for a medical to get her ticker checked out to be sure. She'd been due one two months ago and cancelled because she'd been too busy. Before she could change her mind, she called the doctor's office to book the next available appointment.

TWENTY-ONE

He'd slept in his van after the nightmare because it was too overwhelming inside the apartment. The nightmares were too much and when he was in there he felt as if every ounce of his energy was being drained, which it was. He had no doubt about it. The creature—he wasn't going to call it by his real name because he wasn't strong enough to deal with the consequences —thrived off his energy; a vampire of sorts gaining power from his body.

He kept the Ouija board tucked under the front seat, the planchette in his backpack. It was too dangerous but, when at least he was away from the apartment, he could think much clearer. He was messing around with powerful forces, ones he didn't truly conceive of yet, but he couldn't stop, as much as he wanted to. It was like an addictive drug. And the time he spent inside the attic was unaccounted for. He had no recollection of the last day he'd spent in there and this scared him almost as much as the thought of a beast from the depths of hell breathing down his neck and watching him in the dead of night.

He lay there in his sleeping bag in the back of the van, sandwiched between his worldly belongings, and wondered if he

should forget it all. Burn the board and planchette; forget about
the house, the creature, the power, the evil, and drive out of the
city. He could head toward Coney Island, find somewhere there
to park up. He'd always loved the amusement park, the board-
walk and the beach. Then he remembered it was winter, the
park would be closed, and it wasn't exactly camp-on-the-beach
kind of weather.

The voice whispered inside his head. *You won't have to run
ever again. Whatever you want will be yours.* There was the
attraction. He had never had much of anything growing up and
this thing was promising him the world.

Why had it chosen him? It didn't matter. He knew now that
wherever he ran to, it would follow him. He had no choice but
to do as it wished and set it free.

He hadn't realized he'd been chewing his nails until he felt
the sharp pain of tearing skin. He looked down at the ragged
piece of nail and skin, a thin line of blood running down his
finger. It was stinging, so he shook it. Not sure what he was
going to do next he saw a woman on the sidewalk, laughing at
someone on the other end of her cell. He recognized her as the
cop who'd been going into the house as he'd come around the
side. Afraid to move in case he caught her attention, he watched
her. She was pretty but looked as if she wouldn't take any crap.

For the first time in forever, he felt a stirring in his loins. She
was his type. It was a shame he wouldn't be hers. He hadn't
thought about women and sex since Anya. He wore the guilt
like a cloak because he had liked her a lot. There had been a
time—it seemed like a lifetime ago—that he'd been a regular Joe.
But not anymore. His head was always full of blackness; there
wasn't much room inside it for the normal kind of thoughts men
his age had.

The voice whispered once again inside his mind. *She will be
yours, to do as you please.* He liked the thought of that. He could
take her to the apartment and show her a good time.

He got out of the van and began following her, keeping a distance. He needed to know where she lived; it couldn't be too far away from here. As she cut through Washington Square Park and exited onto Thompson Street, he hung back a little. If she was as good a cop as he thought she was, she might realize he was following her. She stopped at the corner of Sullivan Street and headed up toward Miss Lily's. His stomach was groaning. He never felt like eating in the apartment, but out on the street he'd worked up an appetite. Checking that no one was watching him, he began to stroll up to the bakery. He wanted a fresh bagel and coffee, so he could sit and watch from there. He had a feeling she was close to home, and by the time he reached the doorway of the busy shop, she was already coming back out. He put his head down and waited for her to pass, then went inside.

Watching her through the windows, her saw her walk across the street to a rundown apartment block opposite. He would be a little surprised if this was where she lived; he'd pictured her in a nice apartment over on Hudson. Pulling a crumpled ten-dollar bill from his pocket, he paid for his bagel and coffee then sat on the bench by the window looking onto the building. His mind was working overtime. Was she visiting or was she working? If she was visiting, she'd have had two coffees, yet she only had the one. Maybe she did live here after all, which made it a whole lot easier for him.

He scanned the building but could see no security cameras. He'd have to check the rest of the street for CCTV when he left.

Miss Lily's had just become his favorite new place to hang out, and although he didn't have much money to waste, it was cheap enough. He had no rent to pay, so he could linger with a coffee and look like a struggling student. The area was full of them. NYU was only a short distance from here. He unwrapped the foil from his bagel and began to take small bites, an expert at making his food last. As long as he was eating and drinking, they couldn't ask him to leave. He turned his head to check. It was busy anyway. Lunchtime rush, no one was paying him the slightest bit of attention. And these days that was exactly how he liked it.

TWENTY-TWO

JUNE 1952

"Em, Em! Can you hear me?" Mae turned around to the kid. "Don't just stand there, Bill, go get help. What's wrong with her?"

He shrugged, unable to take his eyes off the pretty lady who was now lying flat out on the chaise longue. Mae pushed him. "Go, now."

She turned back to her friend whose face was now the color of alabaster. Mae felt awful. She didn't know what was going on and bent down to listen and see if she was breathing. She was. She then started gently prodding her to get a reaction but there was nothing – she was like sleeping beauty. Breathing, but unconscious. There were tiny beads of perspiration on Emilia's forehead. Billy barged in through the door again, making Mae jump. He had Beatrice the wardrobe mistress in tow. She took one look at the girl on the chair and shook her head.

"She's passed out. Has she been drinking?"

Mae looked at her. "I don't know, I don't think so. She doesn't smell of booze."

Beatrice went to the tiny sink in the corner of the room and filled up the small glass that was balanced on the shelf above it. Walking back to the chair she threw it over Emilia's face.

Mae gasped. "I can't believe you did that."

Beatrice shrugged and pointed at the casualty whose eyelids were now flickering. "It worked didn't it. Sometimes you gotta be cruel to be kind, kid."

Mae grabbed a dry washcloth and began to pat Em's wet face. Her eyes opened wide, and she stared at Mae confused.

"Where am I? What happened?"

Beatrice spoke first. "You passed out, kid, have you been drinking?"

Emilia shook her head, then gulped. "No, I haven't. I feel terrible."

"Well then, you need to start eating more, skinny is not worth dying for. What if you passed out in front of a bus? Bang, end of story. Look after yourself, eh?" With that, the older woman turned and walked out leaving them all looking at each other. Emilia pushed herself so she was sitting upright.

"I'm sorry, Mae, I only wanted to tell you how wonderful you were."

Mae laughed. "Jeez, you gave me the fright of my life. Look, my hands are shaking." She held up her trembling hands. "Can you stand? I think we should get you home."

Emilia tried to stand. Her legs were as shaky as Mae's hands. Mae grabbed one arm and shouted to Billy. "Grab her other arm, we'll walk her out and get a cab." He did as he was told, gently taking hold of her between them, and they marched Emilia out of the backstage entrance. Billy hailed a cab and helped Mae walk her to it.

"Thank you, Billy," Mae said through the open window.

"I hope you feel better soon, Miss," he said, a small smile on his lips. Then he turned and raced back to the theatre.

The cab driver looked at them in the rear-view mirror. "Where to, ladies?"

Mae leaned forward. "West 10th Street, please."

Emilia placed her head back against the cool leather of the seat. Even though it was warm in the cab, she was icy cold. Her head felt as if it was all a mess inside; she wanted to go to bed, to curl up in a ball and sleep. She watched as the busy streets passed by in a blur, Mae chattering away. She couldn't concentrate; none of the words made sense. As the cab turned into the street, Emilia felt her heart begin to race. Something was wrong and she didn't know what.

Mae paid the driver and got out, running around to Emilia's side, throwing open the door and leaning in to grab her arm.

"I'm okay, I think. You can leave me now. Thank you."

Mae shook her head. "No, you're not. You look dreadful and you can't stand on your own two feet without swaying. Clarke wouldn't forgive me if I left you on your own. Hell, you might not even make it down the steps and through the front door."

They walked arm in arm to the sidewalk and down the steps. Before she could ring the doorbell, the front door was thrown open by a worried looking Missy. "What's the matter, Miss Emilia?"

"I feel a little funny, I just need to lay down for a while."

"Should I call the doctor?"

"Yes!" Mae replied at the same time Emilia whispered, "No."

Missy looked at Emilia.

"Honestly, no thank you. I'll see how I am after I've had some sleep." Emilia turned to Mae. "Thanks, Mae, I'm fine now."

"If you're sure..."

Missy nodded. "She's sure. I'll help her up to bed."

"Is Clarke home?"

"He went to a dinner a few hours ago and hasn't returned. Do you want to wait for him in the library? He'll be back anytime."

"If you don't mind," Mae said, smiling, and walked toward the library.

At the same time, James came running down the stairs, and taking one look at his sister, exclaimed, "Are you ill?"

She shrugged.

"Do you need anything?"

Emilia frowned at him, but he smiled. There was a look of concern etched across his face that she hadn't seen in a long time.

James watched Missy helping his sister up to her room. He then walked down to the library paused to watch Mae standing at the bookshelves, and stepped inside. If Emilia had seen the smile that had spread across his lips, she would have been terrified for her friend, but she was too busy concentrating on getting up to her bedroom, she felt quite ill and in need of her bed.

TWENTY-THREE

PRESENT DAY

Maria passed Miss Green's apartment and paused, wondering if she should knock to see if she was okay. Her phone vibrated in her pocket, and she smiled as she saw Frankie's one word text message: *Outside*. She'd give her neighbor a knock when she got back, maybe offer to make her something to eat.

Maria drained the last of her coffee and walked to the elevator, feeling a lot better. Had she had some kind of anxiety attack in the library? Just because she'd never suffered from one didn't mean she couldn't experience one now. When she reached the car, Frankie had his head slumped forward and a loud snore erupted from his mouth.

"You're such a smart ass, I wasn't that long."

He opened one eye. "Long enough, so what did you find out?"

She climbed into the car, slamming the door. "Gina was right, those articles were accurate. There was a brutal murder there, in July '52. A woman's body was found in the attic, her limbs removed. Her head was nowhere to be found. I don't even know if it ever got recovered."

"So that would make our killer how old now?"

"At least in his nineties. I'm not so good with math, maybe older."

"Do we know any ninety-year-old killers?"

"No... But it's not impossible, you do get those few older people who are still running marathons in their nineties."

"Why would they leave it so long though? I mean seriously, if that is the case, sixty-five years between murders is—"

"A lifetime."

He nodded.

"What was the motive?"

"Don't laugh at me. I think it was devil worship."

Frankie turned to stare at her. "You're shitting me?"

"Nope. Apparently, the apartment wasn't classed as an apartment at the time, it was just an attic bedroom. Well, it had the full works: Ouija board, satanic symbols and a grand grimoire."

"A what?"

"A book of black magic, used for spells, witchcraft and summoning the devil."

Maria could feel her cheeks burn; she didn't really believe in any of this stuff, did she? An image of the woman from the library staring at her filled her mind.

"I'm not saying I believe it. I'm just telling you what I read. So, what are we going to do now?"

"Go and get all the files out of the basement on the murder in '52. Also see if they ever found an ID and her next of kin for our Jane Doe. Old Addison threw us off the case and handed it to Merrick because he had nothing else to do before his retirement and Addison knew it would keep him busy. Merrick did nothing to find the perp and we had our asses chewed and moved on to the next homicide. Maybe we can see if they have the original records from the fifties? Who knows... there might be a mouldy box with your devil bible inside it lurking in the depths of the basement and it might tell us something about our murder of the woman with the rose tattoo."

Frankie drove them in the direction of the station and Maria was silent as she ran through the strange events of the day, including spending time with Harrison. She decided not to tell Frankie about Harrison. He'd only tease her and she wasn't in the mood for it. And that feeling she had... about the house, about being followed... she almost couldn't describe it, but if she did, he'd think she was nuts. It was tense and foreboding, like something was very, very wrong, only she didn't know what and couldn't put her finger on it.

The station basement door swung open to show the dimly lit room and a blast of warm, slightly stale air hit her nostrils.

"Well, if it isn't my two favorite pain-in-the-ass detectives. What can I do for you today?" Officer Layla Allen grinned at them.

Maria grinned back. "We're looking for some case files from three years ago and some from way back in the day."

Layla stepped aside. "In that case I'll let you in. Welcome to my humble abode."

The huge basement had a metal cage blocking the entrance to stop people from getting in and helping themselves to the files that were stored down here. Layla let herself through the door and sat at the counter behind the wire mesh.

"I'm going to need to see your ID, then you can sign yourselves in."

Frankie rolled his eyes. "You're kidding, right?"

She shook her head. "Sorry, doll, it's new rules. No one enters the cage unless they've been officially identified. Then I'll escort you to where you need to be, and if no one else wants me I'll wait with you until you're finished."

Maria signed them both in, tugged Frankie's badge from his

pocket and passed them both over. Layla passed them back.

"Guess you two are the real deal, how about that."

She opened the door and guided them in. Rows and rows of shelving stacked with boxes full of old case files and evidence went on forever. The basement was vast and Maria didn't envy Layla's job keeping everything in order.

As they filed into the first aisle, Layla shut the door behind them. "You can't trust half of those motherfuckers upstairs who come in and mess with the evidence when your back is turned. Well, not on my watch. I've seen *Making a Murderer* and that crap ain't going down when I'm in charge."

Maria laughed. "No one would dare, Layla, they're all scared of you."

Layla dead eyed her. "Uh huh, that's good. So what year are you after?"

"1952."

"For real?"

"For real. Do the records go back that far?"

"Yes, they do. I think we have records that go back to 1950. Anything from before then is stored at City Hall and, before you ask, the reason I know this is because I spend most of my time trying to get this place in some kind of date order to make everyone's life a little easier."

Layla walked along the rows of shelving. Frankie let Maria go first: he was terrified of the woman in front of them. She wasn't as scary as she made out, but Maria wasn't about to tell Frankie that. Layla had a heart of gold, helping out at the homeless shelter in her spare time. After what seemed like forever, Layla came to a block of shelving with old, cardboard file boxes on them. The case file, name and number was written in faded, black marker pen.

"I'm gonna trust you two to find what you need then come and get it signed out. Don't touch anything else apart from the boxes on this unit."

Frankie nodded. "Yes, ma'am."

Layla turned, striding off toward the front entrance.

"Jesus wept, what a place to work."

"I don't know, the only people she has to deal with are cops... She doesn't have to chase killers and look for bibles written for the devil."

They began to look at the boxes which were stacked in numerical order making their search straightforward. Maria found the section full of the case's 1952 boxes and felt her heart begin to race. What if the grimoire was inside it? The thought of it made her feel sick to her stomach. She'd seen enough horror films to know they were made from human skin and written in blood. Her eyes fell on a box pushed behind another; she moved the first one out of the way and saw the name written on it.

EVANS / WEST 10TH ST. – 28-06-52

"Holy crap, it's here. I mean, I didn't actually expect it to be here." She turned to Frankie. "Did you?"

He shrugged. "Suppose not, makes our life a whole lot easier though."

She grabbed the box and dragged it forward. "So, where we going to take this? I don't want to have to explain to the clowns upstairs what we're doing."

"I'd say my place, but Christy is still mad at me."

"We'll take it to mine then. My dinner table can be our temporary office. It's easier anyway. We can get on with it and not have to worry about being called out."

"Well, if that ain't the first good idea you've had all week."

She smiled and stepped to the side. "Big, strong man like you can carry it. You have to come in useful for something. I'll sign it out and deal with Layla." She heard him breathe a sigh of relief behind her.

TWENTY-FOUR

Miss Green lay on the bed not quite asleep, but too tired to get up. Every bone in her body ached and she felt every bit her age this morning. For the last sixty-five years her life had been pleasant. She'd been more fortunate than some and she was thankful for that. What she wasn't thankful for was that note that had been pushed under her door whilst she was out shopping yesterday. It had taken a long time for her to block the memories of that horrific night as far from her mind as possible. Then just like that it was back, boom, the images playing on a loop, over and over again. No matter how many times she told herself it wasn't her problem, she knew that it was, that she was a part of it, and it was her duty to help.

Damn your stupid sense of duty, Missy, you did what you had to and sent it back. This is not your problem. You're an old woman now and it will probably kill you. If that damn demon doesn't, then the fear will kill you; your heart won't stand it a second time. Is this how you want to die? Fighting against something that is an aberration of all things good?

"Shut up, just shut up."

She pressed her hands to her ears trying her best to block

out the noise from her goddamn, interfering, busybody mind. She turned onto her side. The sun was shining through the crack in the drapes. She could feel its warmth on her face and it felt so good.

She liked the light, the heat, the feeling of safety that the sun brought with it every morning when it rose in the sky. She hated the dark and never went out in it if it could be avoided. The dark was full of shadows that you couldn't see, things that came to life once the sun had set. She knew this from experience, which was why every corner in her apartment had lamps. There were no dark corners in here; she wouldn't let anything hide in her home. Unlike the house on West 10th Street. What lived in the dark there was the thing only people with the very worst nightmares could imagine. At least they could leave it behind once they were awake.

She had sensed something wrong in the days leading up to that dreadful night. Not able to describe it or tell anyone, it was more of a feeling. A sense of terrible foreboding that something wasn't right with the dynamics inside the house—and how do you go about telling someone that?

If she'd have voiced her fears, her feelings to Clarke, he could have gone and investigated the attic where James was spending most of his time locked away on his own. If only one of them had gone up there, they would have seen the Ouija board, the candles, the book of black magic. The huge pentagram on the wall drawn in blood. Whose blood it was she had no idea. He had ripped all the paper off the walls, written all over them. They would have realized there and then that they were dealing with a madman, and he could have been taken to the hospital before it got that far; before that beautiful girl was so horribly killed.

She shivered, throwing the covers back, and got out of bed. They'd let it get that far without intervening. Now it was time to go back.

. . .

It was an hour since Missy had made the decision to visit the house, and she was now sat in the back of a yellow cab which was about to turn into West 10th Street. Her heart was racing and her mouth was dry when the driver stopped at the curb. She lifted a trembling hand, passing him a ten-dollar bill. She thanked him and got out to stand on the sidewalk opposite the house.

Despite it being a warm day, the house was dark, there being no sunshine on its side of the street. It didn't look anything like it had the last time she'd been here. Its once grand exterior looked tired and dead, shrivelled up plants hung from the window boxes. In fact it looked as old and decrepit as she felt today.

She had read a long time ago in the newspaper it had been turned into apartments, and that many people had died mysterious deaths or committed suicide in there—she knew it had never been the same since that night. At first, she'd read the papers, clipping out any articles about suspicious deaths and putting them in a shoebox, keeping her own record of fatalities and incidents. Then she'd stopped buying papers, for her own sanity. She couldn't take the worry, the dread, the guilt.

Pulling the gold chain from under her sweater she kissed the crucifix on it and asked God to protect her soul. Taking a deep breath, she stepped forward and heard the squeal of car tyres on the tarmac and a loud honk of the horn. She realized that she'd stepped into the road without even looking. Her heart racing, she jumped back, waving at the driver and muttering sorry. In all her years she'd never once stepped into the traffic without looking; the city streets were mean and unforgiving. It was the quickest way to end up dead or racking up a huge hospital bill.

Shuddering, she crossed herself; it knew she was here and

had tried to stop her. It had tried to kill her. That was the moment the stubbornness and strength that Missy had worn proudly on her sleeve in her younger days returned. She stared at the house and whispered.

"You're scared of me. Well, I'll be damned. You tried to stop me, but it was only a half-hearted attempt. That means you're not strong enough, otherwise I'd be lying crushed under that car's wheels. Well screw you! How dare you. I sent you back once, I'll do it again so whichever dark corner you're hiding in, you better be worrying. I might be much older, but I've still got the stubborn mind of the girl I was last time I was here and you can sense that, you know that I have the power to send you back."

This time she held her head up, looked both ways along the street and crossed to the other side. For a fleeting moment she wondered if some huge chunk of masonry was going to fall from the roof and kill her anyway. Then she was down the steps and looking for the buzzer she needed, but before she could press it the huge, glass door opened and she was greeted by a smiling, much older version of the beautiful girl, not much younger than herself, who she used to dote on.

"You came."

"I had to, my conscience wouldn't let me turn a blind eye."

The two women hugged, wrapping their arms around each other and squeezing tight.

"It's been far too long, I've missed you so much." Emilia whispered.

"I've missed you too. Who would have thought we'd both still live to tell the tale? We should never have lost touch—and you should have sold this godforsaken house and moved away."

They pulled apart and Emilia lifted her sleeve to wipe the tears that were glistening on her cheeks.

"I know, but I couldn't. I felt as if it was my fault; that I had to stay here and make sure it didn't happen again."

Missy nodded. She got that. A sense of duty was a powerful thing, especially when you carried it alongside the guilt that came with it. Then she whispered, "But it did happen again."

Emilia nodded. "I had no idea history would repeat itself. It's been lingering ever since. I can hear it, I can sense it. Although it's not strong enough yet or we would all know about it."

Missy grabbed her old friend's hand. "Then this time we'll send it back, for good."

TWENTY-FIVE

Mikey sat on his sofa, watching an old black-and-white movie. He had no idea what it was called or what it was about because for the last ten minutes he'd muted the volume. He could hear the muffled whispering. Straining he closed his eyes and concentrated, trying to make out what they were saying. It didn't sound as if they were speaking English He knew he should really try and find out where it was coming from because it wasn't him. And he had no one else around to be whispering in his ears. He didn't have friends. He kept to himself, went to work, came home, smoked a little pot and watched TV.

Mikey stood up and crossed to his kitchen to check the window was shut—sometimes noise from the apartment above floated down. Drawing the blind he shook his head, the window was not only shut, it was locked. A loud thud came from the direction of his bedroom. He picked up a carving knife from the block. *If some motherfucker has broken in, they're paying with blood.*

Clutching the knife he crept toward his bedroom door, pausing outside to listen. He couldn't hear anything so he threw the door back and a blast of cold air hit him in the face along with the most gut-wrenching, God-awful smell; the smell of decay. Although he'd never smelt rotting flesh before, he felt pretty sure this was what it would smell like. He gagged, lifting his arm to cover his nose. He couldn't see anything. The room was empty, but he felt it. He felt something huge, full of anger and blackness, charging toward him.

For the first time in his life Mikey screamed, a sound so high pitched anyone outside would have sworn it was a woman. He lifted his hands to cover his face as he fell to his knees. He had never experienced such unbearable coldness that was now enveloping him. He felt as if he was being slowly, crushed to death.

From somewhere inside the building, he heard a door slam and women's voices, chattering. He wanted to call out for help, but he couldn't. Whatever it was had squeezed every last bit of air from his lungs, and his eyeballs felt as if they were going to explode from their sockets.

"God, if you're there, forgive me."

At the mention of forgiveness, the pressure was released, and he fell to the floor, taking in huge gulps of lovely air. Not sure whether he needed an ambulance, a shot of whiskey or a joint the size of the Empire State Building, he lay there, curled up in a ball on the rough, wooden floorboards, big, wet tears rolling down his cheeks. His heart was hammering so fast he could feel the blood being pumped through his brain as his temple pulsated. Too afraid to move, he lay there like a freshly caught fish on the deck of a fishing boat, gasping for air, about to have his belly sliced open and his insides ripped out.

Emilia paused at the bottom of the stairs, turning toward the ground floor apartment that always had the faint smell of cannabis lingering around the front door. Missy followed her friend's eyes, both of them sensing something was wrong. The door opened and Mikey staggered out with a dishcloth, which was turning deep red, wrapped around his hand.

"Oh no, are you okay? What's happened?"

He tried to speak, but his eyes were glazed. All he could do was shake his head. Emilia grabbed one arm, Missy the other, ready to walk him back into his apartment. He shook his head, shivering.

Emilia frowned at Missy. "Well, if you don't want to go back in there you're going to have to come up to my place. I can't have you bleeding everywhere."

She led him towards the stairs, and they were only three steps up when his door slammed violently shut. Emilia and Missy glanced at each other. It was back, and growing stronger, angrier. They walked faster.

Emilia pushed Mikey and Missy into her apartment, bolting the door behind her. She sat Mikey down at the dining table, then busied herself filling a bowl with cold water. Taking a selection of clean dishcloths and first aid kit from the cupboards, she sat next to him and tenderly unwrapped the now heavily bloodstained cloth from his hand. Both she and Missy gasped to see how deep the gaping wound was that ran the full length of the palm of his hand.

"Oh dear, I think you might need more than a band aid. We need to get you to the hospital."

For the first time the man looked Emilia in the eyes and let out a high-pitched laugh. "That ain't going to happen. I pay my rent or I pay the hospital."

Emilia pressed a cold cloth against the wound, then wrapped some dry ones around it and folded his fingers over it.

"Keep your arm elevated. I'm not a nurse, but I do know some first aid."

Missy stood at the sink, watching. "Who slammed your

door? Is there someone down there we can call to come and help you?"

He shook his head. "There's nobody except me in there."

"How did you cut your hand?"

He glared at her. "What are you, the senior citizen's FBI?"

She grinned. "Who told you?"

For the first time he relaxed and smiled. "Sorry, I know you're just trying to help, and I appreciate it. I'm just a little bit shook up."

Emilia removed the cloths, rewrapping fresh ones around again. "Well, I'm Emilia and the inquisitive one over there is Missy. You are Mikey if I'm not mistaken."

"I am."

"So, Mikey, there is no wind blowing through the building because the front door is shut. Do you want to tell me how your front door slammed shut so hard the whole building shook?"

He lowered his eyes. "I don't think you really want to know."

"Well, you can let me be the judge of that. You came out of your apartment looking like—"

Missy interrupted. "Looking like some fool who had scared himself to death and sliced his hand open in the process. Am I close?"

"Missy..."

"I'm right, Em; look at the state of him."

Emilia looked at Mikey who was staring across the table at Missy.

"There is something in my apartment, I don't know what the hell it is. It sure isn't human, that's for real. Now you can blame it on the pot, I smoke it every day and I'm not denying it. But this was no hallucination. Whatever it was, it tried to kill me."

. . .

Mikey looked at the two elderly woman in front of him, waiting for them to laugh at him. To call him crazy. Instead, both of the women were staring at him in horror, and he knew then that he wasn't crazy. He knew that what had happened was as real as he was—and that they both knew what he was talking about.

Missy sat down opposite him and looked at Emilia. "It's getting stronger…" She turned gravely to him. "Have you been dabbling in the occult Mikey?"

Mikey shook his head unable to process what he was hearing. "Damn, I was hoping, you two were crazier than me. I don't dabble in anything except a little weed. Maybe we're all crazy; this stuff doesn't exist, except for in the movies."

"It does in this house… I'm sorry, I had no idea it was able to do that," Emilia said.

"Well, I'd like to know what it was and how it tried to suffocate me when I couldn't see it? I can't get my head around it."

Missy bowed her head.

Emilia spoke. "A very long time ago, my brother bought a Ouija board and found a book of devil worship and witchcraft. He decided to sacrifice a young woman and summon a demon."

Mikey laughed, so loud both women jumped. They waited for him to contain himself. He shook his head.

"I'm sorry—I thought you were going to say it was your dead aunt's ghost, seeking revenge. Are you for real?"

As he spoke, he realized that neither woman was smiling. Instead, they were wide eyed; terrified… The seriousness of the situation all three of them were in came crashing down on his shoulders.

Mikey nodded. "You are… aren't you. It is real. Then we have a problem…"

Emilia could have hugged the man sitting next to her. He'd lived here for years, and she'd never said anything more than good day to him. He wasn't going to leave them alone to fight it. Missy didn't stop herself, she stood up, walked around to Mikey and wrapped her arms around him, whispering, "Thank you," into his ear.

They needed all the help they could get.

TWENTY-SIX

GREENWICH VILLAGE, JUNE 1952

Mae was trailing her finger along a row of leather-bound books. She loved to read almost as much as she loved to act. The door opened and she turned to see a handsome, younger version of Clarke standing there.

"Well hello, you must be James. I'm a friend of your Pa. I don't believe we've been formally introduced."

She crossed the room, holding out her hand which he took. Instead of shaking it he lifted it to his mouth, brushing his lips so softly over the back of her hand that it sent a shudder down her spine. He stared at her, his huge, dark, almost black eyes drawing her in. Her foolish heart began to pump the blood around her body faster. Her stomach swooshed and she felt a sudden rush of warm heat fill her panties. She let out a small gasp, the feelings taking her completely by surprise. James raised his eyebrow, aware of the effect he was having on the beautiful woman standing in front of him and enjoying every second.

She laughed, but her voice quivered. "Well, James, it's very nice to meet you."

She tried to pull her hand away from him, needing to get

some space between them. He didn't let go. Instead, he ran his finger along it, and the pressure in her panties made her squeeze her thighs together. She had never felt such arousal.

She wanted to throw herself at him and beg him to make love to her there and then, and he knew it. He was enjoying watching her squirm, her mind emptied of all rational thoughts. She wanted this man, inside of her, and that was all that mattered. His mouth pressing against hers. He kissed her with such passion that she felt her knees go weak. Pulling apart he took hold of her hand, pressing it against the hard bulge in the front of his trousers. She ran her tongue along her bright red lips. He grabbed her hand, pulling her.

"Not here, upstairs. I don't want to be disturbed. I want to lick and bite every single part of you."

Mae smiled. The thought was almost too much to bear, and she followed him along the hallway toward the back of the house. He led her to a staircase that she'd never seen before and realized it must be the staff stairs. She didn't care. He could take her here on the bare, wooden staircase and she'd have let him.

He rushed upstairs, lifting his finger to his lips. She kicked off her shoes so they wouldn't clatter on the wooden steps. Damn. Cheating on Clarke with his son was wrong, but she couldn't stop it. She wanted to lie on his bed and be fucked. She would deal with the aftermath later; right now she wanted James. Inside her, biting, sucking and doing anything he desired. She let him lead her up the stairs. Unable to shake the trance like state she was in, they reached the tiny attic staircase. He pulled her up the last few steps and opened the door.

The room was in darkness, candles burning on the table in the middle of the room, and it was much colder up here than the rest of the house. He pulled her inside, closing and locking the door behind him.

"I don't want anyone disturbing us, I want you so much."

He kissed her again, crushing his mouth against hers, and

she leaned into him. He then scooped her up into his arms. Carried her into the bedroom, kicking the door open with his foot. Mae's nose wrinkled at the terrible smell. Then she was on the soft bed, and he was removing her stockings.

A loud thud from the corner of the room made her jump.

"What's that? Who's there?"

He laughed. "No one, it's just you and me, baby. Close your eyes and relax, I'm going to eat you up."

The smell of rotting garbage was overpowering; suddenly every bit of passion and lust that she'd been feeling moments before disappeared. Something or someone else was in this room.

She pushed him off. "I don't like it in here... it smells really bad."

James stared down at her. The face she'd thought was dashing moments ago looked nothing like it now and for the first time in her life, Mae felt the cold, hard, reality of fear bearing down on her. She needed to get out of the dark, foul room. Back down into the warmth and the light. She wanted Clarke, needed him. He always made her feel safe and she'd been about to betray his love and trust in the most shameful way that she could think of.

"You don't mean that do you?"

Her mouth was dry and her stomach began to churn. Every lustful feeling from moments ago had turned into disgust. She twisted herself away from him and stood up. Not even bothering about her stockings, she backed away from him, toward the door. He started to laugh and she made a break for the door. It wouldn't open. With what little light there was, she couldn't make out any locks. Twisting the door knob and tugging as hard as she could, it didn't budge.

James was still laughing.

"Let me out or I'll tell your Pa."

He laughed even louder and began to clap. "Now how are

you going to do that, you cheap whore? He's not in and you're locked in this room with the two of us for company. I'm afraid you're not going anywhere, ever again."

In that moment, Mae absolutely knew there was someone else in here. She opened her mouth to scream, but nothing came out. A hand clamped across her mouth, so tight that she couldn't breathe. She tried to bite down on it, but she couldn't. She struggled against the rope which had been looped around her neck. Clawing at his hands, trying to make him loosen his grip. Silver specks began to float across her eyes, and then the room went black.

TWENTY-SEVEN

PRESENT DAY

Frankie downed the last of his coffee, pushed the file he was reading away and stretched. "I'm going to have to call it a day, I want to go home and shower before our dancing lesson."

Maria looked at him in wide-eyed horror. "Crap, is that tonight?"

"Don't tell me you forgot."

"I'm so sorry, Frankie, I did. I have other plans now." She couldn't tell him about the text she'd got an hour ago from Harrison, especially now Frankie was looking at her like a four-year-old when he's told he can't have a candy bar.

"Oh, it's okay. I guess I can go on my own tonight."

"Are you sure? I'll be there next week, I promise."

She waited for him to ask what her plans were, at the same praying he didn't. She didn't want to have to lie to him—she'd never lied to him. She also worried about how he'd take being blown off for a rich man.

"I'll hold you to it." He smiled and stood up, grabbing his jacket from the back of the chair.

"Thanks for the coffee and the food. I'll catch you tomorrow."

"Have fun at your dancing class."

He waved his hand at her and walked out of the door, leaving her feeling bad for letting him down. She might have been imagining it, but she was sure he shut the door a little louder than he usually did.

Maria rolled her eyes. *Shit, Frankie I'm not your wife. You don't need to be so pissed with me.*

Maria looked at the contents of the box that were spread across her table. She'd been relieved to discover there was no Satanic bible to be seen.

The pictures in the box were gruesome, black-and-white stills. The house was gorgeous from the outside: window boxes filled with flowers, the glass on the windows and doors gleaming it was so clean. Who would have guessed what horrors it held inside? Photos of the interior showed it had once been decadent to say the least. Crystal chandeliers, polished wooden floors, gleaming brass doorknobs, huge vases filled with fresh flowers. She would have loved to have visited it back then.

The ground, first and second floors were immaculate; there was nothing to show anything was amiss on any of these photographs It was only when the photographer reached the attic that the tone of the photographs changed dramatically. The heavy, wooden door was pushed open to reveal a glimpse of the pooling blood on the floor. Maria imagined that he'd gasped as he'd stepped inside and began to photograph, shocked by the horror of what he was capturing through his lens. The attic walls had writing all over them—symbols that she didn't recognize—and many dark patches of blood. Once the photographer had captured the surroundings, he'd focused on the body.

Maria couldn't look at it any longer. She shuffled the pictures together and placed them and the typed-up police reports back into the box. She then put the lid on the box and hid it away on the floor of her closet; she didn't want to be reminded about it every time she saw it. The fact that the murder had happened so long ago didn't matter. The horror was still as fresh to Maria. This had been brutal. An act of pure evil.

She wanted to know what the writing and symbols on the walls said. She was going to have to track down either a bookshop or a professor who might know something about Satanic symbols and demonology because this was way beyond her realm of knowledge. It looked like some kind of ritual killing, but at the time, they'd locked the perp up as a lunatic in the nearest mental institution. It seemed no one had bothered to find out what he was doing and why. There were no notes explaining what any of it had meant. They hadn't cared. They had a body and they had their killer. That was all that mattered. Plus, he was from a wealthy family, who would have no doubt paid to have had him taken care of.

The lack of newspaper reports surrounding the case surprised her. There were some, but in her opinion, it had been brushed under the carpet with only minimal coverage the way far too many cases involving the super-rich were. She'd never heard about it and she'd been born and bred in New York along with her entire family.

She walked into the bathroom and began to fill the tub for a nice soak to wash away the horrors. Going back into the kitchen, she opened the fridge, taking out an almost empty, cold bottle of pinot grigio. She poured its contents into a wine glass and took a sip. Kicking off her shoes, she sat down on the sofa, curling her legs underneath her. Today had been one hell of a crazy day.

Just as Maria could feel herself beginning to relax, she suddenly remembered Miss Green. She hadn't checked on her. Taking a huge mouthful of wine, she forced herself to stand up, placing the glass on the table. Leaving the apartment door ajar, she crept down to Miss Green's and knocked on the door, waiting to hear her shuffling along the carpeted hallway, but there was nothing.

Maria stepped forward and pressed her ear against the door. There was no sound. She rapped again, much louder. This was a cop knock that she usually reserved for work, the "no shit answer the door" knock. Still no reply.

"Hello are you there? It's Maria."

A hand touched her shoulder.

"Holy crap!" She screeched so loudly that Miss Green jumped more than she did.

"Jesus, Maria, you're giving me a coronary over here. What's wrong with you?"

Maria laughed. "Geez, I'm so sorry. I've been trying to catch hold of you. Are you okay?"

For a split-second Maria could tell that the old lady standing in front of her was not okay and would probably never be okay again. Then, the reserved, polite and smiling Miss Green took over and she nodded her head.

"I've been to visit a very old friend today; a long overdue visit if I'm honest. Oh, and yes dear, I'm fine. Just a little bit tired, it's been emotional."

"If you're sure, you know if there's anything I can do I will. You just have to ask."

Her friend pushed herself up and kissed her cheek. "I know you will lovely, thank you."

"Oh shoot, my bath. I have to go, I have a date."

The smile that spread across Miss Green's face lit her up. "Well then, don't be wasting your time talking to an old broad like me. Go and get yourself all beautiful, I hope he's the one who's been sending you those gorgeous flowers."

"He is. It's nothing serious; we're just friends—sort of."

"That's how it should be. Now go. Shoo—get ready.

Tomorrow we'll have a nice pot of tea, and you can tell me how it went. I'll be waiting for the full details so don't go disappointing me, Maria. Life's too short to spend it on your own."

TWENTY-EIGHT

Frankie parked in the underground garage. He was home much earlier than he normally was when he worked a late shift. He wanted a shower before he went dancing, so was hoping that Christy wasn't home yet. He spotted her car, but that didn't mean she was home. Like Maria, she often walked to work. He opened the door and walked inside holding his breath. If there was the slightest chance of Christy finding out what he was up to, it wouldn't work. This was going to be his last attempt to put some life back into their very stale marriage. If she didn't care, he wasn't going to stay with her. He had feelings for Maria that ran far deeper than any he'd ever had for his wife. It was wrong, but they made such a great couple.

To his relief, the apartment was empty. He checked each room and noticed the spare room was much tidier than the last time he'd been in it. The bed was made up with what looked like expensive, cotton bedding. He crossed to the bed, stroking the covers. This was nice, much nicer than what was on their bed, and he asked himself why on earth she'd gone to so much bother. Had she said they were having visitors and he'd not heard? That was always a possibility; he did have a habit of switching off when she was talking.

Loosening his tie and undoing the buttons on his shirt he walked into the kitchen to get a cold beer. If he was going dancing on his own he was going to need a bit of a helping hand with his nerves from Mr Bud Light. A loud buzzing noise behind him made him turn around to see Christy's phone vibrating on the kitchen counter. Not really thinking, he picked it up even though he wasn't into the habit of reading the messages on her phone. He saw Adam's picture flash across the screen, and he wondered why his brother was texting his wife. Sliding the screen across he was surprised she didn't have a pass code on it. Then again, she was even worse with technology than he was. He read the message twice, not quite sure if he was reading it right.

Can't wait to finish work so I can bury my head between your legs and taste your honey. xx

Frankie felt a rush of white, hot rage fill his chest as he read it again. All this time he'd been thinking of doing things to make their relationship better, she was screwing around behind his back. With his brother of all people. The dirty, rotten, cheating bastards. Pushing the phone into his pocket he downed his beer and pulled another one out of the cooler and paced up and down the apartment.

He wasn't perfect. Yes, he'd tried it on with Maria the other night, but she'd put him in his place, and he didn't think he'd have had the balls to go through with it. But this... She'd been sleeping with Adam under the expensive bed sheets in the spare room. He stormed in, ripping the covers off the bed. He pulled the pillowcases off and crumpled them all up into a ball which he then began to jump all over. The anger began to subside, and he realized that he was tired. Of all the bullshit, of this crappy marriage. He grabbed another beer and took it to the couch where he sat down. He was numb. Too numb to turn the television on, he lifted the beer to his lips and sipped. His knee twitched as he waited for her to come home so he could see what she had to say for herself.

* * *

The broken buzzer for Maria's apartment vibrated and she checked her watch. He was on time. Eight pm, he'd told her he'd be downstairs waiting for her. That was providing it was Harrison and not Frankie or anyone else. She checked her reflection in the mirror and smiled, tucking a stray strand of hair back into the chignon she'd carefully pinned up. Spritzing herself one last time in Chanel Cristalle, she grabbed her purse off the side and tried to push the butterflies in her stomach back down.

She went to the elevator, pressing the call button, praying that it was working. She didn't want to walk down the stairs and get all sweaty before she'd even seen him. The cranky doors opened, and she stepped inside, briefly wondering if Frankie had made it to the dance class. She felt bad for letting him down, but she was entitled to a little fun as well. What Frankie should be doing was taking Christy with him, not her.

When the elevator opened and she stepped out, she did a double take at Harrison Williams who was dressed in a pair of navy trousers, with a white shirt not quite fastened at the top. Her breath caught in the back of her throat. His hair was styled just a little too perfectly to have been done by himself. He was standing with his mouth open.

"Mr Williams, didn't your momma teach you it was rude to stare?"

He clamped his mouth shut and nodded his head. As she reached him she got a whiff of his aftershave. It was seductive, but not overpowering. She took hold of his arm, linking hers through his.

"Maria, you look beautiful."

She threw back her head and laughed. "You'd be amazed what a full face of make-up can do for a girl. So where are we going?"

"It's a surprise. I can tell you it's definitely not the opera."

She looked at him and smiled. "Good, because I hate it."

They walked out of the building's doors to the waiting limousine and he held up his hands. "I tried to get a town car, but I left it too late. I had no choice."

"We could always walk."

He looked down at her heels. "No, the car is a must. I'm far too lazy to walk where we're going."

"I suppose I can make an allowance, just this one time."

The driver was out of the car and holding the door open before they reached the bottom step. She slid into it and felt the cool leather seat press against the back of her legs. Harrison got in next to her as she spotted an open bottle of champagne and two glasses. One of them was already half full.

"Sorry, nerves. I was scared you might have changed your mind, so I had a glass to calm me down."

Maria looked at him to see if he was being sarcastic and realized he was being serious. He topped up his glass then filled the other, handing it to her. She took it from him and whispered, "Thank you." He smiled at her.

"Phew, that was easier than I'd imagined for the last two hours. I'd convinced myself you were going to give me a hard time."

"I'm not always a bitch."

"Oh crap, that's not what I meant at all."

She laughed. "Well, not all the time."

Sitting back, she watched as the limousine turned onto Sixth Avenue and began to drive into Midtown. This was nice. She'd never been in a limousine drinking expensive champagne, ever. Then and there she decided not to give him a hard time tonight;

if he was as nervous as she was, then she'd go easy on him. She'd thought that he'd be cocky, self-assured and full of himself. It was refreshing to discover that he wasn't. It wasn't really his fault if he had more money than she could ever dream about.

She was going to be a lady if it killed her, for this was one of life's rare, magical moments. If there was nothing more to it, she wanted to be able to remember the night she was wined and dined by Harrison Williams. To be able to store the memory in the part of her brain where she kept her happy thoughts, her special memories to look back on one day. If her mom could see her *now*, she'd probably pee her pants. She pictured the scene from one of her favorite films, *Arthur*. The one when Liza Minnelli was telling her dad about Arthur.

"I take it this bum will be calling you."

"Dad, he's a millionaire."

"You have my permission to marry him."

That would be her mom, she wouldn't care who Harrison Williams was or what his personality was like. For her mom, his bank balance would be enough. Thank God Maria wasn't that shallow, and she hoped that he knew that.

Harrison began to ask her about the library. She tried her best to answer in a normal voice.

"It was interesting, I found a little of what I was looking for."

"Good, that's great. You know I have an office full of researchers, so if you were to let me know exactly what you're looking for, I could get them to look up anything you want. It would save you the time and effort—that's if you were too busy. I know you like the Public Library, it's your happy place."

How much that had changed in one day. She was now terrified to visit and spend time there alone, in case it happened to her again. She didn't want to die on the cold, tiled floor of the New York Public Library, no matter how much she loved it.

The car turned onto West 49th Street, stopping outside the front of the Observation Deck entrance for the Rockefeller Building. Maria looked at Harrison, who shrugged.

"You said nothing too fancy and after your lecture about not visiting the town's iconic buildings I thought you might appreciate this."

She began to laugh, so much that tears filled the corner of her eyes. Shaking her head, she downed the rest of her champagne which was far too nice to waste. Then the door was opened and she was being helped out by the driver who was grinning at her. She thanked him and waited for Harrison to climb out.

Smoothing down her dress she wondered if she should have worn a pair of jeans. Hell, if she'd known they were coming here she would have worn a pair of jeans and Converse. Harrison led her toward the doors which had a sign on them apologizing that it was closed for the rest of the evening. She pointed to it.

"Aw that's such a shame, but I'll give you ten out of ten for being original."

"Come on, they might let us squeeze in if we're nice to them." He pushed open one of the heavy glass doors where the doorman came rushing over, his cheeks burning.

"Sir, I'm sorry. We're shut for the rest of the evening. We'll be open again tomorrow morning at eight am."

"Do you think if we paid a little extra you could squeeze us in? I've waited ages to come here, and I wanted to impress my friend."

The doorman looked across at Maria, smiling.

"Oh, I'm sorry, sir. Yes, I think we might be able to squeeze you in on the last elevator up."

Harrison shook his hand. "Good man, thanks."

Maria watched as Harrison slipped a folded note into the

guy's hand. She had no idea how much it was, but they were led straight to the first elevator.

"Have a good evening, sir. Welcome to the Top of the Rock."

The doors shut and Maria looked at him. "Well, I'll be damned, did you already buy tickets?"

"I got my assistant to pre-book them this afternoon."

She smiled at him. "I don't suppose we'll have much time. I definitely should have worn my sneakers. I hope the queue isn't too long."

They got out of the elevator to an empty floor where the only people were the security guards, leaning against the wall chatting. They waved them straight through. She moved toward his ear and whispered.

"Wow, how much did you tip that guy?"

He laughed. "Probably not enough."

They were stopped by the photographer. Harrison shook his head and Maria looked at him.

"Come on, don't be a spoilsport. I'll buy the souvenirs. Please."

She jumped onto the bench with a black-and-white backdrop of New York City behind them. Harrison rolled his eyes but sat next to her.

The woman with the camera laughed. "Right, you two love birds, give me a thumbs up. That's great, now cross your arms. Uh-uh, now give him a push and show him who's boss."

The camera flashed and both of them laughed. The young girl standing next to the photographer passed Maria a ticket. They walked arm in arm to the next bank of elevators where they were put into another car.

"I can't believe it's so empty, I mean it's never this quiet. I've been as soon as the doors open and there's people waiting in line. Even late at night it's fairly busy."

He smiled at her and shrugged. "I don't really like heights, so I wouldn't know."

Maria looked at him. "Is that why you've never been before, is it some well-kept secret?"

"No, I'm just stating a fact. I'm not petrified of them—I mean I don't have to cling onto the walls or whoever I'm with to make me feel brave."

"Oh, that's a shame. I was hoping you'd want to cling on to me."

He laughed, and the doors slid back revealing another empty corridor. They stepped out and Maria whispered, "At least we don't have to wait ages in line for the photographs." She led them to the heavy, glass doors which opened out onto the observation deck. They were the only two people out there. Maria looked around; it was the two of them and a couple of security guards. Harrison hovered near to the wall, and she grinned at him, slipping her hand into his.

"Come on, tough guy, you need to move away from the wall to make the most of the views." She led him around the entire observation deck and to the stairs to the next level.

"Do we need to? I can see everything just fine from here."

"We're here now, you have to."

He followed her up and watched her as she pressed her face against the toughened safety screens.

"Don't tell me you're sorry you came. Look at our city. It sparkles and shimmers under the moonlight. It's beautiful, a city full of hopes and dreams. A city brimming with romance and character, so much history."

"Even though you deal with the criminals and see it under a different light, you still love it?"

She pointed at the Empire State Building. "What's not to love. Every place, every person has their dark, dirty secrets. You have to see through the darkness to appreciate the light."

"There's one more floor, isn't there?"

"I'm afraid so. Do you really not like it?"

This time he took her hand. "Of course I do, come on."

He led her up the steps to the next floor and she let out a small gasp. Hundreds of candles lit the way to the far end where there was a table with two chairs. Flickering candles were blowing with the warm breeze. It was one of those balmy, hot summer nights, where the heat was almost as intense as in broad daylight. On the white tablecloth was an ice bucket with a bottle of champagne resting in it, next to two crystal champagne flutes. He led her toward it.

"Now, I've done the tourist thing, so you have to do the dining thing. I hope this meets with your approval."

She began to laugh. "Well, it's certainly different. It's beautiful. Thank you so much Harrison."

"Oh, and don't worry, you said you didn't like fancy food. I've had the Rainbow Room prepare us some cheeseburgers and fries."

He winked at her, and Maria felt as if her heart was about to explode. She kept looking around to see if there were cameras, if she was being filmed for some TV show that he was producing. All she could see were the two grinning security guards.

"Am I being filmed, you know for some reality show?"

He looked genuinely shocked. "Of course not, I wanted to let you have a nice, almost normal evening."

Maria took the glass of champagne that he passed to her, and she took a sip, turning around, allowing her mind to take a mental snapshot of the magical scene before her; it truly was one of those special memories that she wanted to lock away forever.

"Thank you, I don't know what to say."

He bent closer and kissed her tenderly on the lips. "Then don't say anything."

TWENTY-NINE

By the time Christy came home, Frankie's burning rage had turned into simmering fury. She waltzed in as if nothing was wrong in her yoga pants and crop top. He stared at her; she had a good figure for her age. She took one look at him, and her pretty face turned ugly. "Why are you home and are you drunk?"

He shrugged as he began to clap his hands together, "Bravo Christy, you had me. You really did."

Confusion in her eyes showed she didn't know what he was talking about, which angered him even more.

"What Frankie, what did I do?"

He pulled her phone out of his pocket, waving it at her. "Did you forget something? Is that what you came back for? You cheating, lying bitch." He stood up, a little unsteady and thrust it into the palm of her hand. She read Adam's message and at least she had the decency to squirm as her cheeks began to burn.

"Don't insult me by telling me it's not what I think, I don't want to know any details. How long has it been going on? What I want is for you to pack your bags and get the hell out. Go stay with Adam in his nice, cramped, studio apartment in Queens. See how much you enjoy screwing him when you have to live with him. All this time I was trying to make it better and you were sleeping with my brother."

"How dare you judge me. I know you've been screwing Maria. You fawn over her like a puppy dog with those big eyes. You make me sick, you hypocritical bastard."

She grabbed an empty mug and launched it through the air. Any other day Frankie would have ducked in time. The beer sloshing around in his brain made his reactions a lot slower and it smacked him full force on the corner of his eyebrow. A gash opened up and blood began streaming down his cheek.

"Oh shit, Frankie! I'm so sorry, I didn't mean to hit you."

He stumbled back and fell onto the sofa. Christy grabbed a dish cloth off the counter and rushed to him. Pressing it against the cut to stem the flow of blood.

"It's going to need stitches, I'll drive you to the emergency room."

He pushed her away. "I've never slept with her, ever."

Adam, who had walked in through the open door, took in the sight before him and muttered, "Oh fuck."

Frankie looked at him. "Take her and get out of my life, you piece of shit. This is how you repay me, all the years I've looked out for you."

Adam held up his hands. "Whoa, Frankie. What's going on, you've got it all wrong."

Christy turned to him, glaring. "He knows Adam. Frankie, I'm sorry—please let me get you to the hospital."

He shook his head. "Yes, Adam, I know. Just get the hell out of my sight before I get her arrested for battery."

Her face turned even paler than it already was. Frankie took hold of the cloth that she'd been pressing against his head, and she let go. She hissed at Adam. "Go wait in the car, I need to stop with you for a few days."

If there was any justice in all of this, it was the look of horror that crossed Adam's face at the thought of having to let Christy stop at his bachelor pad where he screwed every woman he met.

Frankie began to laugh so loud he snorted. "She's all yours now bro, no more sloppy seconds for you."

Adam turned and walked out, back to his car, and by the expression on his face, the dawning realization that his free ride had just ended in the most spectacular way.

Frankie could hear the drawers and wardrobe doors being open and slammed shut. She was never going to fit all her stuff into an overnight bag and suitcase. Good, he'd take it all to Goodwill, that would serve her right.

She reappeared, looking a lot less flawless than when she'd walked in fifteen minutes ago. "I've got some stuff; I'll let you get sorted out. I'm giving you a couple of days and then I'm coming back so we can talk about it. About this, about our stuff."

She was waving her hands around, and he just didn't care. He could see two of her. Damn! She must have thrown that cup with some force because he was clearly concussed.

"Get out, Christy."

She opened her mouth, about to have the last word, then closed it again. Turning, she pulled the case behind her and hoisted the overnight bag over her shoulder. He watched her go, just like that. She didn't slam the door like he'd expected her to. Instead she closed it softly.

He pushed himself off the sofa and immediately felt a surge of stale alcohol and bile fill his mouth. His head was smarting like a bitch so he did the only thing he could think of and stumbled into the bedroom, leaving a trail of bloody handprints and smears on the walls behind him. His bed looked huge now he knew he was going to be sleeping in it alone.

Kicking off his shoes, he clambered onto the white, cotton bedding and closed his eyes. Trying to stop the room from spinning, he should call Maria, get her to come and stick his head back together, but he'd left his cell in the kitchen and he wasn't getting up again. Squeezing his eyes shut, he willed the room to stop spinning and began to drift into a semi-conscious drunken slumber.

THIRTY

GREENWICH VILLAGE, JUNE 1952

James towered over the bloodied mess that minutes ago had been his father's lover and his sister's new best friend. He couldn't see the demon, but he could sense him. It was there.

He needed two more sacrifices to summon it fully. Something that he was more than willing to carry out, although he hadn't particularly enjoyed killing Mae. It had been necessary. He could feel her wet, sticky blood on his hands and face. He could see it dripping from the meat cleaver onto the wooden floorboards.

He dipped his fingers in the spreading pool of blood. Then he drew the biggest pentagram that he could onto the bedroom wall. So absorbed in what he was doing, he never heard the commotion from downstairs. After finishing what he was doing, he decided the best way to dispose of her was to remove her arms and legs. He wanted to keep her head. Even though the terrified look in her eyes took away some of her beauty, she was still pretty. He lifted the meat cleaver and hacked until he had her head. Lifting it up, he stared at her. Kissing her soft lips one last time, he knew he was going to have to put her in a jar and pickle her if he wanted to preserve it.

After wrapping the head up in pages of the *New York Times* to absorb some of the blood and fluid leaking from it, he put it inside the thick, leather Gladstone bag. He went downstairs to hide it somewhere they would never find it if they came looking. As he came out of the spare room, which was used for storage, he heard his father. He was drunk judging by the noise he was making. Fear made his heart beat too fast, and he turned and ran back to the attic. He had to get rid of her body before she was discovered.

As he reached the top step, he heard his father holler. "Mae, where are you? Damn you, don't make me come looking. You promised you'd be here when I came home."

Emilia opened her and she came out onto the hallway, struggling to walk on her own two legs. "Pa, what's the matter? Mae is here, she's in the library."

His heavy feet thundered up the stairs. "She's not there, where did she go?" He looked at his daughter's pale face. "What's the matter Em, are you ill?"

She whispered. "I don't know, I feel as if my head doesn't belong to my body. Mae might have got a cab and gone home. Missy helped me to bed. I left her downstairs."

He watched as his daughter stumbled, her legs gave way as she lurched toward him. Reaching out she grasped hold of the handrail and recoiled. She lifted her hand up, her eyes widened in horror, and she let out a gasp.

"Oh my, is that... is that blood?"

Clarke stared at the red liquid coating his daughter's hand and grabbed her wrist, pulling it toward him. Lifting it to his nose, he sniffed. "Blood."

Emilia screamed and Missy came running up the stairs. He stared in morbid fascination at the blood dripping from her fingers.

Missy took one look and screeched. "Miss Emilia what have you done?"

She whispered. "It's not mine."

Clarke stared up the narrow staircase that led up to the attic. "I need you to call the police, now. Tell them it's an emergency. That much blood, someone is hurt. Real bad," he instructed Missy.

Missy let go of Emilia and ran down the hallway to the telephone in the master bedroom. Clarke rushed upstairs, twisting the doorknob hard. It wouldn't move; it was locked from the inside. He slammed the palm of his hand against the heavy, oak door.

"James, open the door. Are you hurt? Let me in this minute. I command you!"

He was greeted by silence, hammered again and again on the door with his fist. He stepped back and ran at the door as best as he could in what little space there was. His shoulder hit the door and pain shot through his entire body, but it didn't move.

He could hear some noise from inside the attic.

"Open the goddamn door now, James."

The sound of sirens announced the arrival of the police. There was a stampede of heavy boots as four cops ran up to Clarke. He pointed at the blood and the door.

"I can't find my friend, Mae. My son James is in there. Someone is bleeding really bad. There's someone inside and they won't open the door."

The oldest of the men nodded. "Sir, I'm going to ask you to step aside. Do we have your permission to gain access?"

"I don't care if you break down the damn door, do what you must."

The cop hammered on the door. "Police! Open the door now. I'm going to give you to the count of three and then I'm going to shoot the lock off."

There was only silence. The cop pulled his gun from his holster and aimed for the lock on the door.

"One, two, three." He fired four rounds into the door handle, then the burly man next to him kicked the door. It splintered and gave way. As the door opened, the sight that greeted Clarke and the hardened city cops was one that would stay with them for the rest of their lives.

The walls of the attic were covered in an assortment of symbols, daubed in red paint. It was the strong, metallic, sickly smell which made them realize that it was in fact blood and not paint. On the kitchen counter was a gory mess. Clarke could not believe his eyes. He told himself he could face whatever it was that his son had been doing up here.

Guns drawn, the cops stepped into the room, trying to decide what it was they were looking at until one of them retched. "It's a body... there's no head."

A piercing scream filled the air as Emilia, who had followed the cops up the stairs, fell into Missy's arms.

Clarke took one look at the tangled mess of bloodied body parts and let out an anguished cry. Wrapped around the delicate wrist was the twenty-two carat, diamond encrusted bracelet he'd bought Mae for her birthday.

The cops began to search the attic, guns drawn and kicked in the bedroom door. James was standing on the bed, naked and covered in blood. He threw his head back and began to laugh. The sound echoed around the walls. Three of the cops dived toward him.

James didn't put up a fight and they cuffed his hands behind his back. Clarke ran in and, drawing back his fist, hit his son in the jaw as hard as he could.

"You son of a bitch! What did you do to her? My beautiful Mae."

The older cop grabbed Clarke, pulling him away. "He'll get plenty of that where he's going."

"Where is he going?"

James who was rubbing the side of his face, began to scream at the top of his voice. "He's coming, he's coming, he's coming and you can't stop him. He's been summoned."

The cop shook his head. "Greystone Park Psychiatric Hospital. He's nuts."

THIRTY-ONE

PRESENT DAY

Maria opened her eyes then squinted. The sun was streaming through the blinds she'd forgotten to close before she climbed into bed. She smiled as she remembered last night. It had been wonderful. When they'd finished eating, he'd led her down to the Rainbow Room where they'd drunk cocktails and danced to the most amazing singer she'd ever heard. She had no idea who she was, but she needed to find out.

Harrison had been a perfect gentleman, dropping her off at her apartment and escorting her to the front door. He'd kissed her, and going against every rule she abided by, she'd asked if he wanted to come in. He'd declined and said he would love to, but he didn't want to pressure her into anything. She hadn't felt hurt—in fact she'd felt relieved. She was more than a little drunk and didn't want to end the night in some drunken fumble she might regret the next morning. Now it was the next morning, she was regretting not dragging him in. It had been so long since she'd woken up next to someone. It would have been nice to have someone to talk to for once.

She had to get back to work. And that meant she needed to focus on finding who had done the rose tattoo on the victim.

Whoever they were, they might be able to give them a solid lead for identifying them. Maria phoned the first shop on her list but there was no answer and she realized that none of them probably opened until later on in the day. Next moment, her cell began to ring, and she grabbed it from under her pillow. There was no mistaking the voice on the other end.

"Maria, can you do me a favour?"

She held her breath, wondering what the hell Christy was doing phoning her as they weren't exactly friends.

"If I can."

"Can you go check on Frankie? He was drunk when I got home. We had an argument, and he threw me out. I don't want to see him, but he's not answering his cell."

Maria sat up. "He did what?"

"Look I'm late for work already. I can't go and check, and he won't let me in anyway. Please Maria, just make sure he's okay and let me know."

Tucking the phone under her ear, Maria began to pull on her sweats. She ran to the bathroom, all sorts of images running through her mind. Why was he drunk? Why did he throw her out? Why wasn't he answering his cell?

"I'll let you know." She ended the call and rang Frankie.

Shit, you better not have done anything stupid, Frankie. It went to voicemail.

"Frankie, answer your damn phone, ring me as soon as you get this." There was no reasoning behind the panic in her voice; he'd never had suicidal tendencies or talked about it. But she'd been to enough suicides, the majority of them men his age with failing relationships, who had decided they'd had enough of the crap life threw at them.

She brushed her teeth and took a large glug of mouthwash, swirling it around her mouth before spitting it out. Rinsing her face, she still had traces of last night's make-up on, but she didn't care. Tying her hair up she ran toward the elevator, willing her cell to ring so she could hear his hungover voice, deep and gravelly, as if he'd smoked too much.

The judder as the doors slammed shut vibrated the elevator, and jabbing the ground floor button, she prayed that the heap of junk wouldn't choose this exact moment to decide to break down in between floors. Thankfully, it didn't and as soon as it opened, she pelted out through the glass doors and onto the street.

"Damn you Frankie, I hate running," she muttered to herself as she began to make her legs pump faster. A cab would only get stuck in traffic.

As she finally reached Eighth Avenue and ran across it, dodging the cars and onto Hudson; she was increasingly out of breath, her throat dry. She'd not even taken a sip of water yet after all the alcohol she'd consumed last night. She pumped her legs even harder into his fancy apartment block.

Panting, she squeezed into the elevator and turned to the elderly couple who were watching her. "Morning." They nodded, and the lady smiled back. Maria turned away from them; her legs felt like jelly and her stomach was rolling from side to side.

At Frankie's door, she lifted her hand to rap on the door, realizing that it wasn't even shut. She pushed it open and stepped inside.

"Frankie, Frankie!" She was greeted by silence. The first thing she noticed was the bloodied smears on the walls and she let out a gasp. It reminded her too much of the crime scene images she'd been looking at. She began to pray for the second time in as many days. *Please God, let him be okay.* It could be a potential crime scene. Her heart hammered in her chest: this was her best friend. She'd fall apart if anything bad happened. She knew she wouldn't be able to cope without Frankie in her life. She followed the blood along the hallway to the master room, where the door was shut. Pushing it open, she saw him lying on the bed, with blood all over the pillows and lamp.

"Frankie!" She screeched and ran toward him. Reaching out, she poked him in the shoulder and his eyes flew open. This time she screamed and jumped backwards.

"Holy shit, Maria! What are you trying to do, give me a heart attack?"

"Why the hell didn't you answer your phone? And what happened to you? You're bleeding—there's blood everywhere!"

"You should be a cop, has anyone ever suggested that?"

"And you shouldn't be such a smart ass. Christy rang, she said you were drunk and threw her out."

He pushed himself up onto his elbows and groaned. "My head hurts."

Maria looked at the crusted, bloody, black gash on his forehead. "I can see why your head hurts, is that your brain I can see?"

"Are you serious, you can see my brain?"

She started laughing. "Okay, maybe that was a slight exaggeration."

He threw his legs out of the bed and pushed himself up. He held his hand out and she grabbed it, tugging him to his feet.

"Jeez, Frankie. This place looks like a crime scene. What happened?"

"Go make me something to eat while I wash up and I'll tell you all the gory details."

She shrugged. "Do I have a choice?"

"No food, no gossip."

She turned, leaving the room and Frankie to sort himself out, and began to pull out bacon and eggs from the fridge in the kitchen. She busied herself making them both breakfast, and when he finally came in, he looked and smelled much better. The gash above his eyebrow was angry and open, but his clothes were fresh. A trickle of blood was seeping from the wound, and she pulled a cloth out of the drawer, rolling it up she passed it to him.

"You're leaking; press this against it. You need stitches."

"No ER, I'm not explaining to some kid playing at doctors that my wife got me good."

"Where's your first aid kit?"

"Bathroom, top shelf in the cabinet."

Maria passed him his plate of bacon and eggs and retrieved the medical box. Placing it on the table she pulled out some gauze pads and tape.

"You haven't got any strips, we'll stick one of these on and stop off to pick some up. So, what happened?"

She stood there with her hands on her hips and her face stern. Frankie looked up from his food and let out the biggest sigh she'd ever heard.

"She's screwing around with my brother. I found a message on her cell."

"No way. Adam?"

"Yep, she accused me of—" He went quiet, not sure if he should tell her the next part of his story.

"What? What did she accuse you of?"

"Of sleeping with you."

Maria spat the mouthful of coffee she'd just taken a sip of all over. "Sorry, sorry. That's crazy, why does she think that?"

"I don't know, it doesn't matter. She's the one screwing around and then she threw a coffee cup at me."

"You could have her picked up, put her in the cooler for a few hours."

"No way, I'd never live it down."

He had a point. The guys would be rubbing it in for the next three years that Frankie couldn't handle his wife or keep her happy.

"So, what are you going to do?"

He shrugged. "No idea. Go to work I guess. But enough about me, why are you looking so dreamy eyed?

"I am not, I was scared you'd done something to hurt yourself."

"So, you do love me?"

"You know I do, but as my friend Frankie, not as my potential lover."

"Ouch, get that in whilst my cuts and broken heart are still fresh why don't you."

"Just making it clear, we're a team and I don't want that messing up and I better tell you now anyway, I had a date last night and enjoyed it."

She watched him to see how he would react but instead of the fury she'd expected, he grinned at her. "Well, I'll be damned it's about time."

Maria nodded. "I suppose it was."

She hoped that things were going to be okay for the both of them. They deserved a break—and more than a little happiness.

THIRTY-TWO

The cop hadn't given Miss Lily's a second glance as she sprinted by. If she had, she would have seen the man, perched on a stool in the window. Nursing a coffee and watching her every move.

He'd watched her come racing out of her apartment as if she was running for her life. Something was wrong; she looked serious and scared, and he wondered what had gotten her into such a mess. He downed the last of his coffee which was now cold, he'd been nursing it so long. He realised this was his chance to get to find out as much as he could about her. He stepped into the gloomy entrance and blinked a couple of times, his eyes adjusting to the darkness.

He walked across to the row of mailboxes and stared at the names. None of them meant a thing to him. For a start, he could discount all the Mr and Mrs. She didn't wear a ring and she'd only ever taken that cop she worked with in with her. That left eight possible mailboxes, all of them with first and second names except for one, with *MILLER* in black capitals. He stared at them. Which one would a NYC cop use? It had to be Miller. He would place a ten-dollar bet that was her.

The box next to it said *Miss Green*. If he could figure out who she was, he might be able to work out which was the cop's. As he picked up a brown paper package and turned the address label over; out of sight, the elevator doors opened. An old woman came out, dressed all in black with a large floppy hat and an oversize pair of Chanel sunglasses. He stared at her and she stared back.

"Can I help you?"

"I'm looking for Miller, she needs to sign for this."

"Eighth floor, apartment twenty-three."

"Thank you, ma'am."

The old elevator took forever to reach the eighth floor. When the doors finally opened, he let out a sigh of relief and found apartment twenty-three.

The hallway was dark, a couple of bulbs had blown, which would work in his favour. Hers was the last apartment on the right and quite some distance from the elevators. If he tried to ambush her here, it would be unlikely he would make it out without anyone intercepting him. It was risky. There were no surveillance cameras that he could see, and he didn't think this place provided high tech, covert cameras. The whole building needed a serious cash injection.

The hallway was deserted so he pulled his sleeve down and tried the handle. To his surprise he realized the door wasn't actually shut. Pushing it gently he peered through the gap. It was quiet; there was no TV or music playing.

"Hello, anyone home? I have a package delivery for Miller."

The silence that greeted him made his stomach clench with excitement. Checking the corridor to make sure he was still alone, he pushed the door wider and stepped inside. The thought of being inside the apartment of a cop as attractive as her made his legs quiver and his belly roll. It would be a challenge and it was very dangerous, he had no doubt about it, but it would make the result so much sweeter. The demon would appreciate all his hard work in making the final sacrifice the most significant.

Since he'd focused all his energy on making it happen, he felt different. He felt stronger, in control. The voices in his head were still there, only they were encouraging him. At first, he'd been worried they were mocking him, but they were agreeing with his ideas, egging him on.

He had the planchette tucked safely in his backpack, wrapped in a cloth. He didn't dare leave it at the house in the attic, just in case someone went in there and found it. The time was getting nearer; he just needed to make sure he could get her into the house without getting caught.

THIRTY-THREE

Miss Green hailed a cab. She had a yearning to go to church. Not just any church, she wanted to go to Saint Patrick's Cathedral on Fifth Avenue. She felt as if she needed to confess her sins in the Godliest place she knew, not that she had committed many. Chocolate, wine and expensive clothes were her worst vices. Who was she to turn down a designer handbag? She had nothing else to spend her money on and she did have lots of money.

Missy's days as a housekeeper for Clarke Carter had ended when he'd died and left her a lot of money for being a loyal employee and family friend. She'd stayed on after what had happened to Mae, the family thrown into turmoil and shock after her violent murder, and she'd been the one to pick up the pieces. It had been a terrible time; the newspaper reports had been shocking.

Mrs. Carter had stayed at the house on Staten Island and never came back to the House on West 10th Street. Clarke had told Missy over coffee one evening that she referred to it as Hell House, a den of inequity that had torn apart her entire family. Emilia had stayed there. She felt a duty toward her father and that she'd be deserting Emilia if she left. She was adamant it was her fault her friend was dead. If she hadn't taken ill, if Mae had never befriended her, she might still be alive and that had been a huge burden for her to bear.

Missy had tried her best to help Emilia. She had a soft spot for her—always had—but Emilia hadn't wanted any help. She'd wanted to be left alone in her grief, like her father. Clarke blamed himself, although he couldn't have known that James was so mentally disturbed that he would kill anyone in cold blood in the attic.

The house had never been the same after that night; it scared Missy and she wouldn't set foot on the attic staircase. There was always an uncomfortable feeling of being watched. The smell was the worst; from nowhere the halls or certain rooms would fill with the disgusting smell of what she could only describe as rotting garbage. It would fill a room, then seconds later be gone.

The house was always so dark, despite the bulbs being regularly changed, and it was always full of black shadows. The long hallways had filled her with dread; the light which had once filled the house no longer illuminated all the corners of the rooms. It was worst when the house was empty; on the rare occasion that Emilia or Clarke left, she would hear the sound of scratching and dragging. Only once did she summon up the courage to go up to the attic alone. The ice-cold fear that had filled her veins had been enough to send her running back down to her room where she threw herself on the floor and prayed harder than she'd ever done before. She had felt as if whatever it was that was there was taunting them. Time had no meaning for whatever thing James had summoned all those years ago.

The murder three years ago had been almost identical to Mae's, yet nothing had happened since. Who even knew about Mae? Emilia was the only Clarke family member left, since James had died in the hospital. He'd hung himself from the back of door with a bed sheet. Clarke and his estranged wife had both died within months of each other. The only fear she had was that someone or something had been summoned to the house to carry on with whatever the ritual was. Was the monster that lived in the attic strong enough to draw people in? That meant that there had been a shift—and it was dangerous for them all. Emilia needed to leave the house for her own safety, but what about all the other tenants who lived there? Were their lives in danger, too?

The cab stopped on the corner of Fifth and East 50th to let her out at Saint Patrick's Cathedral. She stood and stared up at the beautiful Neo-Gothic styled building. It was breathtaking. It stood there, serene and proud, taking up an entire city block it was so huge. And yet today, she couldn't quite enjoy its beauty. She had more pressing things on her mind: like how a couple of old gals could send one of Satan's soldiers back to the depths of hell, when neither of them was trained in religious studies nor knew exactly what it was they were dealing with.

Maybe she could recruit a priest whilst she was here. If she got a sympathetic one in confession, he might feel duty bound to help.

Or you could speak to one and ask for their help, Missy. Is there any point in faffing around? Just ask.

"Father, I need you to come fight the forces of evil in my friend's house on West 10th Street. It won't take long, maybe an hour and if you don't die trying, I'll make you a lovely pot of tea and the best chocolate chip cookies you've ever tasted."

As long as you don't tell him it's been lingering around, gathering strength since the fifties, you should be good to go. What's the worst that can happen?

The worst she knew was a sympathetic glance, a prayer and not being taken seriously.

She stepped into the cool foyer and smiled at the guard checking purses, but she didn't have one, so he waved her through. What kind of world was this that you couldn't go to church without the fear of some madman coming in with a gun and shooting dead the parishioners?

The church was warm, comforting and busy with tourists all walking around the edges of the pews. She admired the beautiful marble statues, altars and stained-glass windows. There was a mass in full flow, so she made her way to the gift shop; it wouldn't hurt to buy some rosary beads and Saint Michael medals just in case they needed them. She picked up a couple of rosaries and turned to see what was happening at the mass. It was then she noticed the man from the house—Mikey— who had been scared to death. He was now dressed as a security guard and was on purse-checking duty. He must have sensed her staring at him because he looked across at her, not recognizing her until she elevated her hand and waved. He smiled and waved back.

"Yes ma'am, can I help you?"

"These please."

She passed the beads and medals over to the shop assistant, along with fifty dollars. The cashier handed Missy her change.

"Put it in the donation box... Do you know that guard over there? Has he been working here long?"

"Who you pointing at? Mikey or Sasha?"

"The man."

"Mikey, yep, he's been here a few years. Why?"

"No reason. I've met him before, that's all."

The woman shrugged, then turned to serve the next person along. Missy clutched hold of the paper bag containing her things as if it was an expensive brooch off the Chanel counter and headed toward Mikey.

"You didn't say you worked here."

He frowned at her. "No, I didn't. Can't see that it's relevant."

She felt her cheeks begin to flush. "I'm sorry, it isn't. I'm being nosy."

"What brings you here? I can't say that I've seen you here before."

"That damn house brings me here." She looked up to the high ceiling, crossing herself. "It scares me stupid. I just wanted to come and speak to a priest. Maybe confess my sins, ask for some help. I don't know really, but it felt right. I'm glad that I did."

"Good, this is a special place. If you need to confess there is no finer place in this city to do it."

"How were you last night?"

He looked around to see if anyone was listening to their conversation. "Scared. I don't feel real comfortable talking about it here. If you get what I mean."

She nodded her head: she did. It didn't seem right talking about such abomination in a house of worship. "I'm sorry, you're working and I'm keeping you. I'll see you around, Mikey."

"Yes, you will."

She walked off toward the confessionals to wait for the priest to finish the mass. Not sure if it was going to help any, but determined to do it anyway.

Emilia stayed in her room a lot, venturing out for food and drinks. She hadn't spoken more than a few sentences to anyone since that night. She blamed herself and she knew that her father blamed himself.

She felt as if Mae was always going to be here, her soul trapped because of the horrific way she'd died at the hands of her brother. How was it even possible? James was locked up in Greystone Park Psychiatric Hospital for the rest of his life—or so she hoped, because how could they ever let him out of there? Nice, respectable people didn't murder innocent women.

As she lay in bed each evening she would strain and see if she could hear Mae's voice calling to her. She didn't quite know what she was going to do if she did. The thought of it was too much to comprehend. The police had found one of those stupid Ouija boards that were all the fashion up there. She'd heard people say they could speak to dead relatives through them. As far as she knew, the police hadn't taken it away. Why would they? It was of no use to them. Missy had also told her there were lots of symbols painted on the walls. Emilia desperately wanted to speak to Mae. She needed to tell her she was sorry.

She needed to hear that she forgave her and wasn't angry with her.

As she lay on her bed, she realized that she needed the board: if she could use it then she might be able to speak to Mae. She'd only known her a short time, but she missed her. They'd made such a strong connection, it was as if they had known each other for much longer. A loud sob erupted from her mouth. She'd wanted to be best friends with Mae forever; grow old together.

She stood up, pulling on a pair of slacks and a black sweater because she was shivering. She'd decided what she was going to do. Walking downstairs, she went to the library to see if her father was there, but it was empty. She checked the other rooms and there was no sign of him, then she went downstairs to the kitchen—Missy's favorite room. The woman was dressed in her overcoat with a hat, scarf and gloves.

"Well look at you, it's nice to see you up and dressed, Miss Emilia. Would you like me to fix you something to eat?"

"No, thank you. Where are you going?"

"Church, I need to go and say some prayers. Do you want to come with me?" She fixed Emilia with her piercing, hazel eyes.

"No, thank you. I'm not in the mood for church. Have you seen my father?"

"He left about an hour ago, he's gone to meet some business associates at The Waldorf. Would you rather I stayed here with you?"

Emilia shook her head vigorously. "No, I'm good. Thank you."

Missy crossed the room and, pulling Emilia close, wrapped her arms around her. "You need to start living your life Emilia, none of this is your fault. The only person to blame is your brother and he's paying the price for what he did."

She forced herself to smile. "Thank you. Say a prayer for me."

Missy laughed. "I'll be praying for us all."

She walked out of the kitchen and Emilia sat down at the long table. She lifted her hands and hadn't realized how much they were shaking until she tried to clasp them together.

She waited for the heavy, oak front door to slam. She shuddered, despite being dressed for winter, and the house kept warm. For the first time ever, she was alone in the house and not locked in the safety of her bedroom. Rifling through the kitchen drawers, she pulled out a huge butcher's knife. It felt heavy in her tiny hand, but it also felt good, reassuring. Even though she knew her brother was locked in a secure unit, in a padded cell where he'd never be able to hurt anyone else, she still didn't want to go up into the attic without something to protect herself. What if he escaped? It happened. She'd seen headlines in the *New York Times* before about killers who'd been locked up and escaped, going back to their favorite place to kill again.

She went upstairs to the drawing room, needing a slug of something strong to calm her nerves. On the large dresser were several crystal decanters, most of them containing brown liquid. She picked up the one full of clear liquid and tugged off the stopper. Lifting it to her nose she inhaled. It had a faint smell of alcohol, but it wasn't as potent as the assortment of whiskey and brandy in the others. Lifting it to her mouth, she tipped her head back and took a huge mouthful and swallowed. It made her choke so much she let go of the knife, which hit the wooden floor with a heavy clatter. Coughing and spluttering, she used her arm to wipe her streaming eyes with her sleeve. Her throat was burning.

When she eventually regained control of herself, she grinned. The vodka was warming her insides all the way down to her belly; she liked it. This time she took a glass and poured a generous measure out and took small sips of the liquid. It was like a magic potion; her shoulders which were tensed relaxed, and she felt much calmer than she had in months. Why had nobody told her this unassuming liquid would do the trick and make her feel better? Bending down to pick up the knife, she grabbed the decanter with the other hand and carried it upstairs to her bedroom. She was keeping this.

If her father dared to tell her off, she would tell him that if he hadn't decided to screw around with a girl not much older than his own daughter then they wouldn't be in this stinking mess. Emilia gasped. Who had said that? Not her. She didn't talk like that... ever. Then she smiled as she looked in the mirror, realizing that it had been her. With the help of her newfound liquid courage, she had indeed spoken like that.

Leaving her bedroom, she went up the next flight of stairs. There were so many rooms, all of them wasted. Her father slept on this floor, she slept on the one below and Missy slept in a self-contained apartment in the basement near to the kitchen. James had chosen the attic as his bedroom. It had always been creepy; she didn't like attics. She didn't like basements either, but at least the one in this house was used every day. It was the hub of the house and the one place that still felt alive. They'd been like four ghosts that passed in the night, rarely speaking to each other. It had been bad before Mae's murder; now it was even worse.

She walked along the hallway to the far end where the servants' stairs led down, and the narrow staircase led to the attic. She wasn't sure if it was her eyes playing tricks, but this part of the house seemed much darker than the rest. As she neared the foot of the attic stairs, the bulbs in the chandelier began to flicker and she looked up. It stopped, flared bright and then with a loud pop, a shower of hot glass exploded all over her.

Emilia screamed and jumped back, brushing the broken glass from her hair. Her heart racing, she didn't notice the trickle of blood running down her left cheek where a sliver of glass had left a fine slice in her delicate skin. She'd need to tell her pa to sort the lights out—she'd almost died of fright there and then.

Stepping over the pieces of glass, she began to climb the steps with the urge to speak to Mae stronger than ever. As she got to the top, the awful smell hit her. Was that what death smelt like? Was that what her beautiful, Chanel wearing friend now smelled like? Her stomach felt queasy. The door was shut, and she expected it to be locked—a part of her wanted it to be locked so she didn't have to go in. As she reached out and touched the doorknob, a wave of fear rushed through her veins. Gripping the knife tight in her left hand, she twisted the knob and pushed the door open so hard it flew back and slammed against the wall. She felt along the wall for the light switch, pushing it down to illuminate the room, and stepped inside.

THIRTY-FIVE

PRESENT DAY

Maria waited for Frankie. He was much slower this morning than usual and she wasn't sure whether he had concussion or a hangover. Probably both. He took forever getting out of the car as she held the heavy door of Sam's Deli open. She decided it wasn't the time to tease him, and so just smiled and let him lead the way to their usual booth tucked away at the back of the diner.

"Are you hungry?"

"I'm always hungry; gut is a bit off today though."

When Marge brought the coffee pot over, she looked straight at the mess on Frankie's face. "Someone try and knock some sense into you?"

"Something like that."

"Well, I sure hope you gave them something back, honey, they've ruined your good looks."

"You think so? I was thinking it made me look more rugged."

"If that's your brain leaking through that dressing, you're in big trouble, buster. You need every cell you have."

He gave her the finger and she walked away, laughing.

"So, what are we going to do? Did Gina say she could get here?"

As if he'd summoned her out of thin air, she said, "I'm here!" and squeezed into the booth next to Maria. "You're in luck, I wasn't far away when you called. I've come across some more stuff in the archives that might interest you."

Frankie arched an eyebrow at her. "Is that so? That's lucky because at this current moment in time, we're stumped on the *why*. We need a motive. What's the motive for two women being murdered in cold blood, decades apart from each other, and their limbs ripped from their bodies?"

"I think its devil worship at its highest level."

Maria looked at her. "What do you mean? Its highest level, what other level is there?"

"The thing is, I found some articles about how popular devil worship was back in the sixties and seventies, but it was also simmering away in the fifties. I can't help wonder if the first murder in 1952 was some sort of catalyst for the subsequent interest that followed."

Frankie was staring at his coffee cup, his brow furrowed. He looked at the two women opposite.

Gina spoke. "Whoever is doing it must have some knowledge and be into the occult. So, I think the murders are sacrificial offerings to summon the Devil. We need to start looking where devil worshippers hang out."

Maria nodded. "Yes, I think you're right. How would they know what to do?"

Gina put her elbows on the table. "He must have an instruction manual; there are all sorts of books out there."

"Like a spell book or a book of devil worship?" Maria had already thought about this herself. She began typing into Google. She looked up. "Holy crap you can buy a Satanic Bible on Amazon."

"So, it could be anyone, damn it."

Gina frowned. "No, I think whoever is doing this has more than a second-hand copy of a book off Amazon. I mean if you could summon demons for ten dollars, wouldn't we all be at it?"

Frankie shuddered. "Why the hell would anyone want to do anything like that?"

"It's about power, most of the bad crap that happens in this world is because some egotistical bastard is on a power trip."

"I think you're right, it is about power. So, James Carter wanted to summon the Devil in the fifties, only he didn't do a very good job of it." Frankie watched her face.

"No Frankie, I think he did a half decent job. There's something about that house on West 10th that freaks me out. It has a bad atmosphere. It smells bad inside, and I swear to God, I heard hooves clattering around on the wooden floorboards of the attic when I was speaking to the old lady. If he didn't do it properly, then whatever he did summon is trapped, half in this world, half in hell."

"So, this punk three years ago was trying to finish the job?"

She nodded. "Only it didn't work. Why wouldn't it work? Christ, I can't believe we're actually talking about this stuff. Your dad would have a coronary if he heard us."

Gina spoke. "He'd think we were all crazy. But I think I know why it didn't work—or at least not properly, because wouldn't we know if a demon had been unleashed onto the streets of New York?"

Frankie laughed. "Not necessarily, have you seen some of the crazies walking the streets? And we're talking about NYC, how could we tell?"

"I think he needs another sacrifice. It's all to do with the power of three. The mocking of the Holy Trinity is prevalent when there is a demonic presence. Have you ever watched those ghost shows on cable? You can guarantee there will be three knocks, three bangs. When anyone gets scratched, it's normally three red marks that are visible on the skin. Why wouldn't it work when summoning a demon?"

Both Maria and Frankie stared at her, mouths open and eyes wide. He turned to Maria. "You ever get the feeling we might be out of our depth on this one?"

Maria pictured herself in the library, something cold and strong squeezing the life out of her. "It's getting stronger..." she whispered.

"What, you're a psychic now are you?"

"Get screwed, Frankie. When I went to the library, I had this creeping sensation I was being watched and then suddenly I couldn't breathe. Something was squeezing the air out of my lungs, and I thought I was going to die. I was so cold and scared."

Maria expected Frankie to say something sarcastic but he must have realized how pale her complexion was, because instead, he reached out his hand and squeezed hers.

Gina looked at them both. "If it was able to do that it's stronger and it knows that you're onto it. It must be worried that you were gonna work it out and stop it."

It was Frankie who spoke. "If it's worried we're onto it, that means we can do something about it. We can stop it before it gets any stronger."

Maria was stunned he was taking this seriously. "How?"

"I don't know... What do they always do on the TV?" He directed his question at Gina.

"They call in a priest."

"That's it then. We go to the church, grab a priest and get them to go to the house and send it back to where it came from."

Gina began to laugh. "Easy, peasy. Why didn't I think of that?"

He shrugged then pointed to his head. "You either got it or you don't."

THIRTY-SIX

As they left the diner and waved goodbye to Gina, Maria got the feeling they were being watched. She turned around and scanned the street, the cars and the pedestrians. Nobody stood out. There were very few people around, but they were too busy talking into their headphones to give a damn about her. Still, she couldn't shake the feeling and a part of her wondered if it had anything to do with the thing at the house. She was too scared to call it by its name in case she somehow gave it strength.

"We need to go to a tattoo shop on the Lower East side in Orchard St, I've been researching tattoos and I think this is the place," she said.

"You need to go, but I don't. I'll wait outside in the car for you. Where are you getting inked then? Have you thought about this Maria, they don't wash off you know." He winked at her.

"Not for me. I was checking out places that specialize in ones like on the torso from the house."

"Nice work. But how many parlours are there—at least

fifty?" He started to laugh, then stopped and reached a hand up to touch the cut on his forehead.

"Actually, this is the one everyone recommends for those kinds of big colourful tattoos—all the reviews said to go there. And I saw a rose tattoo on their website not too dissimilar to our victim's."

He drove her to Stanton Street, stopping outside a bar called Hair of the Dog.

"This is a sign Frankie, maybe you need something to take the edge off. You've been a grouch all morning."

"My wife is cheating on me, she sliced my eyebrow open, and I have a hangover from hell: I'm so glad this amuses you Miller."

She pecked him on the cheek. "Sorry, that was in bad taste. I won't be long."

She jumped out of the car and hurried around the corner onto Orchard Street where she found the tattoo shop, Floral Glory, nestled between a bookshop and an empty store front. The sign on the door said *Closed* but she knocked anyway, hoping someone was there.

A woman with the most beautiful floral tattoos on both of her forearms opened it. For a moment, Maria was tempted to book an appointment to get one herself.

"Sorry to disturb you ma'am, I'm detective Miller. Do you have a few minutes?"

The woman nodded and opened the door. "Come in."

Pictures of every kind of flower she could name covered the shop from wall to wall.

"How can I help you?" The woman perched on a stool and pointed to another.

Maria hopped onto it. "I don't know if anyone has ever been here to ask previously, but I'm working a homicide from three years ago. If I showed you a picture of a tattoo, would you be able to identify it as being done by one of the artists here?"

"I might be able to... I don't actually do the tattoos. I'm Joy, the shop manager but I'm familiar with all the artists. I take the bookings, run things and have been doing it for five years."

For the first time in forever Maria felt a tiny spark of hope that this might just pay off and give them a huge payback. She took out her phone and found the pictures she'd snapped of the tattoo, wishing she'd brought the actual printed photographs with her. The girl took Maria's phone and held it close to her face, then nodded.

"Yep, that's one of Carly's; she's the owner of the shop. I actually remember her doing this one. It took a few sessions, and the girl was as hard as nails. She never flinched or complained once."

"Thank you, that's amazing. Is Carly around? I need to speak to her."

"You're out of luck, she's gone to visit her friend in Japan and is doing a spot of guest work whilst she's over there."

Every spark of hope that had filled Maria disappeared bringing with it a sinking feeling of despair.

"But I can look at the records for you and see who it was and where she lived."

"You can?"

"Well, I can if she didn't give me dodgy details."

She pulled out a keyboard and began to tap on it with the longest, pointiest set of fluorescent yellow nails Maria had ever seen. She turned the monitor toward Maria.

"Anya Petri, twenty-three years old and lives at 233a Essex Street—-or at least she did. There's a good chance she may have moved since then."

Maria jumped up. She wanted to kiss Joy on the lips she was so damn excited to have a possible lead. Instead, she reached out and shook her hand. "Thank you so much."

"Anytime."

Maria practically jogged back toward the car and clambered inside.

"I have a name and address for the victim. Take me to Essex Street please, we're looking for number 233a."

"Well, if you didn't just catch a break in the case. Good job Maria, all is forgiven."

He high-fived her and headed in the direction of Essex Street. It took them less than five minutes to reach the vintage clothes shop which was number 233. Anya must have lived in the flat above it. There was nowhere to leave the car, so Frankie double-parked and let Maria go check it out.

Maria went inside the shop and asked the woman straightening the clothes how to get to the flat.

"Around the back, but why do you want to go there? It's my flat and I'm here. Can I help you?"

"I'm homicide Detective Miller; I'm trying to trace a woman called Anya Petri."

The woman dropped the coat hanger she was holding and the heavy, black coat slid from it into a pile on the floor.

"You're looking for Anya?"

That feeling of things sliding into place filled Maria with another small hope that she was about to finally be able to identify their Jane Doe. She nodded.

"It's been three years since I saw her, why are you looking for her now? The police did not want to know when I went there and asked for their help."

"When was this?"

"Three years ago, I was back home in Russia, my mother was dying and my father could not cope. I left quickly and when I came back six months later, Anya had gone but her stuff was still in the apartment. I tried to find her but couldn't, so I went to speak to the police who told me she was not a high priority and had probably moved away."

Maria was furious. Of course there hadn't been much to go

on, but if the police had taken this seriously when it was reported, they could have identified her a lot sooner.

"What's your name?"

"Petra Orlov."

"Petra, did you check her Facebook, social media, speak to friends?"

She shrugged. "I did what I could, spoke to the few people who knew her—we both worked at the Russian Bar on 52nd. I felt bad. I left her on her own to pay the bills... I wanted to go and make it right. Only they haven't seen or heard from her since the day after I left."

Maria felt every nerve in her body tense up.

"When did you leave?"

"The first of December."

Maria wanted to punch the air and shout yes as loud as she could. This might be the break they were looking for. If they could identify the victim and trace her last movements, they might be able to place her with her killer, who they could bring to justice—and who could then explain to them what the hell was going on with that house.

"I'm going to take as many details from you as you can give me. I know it's been a while, but the more information you can give me about Anya, the better chance I have of finding her. Do you have a photograph of Anya? Does she have any tattoos or scars?"

Petra nodded and began to log into Facebook where she brought up the profile of a beautiful young woman with icy blond hair and cornflower blue eyes.

"Yes, a big one, roses across the side of her body."

Forty minutes later Maria was heading back to the car where Frankie was snoring so loudly she could hear it from twenty feet away. She felt bad: he looked terrible. His normal tanned complexion was pale, his face was a mess, and he was exhausted, probably suffering from a delayed hangover as well. He needed to go home and sleep, so she decided to keep the latest information from him until tomorrow when he would be feeling better. She opened the door which made him jump.

He sat up, wiping his mouth with his sleeve. "Was I drooling?"

"No, sorry. I didn't realize you were asleep. Look there isn't much we can do right now. I'll go and see a priest at the local church and ask them if they can come to the house with us tomorrow. There's probably all sorts of crap you have to go through to even get them to do that. Why don't you go home, get some rest and you'll be feeling brighter tomorrow?"

"I'm okay, I'll go with you."

"No Frankie, you're not. I have a headache just looking at your face and I can't be bothered. Let me take you home, we'll call it a day. Start fresh in the morning."

She avoided looking him in the eye, in case she'd upset him.

"You don't mind? You won't be mad at me?"

"Hey, of course I don't. Addison has given us free reign for a couple of weeks. We'd be fools not to go a little bit easy on ourselves. One afternoon isn't going to hurt—we can make up for it tomorrow."

He turned the key in the ignition and pulled out. "Yeah, you're right. What the hell, a few hours off will do us both some good."

She smiled to herself. "Actually, I'm going to get out and walk, I want to go shopping."

He stared at her. "Are you ill? You hate shopping?"

She laughed. "No, I need some new clothes. I fancy having a stroll down Fifth and doing some window shopping. I need to do something different, take my mind off this case."

"I'll drop you off."

She opened the car door. "No, you won't, you'll get stuck in

Midtown traffic. It's quicker for me to walk. You get yourself home. If you need me call me, I mean it."

He nodded. She slammed the door shut, waited for him to drive away, then hailed a cab. One pulled over and she jumped in.

"The Russian Bar on 52nd please."

Whether it was still open she had no idea, but it was worth a shot. Pulling the photo out of her pocket that Petra had given her she stared at it. Although not the clearest of pictures, it showed a beautiful, young woman laughing with Petra. Their arms draped around each other, shot glasses in hand, raised toward the photographer. Maria was almost sure that Anya was their Jane Doe, even if the bloodied, headless corpse looked nothing like the image in her hand. After all this time, they had something to go on. They were one step closer to identifying her. Which also meant they were one step closer to finding her killer.

THIRTY-SEVEN

Missy waited patiently for the priest to finish his last confessional; there had only been four and she'd been one of them. When he stepped out of the box, she was surprised to see just how young he was; she'd been expecting an older guy. She stood up from the hard, wooden pew she was perched on and called out.

"Father, have you a minute?"

He looked at her and she would bet his instinct was telling him to say no, but he smiled, showing a set of brilliant, white teeth that any Hollywood movie star would be proud to own and headed in her direction.

"Of course, how can I help?"

For a split second she felt guilty. She was about to involve this young man in something so horrible and detrimental that it might just put him off the priesthood for life. But what choice did she have?

"Thank you for the confession, it's right what they say. It is good for your soul."

He laughed. "Well, as long as I helped. That's what it's all about."

"You might regret ever meeting me today, but I need your help. It's about a matter of life and death and I have no idea who else to ask."

"Well, now Ms—"

"Miss Green, but please call me Missy."

"Well then, Missy, how can I be of service?"

"Is there somewhere we can talk, away from the tourists and photographers?"

"I was just going to grab myself my afternoon Starbucks, you're welcome to join me."

She would rather not have to drink in one of those over-priced coffee shops, but she knew this might be her only chance.

"If you don't mind an old crone cramping your style, I'd love to."

"Great, follow me. I know a short cut."

He led her out of the cathedral across the road and into the Rockefeller Concourse. Missy was fit for her age, but he was a gentleman and kept to her pace. Before too long the steamed-up windows of a coffee shop appeared in sight. He held the door open and gestured for her to take a seat. "You take a seat, I'll grab the drinks. As long as you don't want some fancy crap I can't pronounce."

He laughed. "No, just a plain cappuccino with an extra shot. Don't worry, they know what I like, just point to me when you get to the till."

Missy did just that: when the kid behind the counter asked her name and order she pointed to the priest, realizing she didn't know his name, and the kid said, "You with Father Anthony?"

She nodded.

"We got his drink down, what would you like ma'am?"

"Coffee, just a regular coffee please with milk."

She handed over the money and waited for the drinks. It was like a cattle market: the queue was almost out of the door.

Suddenly, she felt a hand on her shoulder. "You sit down, I'll bring them over." She smiled at the kid who looked not much older than eighteen and thanked him, her perception of the staff in the overpriced shops changing dramatically.

As she sat on the leather bench in the corner, the priest smiled at her.

"Well, this is my first time in one of these shops. I was a Starbucks virgin until sixty seconds ago."

Father Anthony laughed and she immediately felt at ease; he seemed a good man with a normal sense of humour.

"So how can I help you, Missy?"

She felt her stomach lurch at the very thought of talking about it in public, in a coffee shop to a priest. It just didn't sit right.

"I'm going to sound like I belong in a psych unit and you're probably going to wonder if you should call the cops or the emergency medical services. I need you to trust that I'm one hundred percent sane—and also that I'm telling the truth. I wish I could have been long gone before it happened again, but for some strange reason God either has a wicked sense of humour or he needed me to keep an eye on it. Either way, I'm screwed and more than a little scared."

He moved closer, his eyes fixed on her. "I'm listening."

She nodded. "Do you believe that evil exists?"

He smiled. "Missy, I'm not sure if you've noticed the dog collar or not. I'm a priest, my whole career depends upon the existence of evil."

She laughed. "Yes, I guess it does. I'll put it another way, do you believe that a person can summon a demon?"

He nodded. "Yes, I do. I know that they can for a fact."

"You do? Good because this is not some bullshit I'm about to tell you. This is one hundred percent a true story—a horrible story, but I have to tell someone."

"Then you better tell me."

THIRTY-EIGHT

She didn't understand how it could still smell so bad. A professional team had come in and cleaned up the blood months ago. A faded pentagram was still on the wall; it looked as if they had tried to scrub it clean and failed miserably. Mae's blood. In a way, that was all there was physically left of her. Emilia forced herself to cross the room so she was standing right in front of it. Reaching out and placing the palm of her trembling hand against it, she sobbed.

Oh Mae, I'm so sorry. Are you still here or did you go to a better place? I really hope you did.

She pressed her forehead against the cool wall and closed her eyes. Willing an image of her beautiful friend to come into her mind, she tried to concentrate, emptying her head of all thoughts until all she could see inside her head was white. It was then that she heard the sharp scratching of claws on the bare floorboards behind her. Something was coming toward her, something with razor sharp claws, and she could hear the wood splintering.

Her eyes flew open, and she felt the hot, foul-smelling breath of something breathing down her neck as a growl erupted into her ear, a growl so close it felt as if its mouth was touching her skin. Emilia had never felt fear like it.

Afraid to turn around and see what was behind her, she froze to the spot and began to pray like she'd never prayed before. Mae wouldn't growl at her. This was something bad— really bad. Clenching the knife in her fist, she counted to three and spun around, expecting James to be standing behind her, wild eyed and crazy. She swung the knife and it sliced through the air. How could that be? She could smell it. Hell, she could feel it—and she'd heard it.

She looked at the gouges in the wooden floor, sensing the danger. The raw animal enmity. Yet the room was empty, or at least it was to her naked eye. Then she spotted the Ouija Board and planchette underneath the coffee table. Her mouth dry and heart pounding, she lunged for it, grabbing them both before turning and running to the door.

For a fleeting moment she imagined whatever beast or animal it was blocking the doorway and her exit. Then she was through it and stumbling onto the landing. For what good it was, she slammed the door shut behind her, then ran downstairs to her bedroom where she flung the door shut, locking it. Her legs were trembling so much that she collapsed onto the bed, her heart thudding so loudly in her chest that the sound deafened her.

Dropping the board and planchette on the bed next to her, she placed the knife on the nightstand. She wished more than anything that she wasn't alone in the house. Did whatever it was know that she was alone? *What did you do, James? What have you done to our home?*

Sitting on the bed, she drew her knees up to her chest and wrapped her arms around them and hugged herself. The knife lay within reach if she needed it, but what good was a knife against something that you couldn't see?

If by some miracle she didn't die of fright before the morning, she was going to insist on visiting James. She would find out exactly what he'd done tomorrow and find out how to deal with it. Having a clear plan of action made her feel a little better, and when after fifteen minutes no gargantuan beast from the depths of hell had broken her door down, she began to relax a little.

There was no doubt about it, her brother had been messing with things that were way out of his control. Well, there was no way she was going to spend the rest of her life paying for his mistakes. First thing, she would visit her father's friend at Saint Patrick's and ask him for his help. Then, she would go to Greystone and demand that James tell her how to put things right. The atmosphere in this house wasn't just one of grief and despair. It was one of fear—and pure evil.

* * *

Emilia opened her eyes and blinked. How had she fallen asleep? She had waited, locked in her bedroom, for either her father or Missy to come home. The sun was shining through the crack in the curtains. She looked at the clock, it was almost seven. She was on top of her covers, fully dressed. The Ouija board and planchette were on the floor. She must have knocked them off. The knife was still where she'd left it—and she was still alive which was an unexpected blessing.

She had never realized how precious life was until she lost Mae. She got herself up, washed and dressed then unlocked her bedroom door. She tucked the knife under her pillow, not knowing what good it would do against the thing that was hiding in the attic. It made her feel better—not like some helpless damsel in distress.

She hadn't realized just how tough she was until last night when she was faced with the fear of being attacked. She knew she wouldn't go down without a fight. Whoever or whatever was up there would have to give its best shot to kill her.

Hindsight was a wonderful thing, she had no idea how James had got Mae upstairs, but she hadn't known at the time that she was walking up to her death. She was aware that the dynamics in this house had changed and not for the better, so stepping out onto the landing she wasn't sure what to expect. The smell of rotting garbage still lingered, much fainter than last night.

Down in the kitchen, the smell of fresh pancake batter filled the air and Emilia's stomach let out a loud groan. She walked into see the biggest stack of pancakes she'd ever seen.

"Are you hungry, Missy?"

"Yes, I am. I also have a visitor coming for breakfast." Missy turned around, the grin across her face turning into a screech as she dropped the spatula she was holding.

"Shoot, Miss Emilia, what happened to you?"

Emilia frowned and turned to stare at her reflection in the kitchen window, making her do a double take. *Was that even her?* Her face was pale and there were the biggest dark circles under her eyes she'd ever seen. Her hair was stuck up and she looked dreadful.

Turning to Missy she whispered, "I don't know..."

"Well, you need to sit down, eat something and have a think about it because you look like a walking corpse."

"Missy, do you believe in..." She tried to find the right words, but they were stuck in her throat. It was as if she couldn't bring herself to speak them aloud in case what she was terrified of would be brought to life because of it.

Missy sat opposite her and clasped Emilia's hand.

"Do I believe in ghosts, demons? I'd never had much call to consider it, but these past few months I have. A lot. And if you want the honest answer, it's *yes*, something is hiding upstairs in the attic. I haven't seen it, but I've felt it. I didn't want to bother you or Clarke, but it's getting stronger, and I'm scared for us all."

There was a loud knock at the front door which made them both startle. Missy stood up, rushing to answer it. Emilia forked three pancakes from the stack, put them on a plate and carried them back to the table where she drizzled maple syrup all over them. She had a feeling she needed to keep her strength up.

Muffled voices were followed by two pairs of footsteps coming down the stairs. When she looked up, she felt a huge wave of relief to see a priest standing behind Missy. He crossed the room and shook her hand.

"Charles Morgan, pleased to meet you."

"Emilia Carter." She gripped his hand much harder than she meant to. It was huge and warm, and felt safe; she didn't want to let it go.

Missy pointed to a chair and he sat down. He began to talk about the weather, the upcoming masses and a choir concert he was helping to organize while Missy made a pot of coffee and placed it on the table along with the stack of pancakes. Emilia was eating whilst he spoke; he had one of those easy, pleasant voices to listen to—it wouldn't have mattered if he was talking Italian to her. He made her feel safe and she hadn't felt like that in this house since the day before Mae's murder.

She noticed how his hand kept moving up to the starched, white, collar he wore around his neck, his fingers pushing inside it as if it was too tight and he was trying to loosen it. Emilia was fascinated by it because he clearly didn't even know that he was doing it. His cheeks were turning pinker by the minute, as if he was in the middle of a sauna and not their draughty kitchen. There was a fine film of sweat on his brow and he pulled a handkerchief from his pocket to dab at his forehead. The whole time she couldn't stop staring at him, until Missy joined them at the table.

"What's the matter, Father? You look ill?"

He stared at Missy as if he couldn't understand what she was saying. Emilia giggled. It was rude of her and she knew that, but she couldn't help it amid the strangeness of the moment. Both of them stared at her and she stopped as abruptly as she'd started.

"Sorry, I don't know why I'm even laughing because none of this is the least bit funny. In fact, I'm terrified because there is something evil in this house that no one can see. Except for James, I think maybe that he could. I think the only reason it's here is because of him. He's so sick he killed my best friend. Chopped her head off like he was doing something normal then summoned a demon. Why would he want to do that, Father?"

Charles picked up his tea and began to sip it, mopping his brow at the same time before speaking. "I don't know why he did it or how he did it, but he's done something bad. I felt fine before I set foot in this house and now, I feel as if there's a tight band squeezing the life out of my chest. Something is trying to suffocate me—only I won't let it. Whatever evil he has summoned is strong, I'll give it that. But it is not as strong as God. I'm a servant of God and he has given me his blessing to fight Satan and his legion to keep his children safe. That's what I'm here to do. We can't talk here though; I need to get outside, into the fresh air. Tell me... That smell of rotting flesh, how long has it permeated the air inside the house?"

Emilia nodded, glad he could smell it too. "It was never prevalent until after Mae's murder, now it lingers in the air. It comes and goes, sometimes it's so powerful it makes me gag. Other times I can barely smell it."

He stood up. "I didn't come prepared. I wouldn't leave and give in so quickly, but I have nothing on me to protect any of you and I won't deal with it if there's a slight chance you could be in danger."

Missy spoke. "Are we in danger?"

He looked around the room as if making sure no one had

crept in to eavesdrop on their conversation whilst their backs were turned. "Yes, you are. Anyone who chooses to live in this house is in danger. Can't you feel it, hovering in the background like some disease? It's cunning and strong, but it can be dealt with. I need to speak to the archbishop and take some advice and then I'll be in touch with you, Missy. If you need to talk anytime then come to the church, I'm always around and if not, someone will get a message to me."

He crossed the room and made the sign of the cross on both of their foreheads with his thumb. Then, placing both hands on top of their heads, he began to recite a prayer in Latin. Emilia closed her eyes. The warmth of his hand on her head made her feel safe and at peace for the first time since that night.

Why, when her life was beginning to get interesting, did it all have to be taken away so brutally? She was so glad to have had the pleasure of Mae in her life for what short time they'd spent together. She had been like a breath of fresh air to this house and she hoped that Mae had enjoyed her last days as much as she had. Of course, she would give anything to turn back the clock and change it. Even if it meant her pop never having an affair with Mae and Emilia forging such a close friendship for the first time in her life. If she could stop it all before it happened, she would, treasuring the knowledge that she'd known how swell it was to find a friend so special. She felt the pressure removed from her head and opened her eyes to see that Missy was holding a paper towel in her hand. She waved it at her, and it was only then Emilia realized that her cheeks were damp and she'd been crying.

THIRTY-NINE

PRESENT DAY

The taxi pulled to the sidewalk, she paid her money and got out. The bar was all in darkness, and she pressed her face against the glass. Cupping her hand against her forehead to block out the light, she saw movement in the far corner and hammered on the glass. Pulling her ID from her pocket, she pressed it against the plate glass window so whoever was inside would see her badge. The door opened enough for her to squeeze in, and she found herself standing in front of the biggest man she'd ever seen. He crossed his arms against his chest, then nodded at her.

"NYPD Detective Miller. I need to ask you or anyone else who works here some questions about a girl who may have gone missing in December 2019."

He stayed silent and straight-faced, and so she pulled the photograph from her pocket and passed it to him. He studied it and she wondered how long he was going to take when he muttered.

"Anya."

"Yes, Anya. Do you know her?"

He pointed to a bar stool. "Please, sit down."

As she sat at the stool, he moved behind the bar. Maria had never seen so many types of vodka in her entire life. Bottles of every color and flavor you could imagine were lined up against the glass mirror on the oak bar. He unscrewed the cap off one and poured them both a large measure. She took it, not wanting to insult him, and stared at it. He downed his then poured another. Turning to look at her she noticed his eyes were brimming with tears and she wondered how close he and Anya had been. Lifting the shot glass to her lips, she took a sip and immediately regretted it. She coughed and spluttered as it burnt all the way down her throat.

"Sipping is no good, you need to tip your head back and swallow it all. Yes, I know Anya. Very well, she worked here six nights a week. Never missed a shift. One night she picked up some guy and they got drunk in the corner together."

He pointed to a booth. "She never came back... It broke my heart. I liked her, she was a good worker. A kind girl, easy on the eye."

"Did you report it to the police?"

He laughed. "What was there to report? She shacked up with some guy who bought her drinks all night. He made her happy, it's life."

"Could you describe the guy she was with?"

He began to search around under the counter behind the bar, muttering in Russian under his breath. He shouted, "Da!" and passed a piece of paper to Maria: a grainy black-and-white still of Anya with a man. It wasn't the best quality, but it was something.

"That's him. I showed it to the police one night when they came here to drink. I asked them what to do and they told me nothing. She was an adult and I should find myself another girlfriend. Anyway, I didn't like the guy, something about him was off. I have a nose for that kind of thing, I found out from a friend of a friend that his name was Ryan Fletcher, but I could not find him—no one knew where he lived. I think he was what you people call no fixed abode. Do you know where Anya is?"

Maria couldn't tell him she was one hundred percent sure she was dead—and that she had been for the past three years. It was the same girl Petra had showed her earlier and her heart tore at the thought of this young, beautiful life cut short, but Maria also now had a name of the guy who Anya had last been with.

"No, I don't. I'm looking into a cold case in which Anya may be involved and I'm following up what little leads we have. Can I keep this? I'll return it as soon as I can. Does she have any tattoos or birthmarks?"

He nodded at her. "Yes, she has roses and vine tattoo from her leg to her..." He pointed to his chest. "I should have called it in and made more of a fuss? Yes?"

She didn't want to make him feel any worse than he already did. "You weren't to know. Thank you for your help."

She lifted the shot glass and downed the rest of the vodka. He smiled and saluted her.

"Hey, if you find her tell her Viktor wants to say hello."

"I will," she replied, tugged the heavy door open and stepping out into the sunlight, which was so bright she had to blink several times.

So, their Jane Doe was Anya Petri. The tattoo had been a huge step in a positive identification. Poor Viktor carried a bit of a flame for the beautiful girl. Who wouldn't? She was stunning.

The feeling that things were coming together along with the shot of strong vodka made Maria smile for the first time today. She couldn't wait to tell Frankie, but it wouldn't be today. She'd come back tomorrow to show the photographs of the tattoo to Viktor—and she would probably bring Frankie with her when she broke that news to Viktor. He might have looked huge and tough, but it was going to devastate him.

Right now, though, she needed to go back to the station to

look up Anya Petri and Ryan Fletcher; see if there was anything on the system about her, along with Petra and Viktor. Who wasn't to say they weren't all involved in an organized crime group, or had something to do with her murder?

Her phone beeped and she smiled as she read the text.

Busy tonight or do you fancy grabbing a bite to eat? You choose where and when. Harrison x

She did fancy going out for supper— it would take her mind off today. A twinge in her stomach reminded her something was wrong, and suddenly, picturing Frankie's bruised and bloody face wiped the smile off her face. She felt bad; almost as if she was cheating on him. *Come on Maria how can you cheat on a guy who isn't your lover? He's your friend and partner. That's it.* Before she could change her mind, she began typing back.

Love to, Black Tap on Broome @ 8pm. x

Tomorrow she would tell Frankie about Harrison—she might feel better for it. Confession was supposed to be good for the soul. He wouldn't be mad at her; he'd be happy. She was worrying over nothing. Then, she could cheer him up with the news that they finally had an ID for their victim. Tomorrow, they would go back with a warrant to see if Petra had anything that belonged to Anya that they might be able to match to her DNA. But Maria knew in her gut that it was Anya, and that was all that mattered.

She thought about getting the subway, but it was too hot to be stuck down there. Normally she'd walk, but she didn't have the time today. She wanted to get as much information off the system as she could before going home for a shower. She looked like a tramp in her sweats and not her usual work attire. Hailing her second cab of the day, she asked him to drop her at the station.

Maria's head was spinning, and she could feel the beginnings of a migraine in the back of her eyes. She massaged her temples. Frankie had given her a heart attack this morning. All in all, today had been one stressful mess. She was looking forward to a couple of drinks and some food with Harrison. All week she'd been fantasizing about one of the Black Tap's freak shakes because they made the best damn milkshakes in the city. She'd earned one after her run to Frankie's apartment this morning.

When she slipped into the station, no one gave her a second glance—which was fine by her. The department was unusually quiet. She sat down at her desk and began typing in the passwords to get access to the system to run the checks she needed. She could hear Addison shouting down the phone inside his office, even with the door shut. She needed to get out of here before he dragged her in for an update. He'd want to know where Frankie was, and she wasn't about to drop him in it.

Sending everything to the printer, she slipped from her desk and went the long way around to collect her paperwork so she wouldn't have to pass her boss's office window. She waited for the ancient printer to spit out her papers, crossing her fingers in the hope that he wouldn't see her and yell for her to go speak to him. When the printer finished, she scooped the pages up, shoved them into a cardboard file and ran down the stairs, leaving by the rear exit so she wouldn't have to talk to anyone. The thought of a cold shower back at her apartment gave her a good enough reason to keep walking, despite the uncomfortable heat and the tiredness spreading through her bones.

By the time she finally reached her apartment block, she was hot, smelly and needed a glass of wine or a candy bar to boost her energy, probably both. Relieved to be in the cool foyer, she leaned against the wall as she called the elevator. It was quiet in here. Especially compared to the hustle out there today. She'd cut through the park which was busy—it was always busy, just how she liked it. Maybe after they'd eaten, they could sit in the park and watch the world go by. It would be perfect if

Marvin was playing tonight, and even better if Sam was singing along.

She stepped out of the elevator on her floor and immediately did a double take. Miss Green came out of her apartment, dressed as impeccably as ever, but she looked as if she had aged twenty years since yesterday.

"Maria, I'm glad you're here. You left your front door open —what were you thinking? I came home a couple of hours ago and it was wide open. I called out, but there was no answer so I had a quick look inside—it didn't look as if you'd been broken in to. So, I shut it behind me, I hope you have your key?"

Maria felt every nerve-ending in her body spark to life as the adrenalin began to rush through her veins. But she didn't want to scare her neighbor any more than she already was—she quite frankly already looked terrified.

"Thank you, I'm so sorry. I rushed out this morning and can't have shut it properly." This was true: she'd been so panicked about Frankie, she had literally run out and couldn't remember whether she'd shut the door behind her. Still, alarm bells were ringing.

"I do hope everything's okay, honey. I'll catch you later; you still owe me some gossip."

Maria laughed, waiting what felt like an age before the elevator doors finally closed behind her neighbor. Pulling her gun from the holster, she thought maybe she should call one of the cops from the station to come down and check her apartment. Her not very big apartment, which she could clear in two minutes. Deciding against it, she put the key in the lock and pushed open the door. Lifting the gun, she stepped inside.

FORTY

Maria paused for a moment, pushing the door wide open so she had a clear view of the hall. Reaching in, she pressed the light switch, waiting for the flickering light to stay on long enough to illuminate the apartment. She moved from room to room, opening one door after the other, checking under the bed, in the closets and behind the curtains. Nothing looked out of place: there wasn't anything missing. Saving the bathroom until last, she had a fleeting moment of fear, wondering if there was anyone hiding in the tub behind the shower curtain. She grabbed it and ripped it to one side, letting out a sigh of relief. She must have left the door ajar in her panic about Frankie; there was no other explanation for how it could have been wide open. Turning around she saw that the toilet seat was up and felt the hairs on the back of her neck prickle. Stepping closer, she stared into the bowl which was clean. She never left the seat up and always shouted at Frankie whenever he did, so how was it up now? He hadn't been in here today. Had she lifted it up to clean it?

She knew she hadn't. She went into the bedroom to check her drawers, pulling them out one by one. She sat down on the bed, her hands shaking. Should she call it in? Get CSI out to dust for prints. She could hear Addison's voice in her head: *Tell me again why you need CSI, Miller? Because you left your front door open, and nothing has been disturbed except your toilet seat?* Fuck that, he'd think she was going crazy.

She did another check of every room. It just didn't make sense—unless someone had come in and used the john while they had the opportunity.

She went back to the bathroom and took a photo of the offending toilet seat, then shuddered. Pulling on a pair of rubber gloves, she set about immersing the bowl, seat and every other part of it in a bleach bath. It was so strong she felt as if the hairs in her nose had been burned off by the chemical. Satisfied it was clean, she stripped off the gloves and dropped them in the waste basket.

"Are you losing it, you might have spent twenty minutes cleaning a toilet that only you've used?!" she said out loud to her reflection in the mirror. She laughed at the possibility. Feeling better, she turned on the shower and stripped off. She needed to get ready to meet Harrison. At least she didn't have far to go; Black Tap was only three blocks away.

This time when Maria left her apartment, she checked the door was shut tight. She felt nervous about seeing Harrison, but she felt more nervous about coming home late at night to an empty apartment. She checked her watch as she approached the Black Tap: she was a little late, but he'd have to expect that with her job. As she reached the door a little breathless, she waved at Harrison who had somehow managed to grab a rarely vacant window seat. She walked in and her stomach groaned at the smell of burgers and fries with the underlying smell of sweet vanilla. A table behind them was full of students all sipping at the most amazing strawberry pink, cotton candy creations she'd ever seen.

Harrison stood up. He opened his arms and his lips brushed against her cheek. "You look and smell even better than those milkshakes."

Maria giggled. "I'll take that as a compliment because right now those milkshakes are the best things I've ever laid my eyes on. They smell amazing."

She sat down in the window seat opposite him and noticed he looked a little bit uncomfortable surrounded by laughing teenage girls.

"Sorry, I didn't realize it would be so busy or so loud."

"Don't be sorry, I had to stop myself from drooling at the food when it was taken to that table over there."

The waiter appeared and Maria rhymed off her order without looking at the menu. Harrison looked at him. "I'll have the same please."

He took their menus and disappeared.

"Are you okay?"

He waved his hand in front of Maria's face—she hadn't realized she'd been staring into space.

"Sorry, it's been a long day. Yes, I'm fine."

"Do you want to talk about it?"

Instinctively, she shook her head, always the one to act tough. Her eyes betrayed her though and she felt stupid when they began to tear up.

"Hey, talk to me. It's what friends do—and I'd like to think I'm your friend, that you value me enough to be able to tell me what's bothering you."

Picking up a napkin, she dabbed at the corner of her eye and laughed. "I don't know what's wrong with me. I'm so sorry, I guess I'm tired."

She looked at his face and realized that she wanted to talk to him, to tell him all about her messed-up day. The worry of finding her apartment door open and her fear of someone being inside. Before she knew it, she was pouring out the day's events to him. Only pausing when the waiter brought their milkshakes over.

"Did you call the cops, Maria?"

She laughed. "I am the cops. No... I didn't."

"Why not?"

"I couldn't be sure if I'd left the door open and the toilet seat up. I was so scared about Frankie I ran out of there. My head was all over the place. I'm probably being paranoid."

"Well, you're not going home tonight. When we leave here, we're going to my apartment. I have a spare room you can stop in. I'll go with you tomorrow to yours and we'll check it out, I have a friend who can fit a camera on your front door and extra security measures. I want you to be safe."

He reached out and stroked her cheek. For the first time in a long time, she knew that this was what she wanted. She didn't want to be alone tonight. She wanted to spend the night with him. Preferably in his bed, with his arms wrapped around her, feeling safe and loved.

"Would you not mind?"

He laughed. "For a moment I was expecting you to give me a whole load of crap about not needing a man to keep you safe. I can think of nothing that I would like more. It would be my pleasure."

"Thank you, that's great." And in that moment, she realized that it didn't matter what the hell Frankie would think when he found out she'd stopped at Harrison's . This was her life, and she was tired of being lonely.

* * *

He sat there cross-legged, not daring to breathe. It was amazing how she hadn't checked the crawl space in the hall closet. It was tucked away at the back, behind the rack of coats. He was lucky that he had found it, but he'd known there would be someplace in the apartment to hide. It was tiny, and he could only just fit inside. He had managed to stretch his legs enough that he didn't get cramp, but he didn't know how long he'd be in here for. He hoped it wasn't too long.

However, he was furious with himself. All he'd done was pee. Habit had made him lift the seat and he hadn't even considered to put it down. He wouldn't make that mistake again. If she left the apartment he would make his escape through the window next to the fire escape. He should have got out when he had the chance, but he'd wanted to see her relaxed.

Stupidly, he'd also left the door open when he'd gone in, but that was how he'd found it and he didn't want to arouse her suspicions too much. She could have come back at any moment, so as soon as he'd found his snug hiding place, he'd crawled inside. The warmth and the dark had made him feel safe and he'd drifted off, awaking to the sound of someone throwing open doors and slamming around.

At first he'd felt disorientated, wondering where he was— and then the closet door had been thrown open and he'd smelled her perfume. Chanel. It all came back to him. He was taking a huge risk; one that was worth it in every sense. Even if she dragged him out and shot him, at least he'd die looking into her eyes.

Finally, he heard the shower turn off. It had taken every ounce of his self-control not to sneak out and take a peek. He didn't know what he'd do if he saw her naked body. He wasn't a sexual predator. Anya had slept with him of her own accord, but would the sight of a naked woman whose apartment he was hiding in be too much for him to bear? So he stayed where he was, pins and needles beginning in his feet and legs. He shifted slightly, hoping that she was going to go back out soon or he'd have to risk it all.

The closet door opened again and he got a stronger smell of the perfume; she must have been about to go out. He could see her bare ankles, the heels she was wearing not too high—just enough to accentuate her slender calves—and he felt himself getting hard. He imagined what else she was wearing. He didn't think she would be the kind to wear a short skirt; she would go for a knee length dress. Something black. He didn't care what to be honest: she would look good in anything and he couldn't wait to get her back to the apartment. The beast was getting restless; it had been waiting for an eternity to be set free. When it was, he would have the power to attract any woman he wanted—women like Maria would flock to him and be ready to satisfy his every need. This city wouldn't know what had happened and he would be there for the ride.

FORTY-ONE

Emilia bid goodnight to Missy. They hadn't spoken much after the priest had left, both afraid that the monster who was half living in their world and half in the underworld could hear them. They didn't want to let it know what they were planning to do.

She hoped that Father Morgan could help them, but if he went to the archbishop, he had to make him believe him. How long was that going to take? She wanted this resolved, now. She wanted her home back the way it was: warm, peaceful and as happy as a home could be under these terrible circumstances.

What had happened to James? She didn't understand why he had done this; it didn't make any sense. As she went upstairs to bed, she couldn't get the image of Mae out of her head. She wanted so badly to speak to her and ask her forgiveness.

She went into her room and shut the door, turned the key in the lock and looked at the Ouija board. What did she have to lose? It was a stupid child's game; nothing more. James was mentally unbalanced. He did what he did out of pure hatred and jealousy. She picked up the board, placing it on the bed, and took the planchette from the drawer where she'd hidden it.

Not sure if there was some sort of protocol to using one of these things, she lit the candles on her dresser and turned off the lights. She placed the planchette on the board, not realizing her hands were trembling until it began shaking.

Now what? She didn't know what the hell to do with it. Did it move of its own accord? She waited, staring at the board, willing it to move with all her might. She pictured Mae's smiling face and waited. Nothing moved, nothing happened. Tutting, she stood up and walked across to blow out the candles.

The sound was faint, like a scraping fingernail against a chalkboard and she felt the hairs on the back of her neck stand on end. She turned back to the bed to see the planchette edging its way across the board. A screech escaped her lips as her hand flew to her mouth. *How?* How was that happening? Her feet froze to the floor. She willed herself to go back to it, but a voice in her head was whispering, *Get rid of it, burn it, throw it out of the window. Whatever you do, don't try and communicate with it.*

The planchette moved to the H then I, E, M, M. *Hi Emm.* She gasped, and ran back to sit on the bed, careful not to disturb the board.

"Mae, are you there? Oh Mae, I'm so sorry, I miss you."

The pointer began to spell out more words and Emilia grabbed a journal and pencil off the desk.

I, M, I, S, S,Y, O, U.

Emilia stared at the words and let out a sob. "I miss you too Mae, I'm sorry. Where are you?"

H, E, R, E, R, U, N.

She scribbled down the words *hererun*, where was *hererun?* A loud knock sounded to her left and she whipped her head round to see where it had come from and who had made it. There was no one or nothing there. Then, an even louder thud made the floor vibrate, and a foul stench hung in the air, making her gag. Where was it coming from?

She sense movement in the corner of the room once again, and yet she couldn't see anyone. Picking up the planchette, she lifted it to her face to study it, unable to work out how this simple, teardrop shaped piece of wood with a piece of glass in the middle could move on its own. Holding it to her left eye, she peered through the glass, wondering if it was like the magnifying glass her pops had on the library desk.

The room loomed larger through the lens, the walls much closer, covered by a dark, moving shadow. She lowered the planchette. Now, she couldn't see anything.

A scrabbling noise behind her made her turn her head, and she lifted the planchette again, closing one eye, whispering, "Mae is that you? Where are you, I can't see you." Movement again. There was something there. An overpowering smell of rotting garbage seeped into her nose, and she dropped the planchette on the board. It began to move again.

I, T, S, H, E, R, E, R, U, N

Itshererun. She breathed out a white plume of smoky breath and cried out in fear, as she realized what her friend was telling her. The candles flickered wildly then the flames extinguished, just as she had split the words up. *ITS HERE RUN.* A growl, low and guttural, filled the room and Emilia threw the board off the bed. The words were screaming in her mind: *It's here, run.* She ran for the bedroom door, throwing herself through it. She screamed at the top of her voice and ran down the staircase as fast as she could, bringing Missy out of her room.

Emilia grabbed her hand. "There's something in my room. We have to leave, now!"

Missy stared up the staircase while Emilia began to pull her away as hard as she could. Before they could tear her gaze from the top of the stairs, they saw a huge, black cloud begin to form into two, cloven-hoofed feet.

"Missy, move, NOW!"

Missy let Emilia tug her toward the front door, and they ran out onto the sidewalk, the door slamming in the wind behind them. Emilia kept tugging on Missy's hand until they were running across the street to the opposite side. Emilia looked up to see a black, shadowy figure at the second-floor window. It was her bedroom window it was staring out of.

They hammered on their neighbor, Mrs. Smith's front door, knowing she would open up to them, even though they were screaming to be let in. The poor woman opened the door to a pair of screaming banshees, wild eyed, their faces stricken with horror. Mr. Smith appeared with a gun, thinking they were being chased.

Mrs. Smith slammed the front door shut. "Child, what on earth is wrong with you?"

Emilia couldn't speak, her voice was hoarse. Missy glanced at their neighbors who looked as petrified as they did.

Composing herself, Emilia whispered. "There's something in the house."`

"Like what? You mean there's an intruder, someone has broken in?"

"No, I don't know what it is. It's a monster."

"Honey, the only monsters in this world are the bad people who do bad things to good people. Like your—"

Mrs. Smith stopped talking, a faint redness creeping up her neck.

Emilia looked at her. "Like my brother, you're right. He is a monster. But this isn't a human being I'm talking about. I was using the Ouija board to speak to Mae, but something else was there. It smelled terrible, it made the room freezing cold, and it growled louder than a grizzly bear."

Mrs. Smith led them into the drawing room, closing the door behind them as Mr. Smith spoke to a police officer on the phone.

"Honey, you shouldn't be playing around with one of those boards, they're evil and bring forth spirits that have no place in this world. I read that your brother used one as well as painting satanic symbols all over the walls. If what you're saying is true I think he may have summoned more than your dead aunt from Milwaukee."

Missy looked at the woman and Emilia felt her knees give way as she slumped onto the couch. She was relieved that Mrs. Smith believed her, it meant that she wasn't going crazy.

"What do we do about it because it's getting stronger and it's taking over the house!"

Mrs. Smith checked to see her husband wasn't listening. Then she whispered, "I can help you to get rid of it, but it won't be easy. We mustn't let David know either because after the last time I chased an evil spirit, he made me promise I wouldn't ever do anything like it ever again. What made you come here? You are lucky you did hammer on our door because Mrs. Fitch is a good Christian woman who would have shut the curtains and turned her television louder." She winked at them.

"I don't know, I felt drawn to your house. It has always seemed like a safe place to be... Why did he make you promise?"

"It nearly killed me, honey, but I survived. Damn it, I knew there was more to this than your brother flipping his lid! He's been meddling in stuff he had no right to meddle in. Have you called in a priest?"

"Yes."

"What did he say?"

"He got sick and had to leave; he rushed out of the house and said he had to speak to the archbishop."

Mrs. Smith chewed her bottom lip. "That will take a long time and the church, well... although it survives by preaching to its flock about the fight between good and evil, it has kind of a hard time actually believing that those kind of evil spirits and demons truly exist. Some priests are good and will help, others won't. Do you think he will help? Because it would make it better if we had a man of God standing with us?"

Emilia didn't like the way this conversation was going. What did she mean by "standing with us"?

"I don't know, I thought I could trust him, but he ran away."

"Fear can do that to anyone, sometimes what you need to do is stand your ground and fight it head on. These demons, entities, whatever you want to call it, they feed off fear. They invoke it especially for their own pleasure."

Emilia stole a glance at Missy who was looking paler by the minute. She had spoken no more than a few words for the last couple of years to the short, round woman standing in front of her. Yet here she was giving them shelter and talking about fighting a demon with them. Any moment now someone was going to shake Emilia awake from this nightmare, and she'd be relieved to discover it had all been a horrible dream. That at this very moment in time, Mae was taking her final bow on the stage. That James was back on Staten Island and the house on West 10th Street wasn't the home of a beast from the depths of hell.

"I don't suggest we deal with it tonight; they like the dark and gather more strength. Daylight is their enemy, so we will gather what we need tomorrow morning, including your priest. I will wave Mr. Smith off to work with his lunchbox just like I do every day, and then we will prepare to do battle. Is this agreeable by you?"

"Yes, thank you. I don't expect you to put yourself at any risk though, Mrs. Smith."

"I can no longer live across the road from a house full of evil and ignore it than I can a starving child begging on the corner of Fifth. It's my calling; my mom had the gift and so did her mom. Mr. Smith doesn't understand it. He thinks it's all a bit of game. I've been cleansing houses and speaking to dead people since I was eight years old. I do God's work, and not all spirits are bad. Some are lost, or lonely; some are shocked and don't understand that they're dead. A guiding hand and a soothing voice can send them on to where they need to go. Most of the time they're thankful to be able to speak to someone who can still hear them. Some of them are a bit grumpy. You get used to it. I like to think that I do God's work on earth for him. A bit like a shepherd, only instead of a flock of sheep I gather lost souls."

Emilia stared at the woman. She was being entirely serious. Mrs. Smith smiled at her, and Emilia saw a flicker of golden light in the iris of her chocolate, brown eyes. It was warm, loving and for the first time since Mae's horrible death she felt safe, in this room with the friendly woman standing in front of her, smiling.

Emilia nodded. She understood that somehow, she had been led to this house. Out of all the brownstones in the street, she ran to this one, a safe haven from the horror that had taken up residence in her home.

FORTY-TWO

PRESENT DAY

Frankie opened one eye and groaned when he moved his head. It hurt like a bitch. It was throbbing and he wondered if Christy had chipped his skull when she'd thrown the oversized coffee cup at his head. For all he knew, he had swelling on the brain—it sure as hell felt like it.

He could check whether Maria was up yet; he didn't want to spend the morning feeling sorry for himself. He'd rather be up working and trying to find the killer before Addison hauled them off the case and gave it back to the cold-case team. It would be mighty fine if they solved it, prove just how good Miller and Conroy were. It sounded good. Miller and Conroy could be one of those fancy detective series on the television. The modern equivalent of *Cagney and Lacey* or *Starsky and Hutch*.

He sat up feeling a little dizzy. For the second time in less than five minutes, he questioned if he had some kind of permanent brain damage. When he'd showered and dressed, he put some bagels under the grill and called Maria. She sounded even groggier than he did.

"Urgh, what time is it?"

He looked up at the oversized kitchen clock Christy had insisted they had to have from Macy's that he hated. It was like looking up at Grand Central's huge clock which looked great on the side of a huge building, but not in his freaking kitchen.

"Eight."

"What do you want?"

"Oh, that's real charming, I was going to ask you over for breakfast. I thought we could get an early start."

"I'm not home, hang on."

Her voice went muffled and he knew she'd clamped her hand over the mouthpiece. What was worse, she was talking to someone else, and he felt his stomach drop. She came back on the line.

"I can be at yours in an hour, I need to go home first."

"Where are you?"

There was a pause. He knew it really wasn't any of his business where she was, and Maria was also probably thinking the same.

"At The Plaza."

He began to laugh. "Yeah right, you spent the night at The Plaza."

"Why is that so hard to believe?"

He laughed even harder. "Because you'd never pay Plaza rates for a room, Miss Tight-Ass."

"Screw you Frankie, I'll see you at nine."

She ended the call. She was being serious. *Holy shit, Maria, who did you screw to get a night there?*

A bitter taste filled his mouth. He knew exactly who she'd spent the night with. Harrison Williams probably had a whole goddamn suite at The Goddamn Plaza. He clenched his fist: he wanted to smack the smug fool in his mouth and knock his row of perfect white teeth out.

For the next twenty minutes, Frankie slammed around his apartment until he calmed down. He knew he had no right to feel so angry because Maria had gone out on a date. What she did in her own time was nothing to do with him. They worked together, they were partners. That was it. They weren't lovers. They'd never slept together. The voice in his head whispered, *Yes, but you wanted to didn't you? Now Christy has been screwing around, you're a single guy and after years of being single the woman you've been in love with for a long time has found herself a very rich lover. So where does that leave you, Frankie? Out in the cold, that's where.*

This time, it was Frankie who picked up one of the stupid cups, another thing Christy had spent a small fortune on. The clock began to chime, and he launched it at it, ducking at the almighty crash and as shards of glass flew everywhere. He stood tall and looked at the mess. *Jeez*, it was going to take him an hour to clean it up. But for the first time since he'd woken up, he smiled. He would put the clock and pieces of broken glass in a paper grocery sack and mail it to Adam's house as a house-warming gift.

Maria smiled as Harrison fiddled with his tie. "So, do you always bring your dates here? Is this like your own personal suite?"

He smiled. "My mom's in town; she's on her twice-yearly visit with her entourage of friends. I booked this suite for her, but she insisted on stopping with me. I love her, but Christ, she drives me mad. I didn't want to subject you to a grilling by her and the two ugly stepsisters."

She laughed. "I could have handled your mom."

"Oh, I have no doubt about that, however I really like you and I don't want her putting you off agreeing to another date with me. Which you would—I'm sure you would after meeting her."

Maria got out of the bed, slipping on the fluffy white robe

emblazoned with the hotel's logo. She crossed the room and began to fasten his tie for him. He let her and she enjoyed being so close to him, smelling of mint and lemon shower gel.

"I need to shower and go home, I have work. Thank you for last night, I enjoyed it."

She turned to walk away, and he tugged her back, pulling her face toward his. He kissed her and she felt her stomach flutter. As much as she wanted to go back to bed with him, she had to go to work. She pulled away, her cheeks flushed.

"Sorry, I do have to go. Could I have a lift please?"

He laughed. "I don't know what shocks me more, you asking for a lift or the fact that you stayed the night."

"Yeah, well it must have been the milkshake overload. All that sugar made me lose control of my senses." She turned and walked into the huge bathroom. He shouted after her.

"I have to go, I'll have the car drop me off and come back for you. Is that okay?"

"Perfect, thank you."

Maria turned the shower on. She had a lot to do today, and even though facing Frankie was going to be difficult, she wanted to get it out in the open. She didn't know how long this "thing" with Harrison might last, but she sure as hell wanted to enjoy it. And she couldn't if she was sneaking around behind Frankie's back.

As she got in the elevator, she smiled at the elderly couple who were bickering over what to eat for breakfast. She couldn't help wondering how long they'd been married. She felt a little over-dressed for this time of day and was relieved to reach the lobby and out of the entrance doors. She felt overdressed—and a little bit like Vivienne from *Pretty Woman*. As she walked down the red carpeted steps, she saw Harrison's driver jump out of a stretch limousine. He opened the door and nodded as she slid inside the car.

Not quite believing her ride was so luxurious she stared out of the window watching the hordes of New Yorkers on their way to work. She would make it up to Frankie and buy him lunch. And she wanted to do everything possible to find the man on the still with Anya. It was going to be a long day, but it was what she loved. The car stopped outside her apartment. "Don't get out, I can manage. Thank you."

The driver shook his head. "Ma'am, it's a long, boring day driving around. If I get out, I can stretch my legs." He was out of the car and round to her side before she could object. He opened the door, and she stepped out.

"Thank you, what's your name?"

"Benjamin."

"Thanks, Benjamin."

"You're very welcome, ma'am. I hope to see you again soon." He tipped his hat at her and she laughed.

As she made her way up to her apartment, she wondered if she would see him again. Now she'd given in so easy to Harrison Williams, would he still be interested in her? It didn't really matter; she'd had a good time and that was what counted.

Opening her front door she inhaled and wrinkled her nose. It smelled terrible. Had she left food or milk out? She didn't think so, yet it smelled like rotten garbage. Closing the door behind her, she kicked off her heels and went to the kitchen in search of the foul stench. It was surprisingly cold in here; she must have left the air con on high. A shudder racked her entire body as she checked the bin and cupboards to see where the smell was coming from. There wasn't anything obvious, although the fridge didn't light up and there was no blast of cool air as she opened it slightly. The power must have gone. All her food must have gone off. Annoyed, she checked the plug and saw it had been pulled out of the socket. *What the hell? How did that happen?*

Furious, she plugged it back in, the light illuminating again. As she opened the door wide, she let out a scream of horror. On the shelf was a decomposing head. The skin was marbled black and green, and two eyes were staring at her. Maria cupped her hand over her mouth and nose. Panic filled her chest. Where was her phone? Realizing she'd left her purse in the car, she turned to run out of the apartment to Miss Green's and slammed straight into a man. She froze with fear at the sight of this complete stranger standing in her kitchen.

His fist shot out and he punched her so hard in the side of the head that her vision blurred. Stumbling, she grabbed the nearest thing to her, which was a glass vase, and threw it at him. He ducked as it whistled past his head and smashed against the wall sending shards of glass everywhere. He lunged for her and she side-swiped him with her fist, unsteady on her feet. She was almost past him when he stuck his foot out and she fell forwards. She tried her best not to go down, knowing that if she did, he'd be at an advantage. But then he threw himself at her and they both landed on the carpet with a heavy thud.

Maria felt her breath whoosh from her body as he straddled her back. Opening her mouth to scream, the sound was cut off by the tautness of the rope wrapped around her neck. She gagged as she choked, clawing at the rope with her fingernails to loosen it. He pulled tighter until she saw flecks of silver floating around in her eyes and then with a final squeeze everything went black.

FORTY-THREE

Missy paused. Had that loud thump and crash come from Maria's apartment? Concerned rather than nosy, she pressed her ear against the wall. She couldn't hear anything, and if Maria had hurt herself, she'd be shouting for help.

It had occurred to her that if she had asked her, Maria would have come to help them. The last thing she wanted though was to put her in any danger; she already walked that line every single day. Gathering what she needed, Missy slung the heavy purse over her shoulder and turned to look around her apartment. She couldn't complain: she'd had a long, happy life. It was far more than Mae Evans had, and she felt truly blessed that God had seen fit to let her do so. If she died today, then so be it. She was going to die sometime—that was one thing there was no escaping from.

She placed the smooth, ivory envelope on the sideboard and walked out of the front door, closing it behind her. She decided to take a town car to West 10th—she could afford to splurge. As it stopped outside, she bent forward and tipped the driver a hundred dollars.

He looked down and shook his head.

"I can't take this, ma'am."

"Yes, you can. Thank you."

She got out and stared across the road at the house that had once belonged to Mr. and Mrs. Smith. What she would give to have Mrs. Smith fighting their corner once more. Only she was now older than Mrs. Smith had been the first time around. Missy wondered if Mrs. Smith was watching over her now. Since that dreadful day, she'd never really felt alone, even when she was. This thing—beast, demon, monster, whatever it was called—had inflicted far too much suffering on innocent, unwitting victims. It was time to end it for good.

The house stood tall and proud, cloaked in a veil of shadows. Had it always been so dark? She didn't think that it had; she remembered the days the sun was so bright it would burn through the windows. The heat would be far too hot, making the rooms stuffy and unbearable until she'd thrown them open to let the air flow through. No, the house hadn't always been one full of black shadows, cold draughts and foul smells. It had been a happy, warm, loving home. Her home, her happy place —until that night. None of them had ever felt safe again in there.

She hadn't been able to wait to move out. The day she left, she'd been guilt ridden because Emilia had insisted on staying on, even after Clarke's death when she could have gone back to the family home on Staten Island to be with her mother. How had she spent the last sixty-five years living in the grasp of such evil? It was something Missy didn't think she'd ever be able to comprehend.

She turned around, finding herself standing at the foot of the steps to Mrs. Smith's Brownstone. She reached out and touched the gatepost, which was warm, and her hand felt as if it was heating up. This house was the polar opposite of Emilia's; it emanated light and peace from every single brick and the sun always shone on this side of the street. She placed both hands on the bricks, absorbing the goodness that this warm, happy, building emanated.

"Mrs. Smith, I don't know if you're here..." she whispered. "It feels as if you are. Please send us your strength. You helped us to send it back once, please help me again. I don't know if I'm strong enough to do it on my own."

"Good morning, Miss Green."

The voice—so loud and unexpected—made her jump, and she turned around to see Father Anthony standing there smiling at her. He was dressed in a pair of faded jeans, with a short-sleeved, black clerical shirt. His pristine white collar was so bright she wondered if he'd worn a new one just for the occasion. This made her smile. He was going to need more than that if he was to go in the house with her.

"Father, you scared the life out of me."

"Sorry, I didn't know how deep in thought you were until you jumped that high off the ground. You'd have cleared a hurdle."

She laughed. "At my age that would be quite something. What are you doing here?"

"I've been doing some research. After what you told me, I couldn't stop thinking about it. I spoke to the archbishop and an old friend who has some knowledge on these matters."

"What did he say?"

"Well, I'm not sure you would want me to repeat such bad language."

"He thinks I'm a crazy old fool?"

"Yes."

"What about you? What do you think?"

He looked over at the house and crossed himself without even realizing, which confirmed what Missy suspected.

"This is not something we can go into lightly, you understand that don't you? I fear that if you go in there alone and call it out, you won't necessarily remove it."

"And?"

"And, there is no other way to say this... you will die."

Missy laughed—not just a small laugh. It was a real, came-from-the-heart, belly laugh.

"What's so funny?"

She shook her head. "Nothing, I'm just nervous and yes, I have known all along that one day it might kill me."

He folded his arms across his chest and arched an eyebrow.

"Bless you, thank you for coming to see me. I guess I've already resigned myself that death is inevitable... I'm just hoping that the big guy in the sky takes pity on me and lets me in. I don't want to spend all of eternity with a beast that smells like a rotten side of beef."

It was his turn to smile. "I admire your bravery, but really what we need to do is get your friend out of that building. I want you both somewhere safe, where you can be blessed and out of harm's way until I'm fully prepared to go in. Just a few hours will do. It's not much to ask, is it?"

Missy decided not to argue with him, for what difference would another few hours make? It had been here a long time. She pulled out her cell and rang Emilia.

"Grab a few things, I want you to come outside and meet me. It looks like we might have a backup plan."

Emilia didn't respond and for one dreadful moment, she wondered if her friend would do as she'd asked. She was probably more exhausted and tired of this than Missy was. Then the front door opened and she saw Emilia and Missy waved to her. Startlingly, there was a loud crack, as though a bolt of lightning had struck the chimney of the house. Missy looked up to see chunks of masonry begin to cascade down and one of the large chimney pots balancing on the edge of the roof. In a matter of seconds, it was going to collapse directly onto Emilia.

Father Anthony began to run across the road, but it was too far. The heavy, stone chimney came crashing down. Missy screamed. Unable to look, she turned her head away. Not seeing the pair of strong arms that wrapped themselves around her friend's frail shoulders, dragging her back inside the entrance of the house. The chimney pot whistled past Emilia's head, hitting the concrete steps with such force it shattered into a million pieces and took a huge chunk out of them. She heard Father Anthony's voice as he shouted.

"She's okay, she's not hurt! You stay there."

Not about to argue with him, she watched as he clambered over the shattered chimney pot to help Emilia over it. Behind her was Mikey. He waved at Missy, and she mouthed, *Thank you*, to him. The two men towered over Emilia as they half led, half carried her across the street to where Missy was standing.

"It's scared, so it's trying to fight back the only way it can," Mikey said. "We need to send that mother-fucker back to where it belongs once and for all. So, what's the plan?"

Sirens blared in the distance and there was quite a crowd gathering to look at the mess across the road. Father Anthony hailed a passing cab and bundled them all into it.

"Saint Patrick's Old Cathedral, please."

They sat in silence until the taxi stopped outside the church. If the taxi driver thought they were an odd bunch, he never said anything. Two old women, a black man and a priest. Missy smiled. There was a joke in there somewhere. As it was, they were an unlikely bunch, united through fate to do God's work and she found a small measure of comfort in that thought.

Father Anthony paid the cab driver and ushered them out. Instead of walking to the huge front doors, he led them through a locked red door. Missy looked around at the beautiful, leafy garden. It was like they'd stepped through a doorway in time, back to when there were no cars polluting the city streets. A narrow, twisty path edged with trees and shrubs opened up to an imposing, rough, cut-stone building that mirrored the cathedral. It too had a blood-red door steeped with shiny, green Boston ivy growing around it.

Unlocking it and stepping inside, he shouted, "Father, I have some visitors. Is it okay to come in?" They were greeted by a gruff voice and Missy wasn't sure if it had sworn at them.

Father Anthony smiled. "He sounds like an ogre, but he's not. He hates being disturbed, but I think he will want to hear what we have to tell him."

Missy wasn't so sure. But right now, they needed all the help they could get and if she had to talk to a miserable priest, then she would.

Father Anthony led them into the most beautiful, oak panelled library that Missy had ever seen. She'd thought the library at Emilia's house had been wonderful, the hours she'd spent in there choosing which books to read were too many to count. Here, floor-to-ceiling shelves and glass display cabinets were full to the brim with books. A grey-haired man wearing a roll neck sweater and fingerless gloves despite the warmth of the day outside was sat at the desk near the window. He peered over the top of his wire-rimmed oval glasses and Missy wondered where she'd seen him before. He looked so familiar— or was it because it was the middle of summer, and he was dressed like Ebenezer Scrooge? He looked at them in turn, spending the longest moment staring back at her.

"What are you doing bringing this band of trouble to my door, Anthony?"

He was blunt and Emilia looked at Missy, her face a picture, which in turn made Missy smile. Mikey, who hadn't spoken a word since he'd dragged Emilia out of harm's way looked at Missy as if to ask, *What the hell?* She shrugged. They couldn't argue with the man. But they were trouble—and he didn't look the least bit interested in them.

"I think you're going to want to hear this lady's story. This is Emilia Carter. She lives in the house on West 10th Street."

Missy wondered how on earth that was supposed to explain anything, but for the first time, the old man's eyes opened wide as he sat up straighter.

"The house?"

Anthony nodded. The man stared at Emilia as if she'd suddenly grown another head or a pair of wings.

"You're Emilia Carter? Well, I never—you still live there. How long has it been?"

"All my life. Why, what do you care?"

He laughed and his face broke into a smile; he didn't look quite so terrifying.

"I care more than you would ever know. You don't remember do you? I completely understand why. I've been keeping a watch on that house since 1952. I didn't know if it was a rumour or if that meddling Mrs. Smith had only made things worse."

Suddenly Missy remembered why she recognized him: he was the priest who had paid them a fleeting visit. He looked a lot different now, and then she caught sight of her reflection in the large mirror on the wall above his desk and had to do a double take. For a split second she was looking at her much younger, prettier self. She blinked and that woman was replaced with the grey-haired, wrinkled woman she was today. That was what life was like, it went in the blink of an eye. A wave of sadness engulfed her; she'd wasted so much of her life being afraid. She turned to Emilia and wondered if she felt the same. It was a testament to God and their stubbornness that they were both still alive.

Emilia was staring at the man, who pointed to the couch. "Please, sit down. Forgive my grouchiness, I'm no longer a morning—or a people person come to think of it. I spent a good many years of my life doing God's work until it got too much. Now I take care of the library—it's my pride and joy. There are books in here the Vatican have been trying to get hold of for a long time. They're not getting them, I can tell you that. Well, not at least until I die—then I can't do much about it. I also have some books in here the big guys don't know about and wouldn't be too happy with."

It was Mikey who finally spoke.

"What has this got to do with the situation we're in now and why would you be watching that damn house? Who are you?"

Anthony stood up, his face burning. "Sorry, how rude of me —it's about time we had a formal introduction."

Missy shook her head, they were all a little bit highly strung today. She crossed the room to where Father Morgan was sitting and held out her hand.

"Missy Green, former housekeeper for Miss Emilia and the gentleman is Mikey, who is a current tenant in the house. What's your name, because I refuse to spend the next hour calling you Father?"

"Missy, Mikey, Emilia." He nodded at the three of them. "You can call me Charlie. If you aren't an unlikely bunch of heroes, I don't know who is. You don't look anything like Venkman, Stantz and Spengler." He began to laugh so hard at his joke it made him cough.

Emilia and Missy stared at the man as if he was speaking a different language.

Mikey started laughing. "We aint, afraid of no ghost. Man, we definitely don't look like Ghostbusters and that's because we aint."

"You might not think so, but I have bad news for you. I guess you've heard the saying God works in mysterious ways. Well, it's true, sometimes he has a sense of humour. This is likely why he's chosen you three to take a stand. I take it the entity your brother summoned on that fateful night never actually went away? That you couldn't see it, but you knew that it was there? Lingering in the background, biding its time. You've been living under its shadow for a long time, but that's what they do. They're like a cancerous tumour sucking all the spirit out of your body, your mind; it's probably been oppressing you all your life."

Emilia began to blink fast as a tear fell from the corner of her eye. Missy reached out and clasped hold of Emilia's hand.

"I should have known. I should have investigated it myself. Instead I trusted that Mrs. Smith had done the job for the church. She prided herself on helping the people the church wouldn't. I was too young and inexperienced, too scared. I'm sorry."

"Why wouldn't the church want to help anyone living with such a horrible thing?"

"It would open up the floodgates for every crackpot in the entire world. Of course, the church is well aware these demons exist. But to publicly announce it would cause panic and every mentally ill person who needs a psych evaluation would be dropped at our door. We don't have the capacity to fulfil that role. What we do is take each case on its own merit. We have to investigate, send out a psychologist to assess if the person is off their meds or not. When we have proof, the archbishop then gives his blessing for an exorcist to step in."

Emilia's body shook and her voice trembled. "If I'd have asked the church to help, would they?"

"In this case, at the beginning probably not. I'm sorry, I should have been honest with you, but I was young and very inexperienced back then."

"Why?"

"Your brother displayed all the signs of classic psychosis— the police reports said as much. That he was having a psychotic episode on the night he killed Mae Evans. They didn't believe it had anything to do with devil worship or summoning a demon despite the pentagram drawn in blood and the presence of the Ouija board. The cops prefer things to be cut and dried. They would have been torn to shreds by the papers if they hadn't sent your brother to Greystone."

Emilia sat down, wringing her hands and Missy's heart went out to her.

"Why didn't you speak to us or the police if you thought there was something going on?"

"I did, I spoke at great length to your father. It was him who gave me permission to see copies of the psychiatrist's reports. On paper it seemed as if the police were right."

"But...?"

He let out a loud sigh. "I didn't think they were telling the whole truth; something about it wasn't right. I went back into your house with your father and I couldn't get any further than the first floor. I felt as if I was going to have a heart attack and die. I became clammy... dizzy and sick. I'm ashamed to say that I ran out of your house and tried to go back but I couldn't. I was scared and fascinated so I began to research it as much as I could from a safe distance. Mrs Smith told me that I should stop being a dress-wearing bible basher and face the truth. That there were things in this world beyond the church's control."

Missy looked at him. "She was right. She had to battle to close the portal that James opened up. She told me afterwards that she'd had to call on all her spirit guides to help her fight it. If you'd helped her would it have made a difference?"

He shrugged. "Mrs. Smith did a very good job, better than I would have done. I wasn't a trained exorcist back then."

"But you are now?"

"Yes, although I've stepped back from that line of work. I'm too old to be fighting with anyone, let alone a demon."

"Are you going to help us?" Missy needed to know. For the love of God, he didn't look any younger than she was.

He paused, looked at Anthony and nodded. "I'm going to advise you."

Mikey began to laugh. "And what the hell good is that going to do? Pardon my language, Father."

"I have been teaching Anthony everything he needs to know."

Missy stood up. "Forget it, the church didn't help last time. We don't need your help this time. You're telling me you've had a vested interest in that house for all these years, yet you're going to hide away in the comfort of this house and let us do the rest.

"For Christ's sake what's the worst that can happen? In case you haven't noticed, between the three of us we're ancient, we all got to die some time and I'm afraid it could be anytime. Why the hell would you want to send Anthony in to do a job you could do with your eyes shut. You're putting him and us at risk." She turned to Anthony. "Have you done this before, Anthony?"

"No, but I can. Charlie has taught me well."

"Jeez, what a pair of assholes. No offence guys, but I think we'll manage. Emilia, Mikey, let's go."

She turned to walk out of the door when a voice bellowed at her.

"Stop."

She turned around and felt her heart sink. Charlie wasn't sitting in a conventional chair. He wheeled himself around from behind the desk and she stared at the missing gap where his right leg should have been. Now she felt like an asshole. She hadn't noticed. How would he even get up to the attic?

"I have an unfortunate disadvantage due to the diabetes I developed in my seventies and yes, you're right, I'm pretty sure that at some point in the near future one or all of us are going to die, but not at the doing of a demon. I would like nothing more than to go in there and do battle; it would be fun to have one last showdown with one of Satan's creatures. I'm also no fool. I'm a weak link in the chain and it would seize the moment the minute it sensed I had entered the house. This is between

Emilia and you. The pair of you fought it the first time and did a pretty good job of sealing it inside the portal. Whoever decided to reopen it knew exactly what they were doing. "

He waved an old, cracked black leather book at her. "The ritual requires three sacrifices. Now I don't know why a third wasn't done after the last one. Maybe it's because they got cold feet or got locked up for something else. What I do know is that it's getting stronger, which means something is happening. I wouldn't be surprised if another sacrifice was imminent."

Mikey looked at the priest and sighed. "I can't believe I'm hearing this. Sacrifices, demons, Ouija boards... that's some bad shit going on there. How do I live in a house of evil for ten years and not know any of this?"

Charlie shrugged. "Some people are oblivious to it all and some people are very sensitive. It's life. Some people like mustard on their hot dogs, others don't."

The room fell silent as they all reflected on the fact that this was all very real. It was Emilia who broke it.

"I've had enough of this. So, Charlie, what the fuck do I have to do to claim my house back?"

FORTY-FOUR

Maria could feel the soft, sagging mattress under her. How had she got into bed? Had she passed out and Frankie had found her? She tried to open her eyes, but one of them was sealed shut. Blinking the other, she tried to focus on the darkness that surrounded her. The air in the room was heavy with the stench of decomposition and she felt her stomach clench; her gag reflex kicked in. As the back of her throat filled with bile, her tongue moved forward, but she realised she couldn't move her mouth or her tongue to be sick. She lay still, trying not to breathe too deeply because then the smell would penetrate her nostrils again and make her sick. The gag would result in her choking to death on her own vomit.

Her chest began to fill with the fluttering wings of panic. There were only two times in her life she'd ever felt like this, both in her childhood. She didn't panic. As an adult it was one of her rules. The alarm bells were ringing in her head. She was in a dire situation that was going to end very badly if she didn't stay calm.

She closed her other eye: she would pretend she was still unconscious. She needed to think. She wasn't in her bed because that was much firmer, so she was in an unknown place —one that smelled strongly of death—with a gag in her mouth. She knew it was futile, but she still tried to move her arms and legs as slowly as she could without alerting her captor to the fact that she was awake. The rope bit into the soft, flesh of her wrists and fear rushed through her veins. She was not only tied and gagged but spread-eagled on the bed. She was cold, and thankfully not shivering so at least she was still fully dressed; she still had some dignity. If her asshole colleagues were going to find her body, she'd still have some pride. Bad enough to die this way, never mind being gawped at and photographed a thousand times by the jerks she worked with. This thought alone was enough to focus her mind: it wasn't going to happen, not like this.

Maria hadn't really got a good look at the guy who had been in her apartment. She couldn't be sure if it was the same guy that was in the still with Anya. She tried not to shudder at the thought of Anya's decomposing head in her cooler. Anya. Jesus, Maria knew exactly where she was, and she had to stifle a cry. She was in the attic apartment of the house on West 10th.

There was movement in the corner of the room. She didn't dare to open her eye. She waited for him to come closer; wondered if he had an axe and how much it was going to hurt. A loud long scratching noise filled the air and a vision of Freddy Krueger who'd terrified her to death as a teenager filled her mind. The sleepless nights she'd had because of those films were too many to count. And now an asshole like that was going to kill her.

She was too scared to move. The only thing she could do was headbutt him if he got near to her and hope she could untie herself in record time. She waited, not daring to breathe out. The scratching didn't happen again, but the smell seemed stronger, more potent, and it made her eyes water.

After a few minutes, she gently tugged her arms against the

rope. To her relief, there was a little movement. If she could work up a sweat, she might be able to make her skin slippery enough to pull her wrist free. She was glad of the gag in her mouth because it stopped her crying out in pain at the friction burns the rope was causing as it rubbed the skin from her wrists. She paused when she heard a low growl that sent a shiver down her spine. It sounded much, much bigger and more terrifying than a dog. She carried on, writhing both wrists against the rope. The soft, tanned skin of her wrists was now a burning, red mess. Any minute now she would break the skin and the blood would begin to seep through. She didn't care: if it gave her enough moisture to pull her wrists free, she would deal with the mess later. Friction burns were the least of her worries; a homicidal maniac was her main priority.

To distract herself from the pain, she tried to remember the layout of the apartment. There was a kitchen/living area not too dissimilar to hers. The bedroom was off the kitchen. It was on the top floor, would have to have a fire escape. If she could make it to the window and climb through... She had no weapon on her, but if she had to, she would fight with her bare hands until she found something suitable to kill him with because he wasn't getting away a second time. This time she would finish it for good. No more women were going to be killed in this apartment. A door closed from elsewhere in the attic apartment and she felt her heart skip a beat. If he was outside the bedroom, then who was inside?

FORTY-FIVE

GREENWICH VILLAGE, OCTOBER 1952

As the police entered the house on West 10th Street, guns drawn, Missy and Emilia grasped each other's hands and watched on from the safety of the window opposite. Every single light was flicked on in turn as they searched each room. Emilia knew it was pointless. The cops would never find the thing that was hiding in there. It didn't care about their guns or harsh language. They would come out of there scratching their heads and rolling their eyes at the two crazy broads who'd over-reacted to a noise.

The house was lit up like a beacon, every window glowing brightly, casting out the shadows. Mr. Smith was watching in fascination from the front step. Mrs. Smith whispered, "As soon as the cops leave, I'll take you both back over."

Emilia released a small cry, and she felt the warmth of Mrs. Smith's arm as it wrapped itself around her.

"The cops will never find it in a million years. They won't be looking for it—they're looking for a man made of flesh and blood. Not a monster made of smoke and shadows. Father Morgan might help us, but don't rely on it.

"Normally I wouldn't ask; the church is a pain in the ass

when you need instant action. They have more pull than The White House, yet need everything in writing, so I'm not holding much hope. It might just be us girls."

The officers spewed out of the front door, faster than they went in. Their faces confused, they shut the door behind them and scrambled to get onto the sidewalk and as far away from the house as they could.

Mrs. Smith watched them and nodded. "Uhuh, something went down in that house, but I bet your bottom dollar they won't spill." She left the two women, and they watched as she marched down her steps to where the cops were standing.

Emilia turned to look at Missy. "I'm scared."

"Me too, but we have to do what she tells us otherwise we won't be able to live in the house and we can't let it scare us away. That's what it wants. Didn't she say they live off fear? Well maybe it's time we took a stand."

"You think so? You think that we can fight a monster made of smoke and shadows, Missy?"

"Yes, I do. We have to. What choice do we have?"

Mrs. Smith was pointing her fingers at the chest of the cop in charge and Mr. Smith ran over, grabbing his wife's arm, gently pulling her away. Missy watched them for a little while and then turned her full attention back to the house. All the while they had been arguing, the lights had been turning off one by one, the top two floors now all in blackness even though the house was empty.

"Father tell these poor, terrified ladies what you told me?" Mrs. Smith returned to the room with Father Morgan in her wake.

He looked as if he wanted to be anywhere other than standing right here, and glared at Mrs. Smith. "Well, I, um, I'm not sure that I can do anything to help tonight. I need to speak to the archbishop. This isn't something I can just go in and flush away."

"Basically, he's saying he's a coward and won't do anything unless he's been given permission."

"No, not at all. It's just... you know Amanda that it isn't that straightforward; there are certain protocols that have to be followed."

"For Christ's sake Charlie, grow a set of balls and help these girls out, will you? Look at their faces, how can you turn your back on them?"

He shook his head. "I can't help, you know that, and neither should you."

"Right, well the least you can do is to keep Mr. Smith entertained whilst I go and do it."

"Amanda, you promised no more."

"I did, until it happened on my own doorstep. Charlie, you might be afraid to break the rules, but sometimes they must be broken. I can't ignore it and besides, I feel as if it's taunting us, taking up residence in the house across the street."

He shook his head and left them to it. Missy expected to see him leaving and walking down the street as fast as he could. Instead she heard the muffled voices of him speaking to Mr. Smith.

Mrs. Smith turned to them. "I was wrong, we can't wait until the morning. We must fight it now. Give me a few minutes, I need to call on all of my spirit guides to help me with this and it might take a little while for them to get here." She sat down on a chair and closed her eyes.

Emilia wondered if they were in a strange dream. She didn't have a clue what a spirit guide was, but it sounded very important.

·   ·   ·

"They're here." Mrs. Smith opened her eyes, nodding. "All of them. And they agree with me. We can't wait any longer; it needs to be brought out of the house, out of its hiding place to be sent back to hell. Once that's done, we will go back inside the house and seal the portal."

Missy looked at her. "What do you mean it needs to be brought outside? How do you do that and isn't it dangerous for you? What's a portal?"

"Well, I'm not going to lie. This is very dangerous, but I'm afraid it's our only option. If Mr. Smith knew what I was about to do he would probably divorce me, he would be that angry. I'm going to draw it out. It won't be expecting a house full of guides and angels. That's good though, we'll have the element of surprise. A portal is a doorway between our world and another, in this case between our world and hell."

"You can't do that. What about you and Mr. Smith? You'll be putting yourselves at risk."

"Honey, it won't be the first time and it won't be the last. Besides Mr. Smith is oblivious to any of this. He'll be watching that television set we paid an arm and a leg for. He plays along with me, but he thinks I'm a little bit crazy."

Missy wondered if the woman was nuts, but what choice did they have?

She stood up, clasping hold of their hands. "We will do this outside of the front door and hope for the best. Whatever you do, don't break the circle. Keep tight hold of each other's hands." She began to pray. When she'd finished, she went to the dresser and pulled open a drawer. She returned with two sets of rosary beads and placed a set over each of their heads.

"Do you believe in God and all things good?"

They both nodded.

"Then we're ready. Now this might be easy, it might go without a fight because sometimes they do. When they realize there is someone who isn't going to let them through, they cower and back down. Others, who are stubborn, will hang on for dear life. Are you both ready?"

The horror which filled Missy's veins turning her body into a quivering wreck was too much to comprehend. What choice did they have? It was unlikely they would ever find another person so kind and brave to help them. "Yes, I'm ready."

Mrs. Smith smiled at her. "Then let's get over there quick whilst we're ready to fight."

They all left the safety of the house and crossed the road which was now deserted once more after the flurry of police activity. The three women stood in a circle and held hands. Mrs. Smith nodded at them.

"Demon, I command you to come to me. I know you can hear me, I'm sending a beacon of light for you to follow. I have the girls, they are waiting for you."

Panic filled Missy as she tried to pull away from Mrs. Smith. She was offering them up to that monster.

Mrs. Smith had such a tight grasp on her arm she couldn't move. Looking at her, shaking her head she hissed, "Don't break the circle."

Missy who had never been so scared closed her eyes. Could she trust Mrs. Smith? What if she really was offering them up?

Her fingers, which had gone numb they were so cold, began to tingle as a warm, pleasant feeling began to spread up them. The warmth spread up her arms and began to envelop her entire body, and she felt calmer than she had done in months. She opened one eye to peek at Emilia who had the same blissful expression on her face that she was sure if she looked in a mirror, she would see reflected back at her.

Mrs. Smith smiled and called out again. "Demon, you have been called. It is your duty to come out of the shadows. I command you to show yourself."

The light by the door began to dim, getting darker by the second and Missy's heart began to beat faster. The air was getting heavy, oppressive. A huge thump on the sidewalk in front of Mrs. Smith made the ground shake. Missy looked around. She couldn't see anything, but she could feel hot, fetid breath on the back of her neck. The smell of rotting flesh was overpowering, and her knees began to buckle.

"Tell me your name, demon? I've invited you into my circle, and so you have to tell me your name."

It growled, a sound so low and guttural that it made Emilia squeeze Missy's hand so tight she thought it was going to fall off. Missy squeezed back. She had never felt fear like this and prayed to God that she would never again.

"Are you shy, demon? You are not welcome into my house or the house you've just come from." Mrs. Smith paused. "Ah, I know you. I don't need your name, I already know it."

The street was so dark that Missy could no longer see Emilia or Amanda even though they were standing inches from each other. There was a roar so loud that Missy's instinct was to cover her ears, but Mrs. Smith wouldn't let go of her hand, and then a blinding, golden light filled the space in front of them. Clearing the darkness, it was so bright and warm it felt as if the sun had just risen inside the entrance to the house. The feeling of love and warmth that enveloped them was enough to make Missy's eyes fill with tears; it was pure, beautiful.

Mrs. Smith whispered. "Thank you all so much."

She let go of Missy's hand and turned to Emilia. "You can open your eyes now. It's gone. Back to hell. You're safe."

Emilia stared at her. "How?"

"I had a lot of help from some special friends. Now you have to go and seal the portal before it comes back."

"But how do we seal the portal? I don't understand."

"Oh my." Mrs. Smith gasped and reached for her chest.

Missy managed to catch her as she collapsed into her arms. The weight of her was too heavy to bear and Missy began to fall toward the floor, doing her best to keep hold of Mrs. Smith, who was dead before they hit the floor.

This time Emilia began to scream so loud that it brought Mr. Smith running from his front door to see what had happened.

FORTY-SIX

Frankie was pacing up and down the hallway. While the CSIs were working Maria's flat, the elevator doors opened, and he saw the huge bunch of white roses before he saw who was holding them and knew it was Harrison Williams. Frankie ran toward him, barrelling into his chest and crushing the roses. Harrison yelled as he was pushed back into the elevator.

Frankie had his elbow pushed tight against his neck, choking him. "I swear to God, if you've hurt her, I'll kill you with my bare hands. Where is she asshole? I'm giving you thirty seconds before I haul your ass in for kidnap."

Harrison's face paled visibly as he tried to shake his head. Frankie moved his elbow so he could speak.

"What are you talking about? Where is she? I haven't seen her since this morning. My driver brought her here... I've been in meetings all day. Jesus Christ, I wouldn't hurt her—I like her."

Frankie stepped back, the roses which were now a squashed mess of petals and leaves were all over the floor. He ran his hand through his hair. "I don't know, she's gone. There's broken glass and blood in her apartment."

Harrison pushed Frankie out of the way and ran toward
Maria's apartment where he was greeted by an angry-looking
CSI.

"Buddy, you can't come in here, it's a crime scene."

"I need to see."

"No, you don't. If you trample over my scene, I'll shoot you.
If you care about Maria, you'll let us do our job. If you compromise any forensic evidence, then you're going to slow down any
chance of us figuring out what happened."

Harrison's shoulders sagged. "What can I do?" he asked
Frankie. "I have people I can contact. What do you need?"

Frankie grabbed his arm. "How fast can you get a cell site
analysis?"

"I need to go to my office. I have a tech guy there Joe. He
knows how to do all sorts of stuff including tracing mobile phones."

Frankie ran to the elevator. "Come on then."

As Harrison rushed to the limousine, Frankie shook his
head. "No way, we'll go in my car. That thing is way too slow."

Frankie ran toward his car, pressing the fob to unlock the
doors. He threw himself in, and Harrison followed suit.

"Buckle up, this won't be no fancy, slow ride."

Harrison tugged the belt across his shoulders and pushed it
into the clasp. Frankie did a U-turn and sped off down the street
to a symphony of blaring horns. Harrison pulled out his cell and
began talking to his guy on the other end. When Frankie
screeched to a halt outside the Manhattan Media Corporation,
Harrison muttered, "Thank Christ we're here in one piece."

Harrison took them past security, and the bank of public
elevators, to a smaller set of doors at the end of the corridor. He
pressed his thumb against the keypad. Frankie watched in awe
as the doors slid open to a much smaller, more intimate elevator.

Harrison shrugged. "Private elevator, perks of the job. I
haven't got time to make small talk with everyone who works for

me. Don't get me wrong, I do talk to them, just not first thing in the morning. I hate small talk at the best of times."

Frankie looked at the highly polished cherry wood and brass fittings and felt a grudging respect for the guy standing in front of him. Frankie didn't do small talk either, except with Maria— he could talk about anything with her. A sharp pain tugged at his heart at the thought of her name. For a moment he'd forgotten about her. Now it was back, the churning stomach was on double time and he felt queasy.

The ride up was smooth and fast. Frankie felt his ears pop and knew they were high. The doors opened into a large room filled with people, computers and television screens. Nobody looked up from what they were doing—they knew better than to speak to their boss unless he spoke to them. This was where the behind-the-scenes magic happened.

Harrison pressed on, through a set of double doors to a smaller metal one, where he held his thumb against another scanner, opening the door. It was a small office with almost as many computer screens as the huge one. A kid who didn't look any older than twenty typed away on a keyboard. His fingers were flying across the keys so fast Frankie got dizzy just watching him. He looked up at Harrison. His shaved head and Iron Maiden T-shirt made him look like an extra off *Prison Break*.

"I need a number."

Harrison pulled out his cell and rhymed off Maria's number.

"How can you track it?" Frankie had to ask; he was a geek when it came to anything technical.

Joe rolled his eyes at him. "Mate, anyone can track a phone. It's not rocket science. There are all sorts of apps out there. Is it an iPhone?"

Frankie was surprised at his British accent. "Nope, it's a

cheap cell. Maria is too tight to pay contract fees for one of those."

"Ah, that might make it a bit trickier. Still, I can do it, I'll use CCSS7. It might take a little longer if it's not an up-to-date mobile."

"What's CCSS7, I've never heard of it?"

"Well, basically it's a network interchange service that acts as a broker between mobile phone networks. By hacking into the system, I can track the location based on the mobile phone mast triangulation. It will even let me read their text messages, and I can log and listen to phone calls by using the number as an identifier."

Harrison nodded at Joe. "Let's just hope she has her phone with her—it definitely wasn't in the apartment, Frankie?"

Frankie wasn't sure, but he hadn't seen it. "I don't think so, she never goes anywhere without it."

"Well, let's hope this works then. All we need is a location."

Harrison stood watching Joe over his shoulder until the kid turned to look at him.

"Boss, you might pay the wages, but back up. I can't work with you breathing down my neck, you're putting me off."

Harrison stepped back and looked at Frankie, who was surprised to see Harrison do as he was told. He didn't strike Frankie as the sort of guy who did what someone else told him very often. Maria must mean something to him if he was willing to be so compliant.

Joe let out a whoop. "I'm in and this mobile is somewhere in a one mile radius of West 10th Street. I can get you her last messages up if you want."

Frankie felt the contents of his stomach threaten to spew out of his mouth all over the fancy computer system that Joe was sitting behind. The blood drained from his face and Harrison watched him, horrified.

"What, what the hell does that mean? It's bad, isn't it? What's on West 10th Street?"

"A murdering son of a bitch, that's what. I have to go, wait here. I'll contact you when I have her."

"No, I'm not waiting here. You can't get out on your own, you have no security pass or access to the elevator. You need me to get you out of this building."

Frankie knew he was telling the truth. "Move your ass then."

FORTY-SEVEN

PRESENT DAY

Charlie wheeled himself as close to Emilia as he could. His office at the side of the Cathedral was the safest space she'd been in for a long time.

"I think you know what you need to do, whether you know how to do it is an entirely different matter."

She shook her head as it all came rushing back—that last evening when she'd been chased from her own home to Mrs. Smith's house across the street. A terrible slideshow of complete and utter fear filled her heart as the images flashed across her mind. She gasped.

"We need to seal the portal, we never did... After that night when poor Mrs. Smith died in Missy's arms, we didn't do it! We were supposed to, but it all went horribly wrong. Mr. Smith was so angry with us for coming to them for help. By the time the emergency medical services and cops had been, we forgot all about going back to do the ritual."

"Yes...When we finally went home, we were so exhausted, no wonder we forget. The house felt different, too. Lighter, happier, free of that goddamn smell. It had worked. For so long, I didn't notice it creeping back in. And even when I had, I left you. I'm sorry, I left you to deal with the consequences and you've spent all those years locked inside that prison."

Emilia sobbed so loudly it made them jump. "What do we need to do? I don't care if I die trying, I've had enough. I've lived under the shadow of that beast for far too long. I'm ready to fight it single handed."

"Now that's what I like to hear, fighting talk. I believe you're ready to do this, I truly do."

He turned, wheeling himself toward a glass bookcase stuffed with cracked, antique, leather books. He opened the door and pulled one out, handing it to Emilia. "You need this, holy water and salt. Go to the attic. The portal has to be in there. My guess is that it's inside the pentagram. Make the sign of the cross with the holy water, then seal the area with salt and repeat the prayers. First of all, Anthony must go through the entire house, blessing each room with holy water. It will help to remove all the negative energy and stop it from leaving the attic whilst you go up and seal the portal. The page in the book I've marked are the prayers you need to say."

She looked at Anthony. "Will you even need to be there?"

He smiled at her. "I'll be there to bring in the light and watch your back; I'll be your support."

Missy narrowed her eyes at him. "Shouldn't it be the other way around, shouldn't we be watching your back?"

"In some cases, yes, the church leads the way. In this case, I believe that Emilia's strength of character and the fact that she knows it so well will be to the advantage."

"So, yet again, the church is copping out and letting a couple of seniors do its job?"

"To the contrary Missy, for once the church is being devious and playing evil at its own game. You must trust me on this one. Anthony will go in and do the prayers to cleanse the house. You will go to the attic and deal with the portal."

"Let's go, *now*—I want it finished."

Mikey looked at them both. "What am I to do?"

Charlie spoke. "You're the hired muscle: you make sure Emilia can get to the attic at all costs. Now gather round, I need to bless you all. Come, come, join hands and close your eyes. I want you to believe in the power of good and God more than you've ever believed in anything else."

FORTY-EIGHT

Maria's wrists were on fire. She could feel the wetness of the blood as it seeped down her arms from the rope burns. Gritting her teeth, she managed to tug one arm free. It was better than nothing. At least she could punch or poke his eyeballs out with one hand.

Silent tears were running down her cheeks. She'd never felt such intense heat and pain as she writhed the other wrist against the rope. She also knew there was something in the room with her, something she couldn't see, but she could sense. When she got out of here—*if* she got out—she had no idea how she would explain it to the guys, to Frankie.

Frankie. The pain in her heart at the thought of never seeing him again was like someone had taken a knife and physically plunged it into her heart. She loved him—despite the fact that most of the time he drove her nuts—and had never told him she did. They were connected on a deeper level. They'd been through a lot.

How ironic that after all the attempted drunken fumbles, now he was finally a free man, she'd met Harrison. Not to mention it was quite likely she was going to die before she got the chance to make a life with either of them.

Maria stifled the sob which wanted to explode from her chest. This was so wrong. She'd spent the last ten years of her life hunting down homicidal maniacs to get them off the streets of New York to make it a safer place. Yet here she was in the world's smelliest apartment, waiting for a killer to come and chop her head off.

Well, not today, Satan. This is not going down on my watch.

Her wrist slid free from the rope, and she smiled to herself. She didn't touch her wrists, as tempting as it was to rub them because she knew they were a bloodied mess. She wiped them across the bedcover to remove some of the blood: she needed her fingers to be dry. Sitting up, she began to unfasten the ropes around her ankles, praying he wouldn't come back before she'd set herself free and found a weapon.

Her eyes had adjusted to the darkness inside the room; she could make out a chest of drawers and a wardrobe on one side. The other wall had nothing against it. It was a huge expanse of white with a freshly painted pentagram filling the middle. Her heart, which was already racing, began to hammer against her rib cage. She didn't want to believe in this crap. It was far easier to accept it had nothing to do with angels and demons. Humans were more than capable of committing acts of heinous behavior of their own free will. They sure as hell didn't need the excuse of being possessed by demons to do so.

A scraping, creaking noise began to fill the room. Maria's fingers began working even faster to loosen the knots in the rope as she tugged one foot free. She looked up toward the penta-gram and felt her entire body prickle with fear. On the inside of the plaster, a huge, shadowy shape pressed forward against the inside of the dry wall. She watched in fear as the plaster bulged and start cracking. For the first time in her life, Maria felt the realization come crashing down on her that she was wrong. There were things in existence that couldn't be explained.

Freeing herself fully from the ropes, she ran toward the door, desperate to get away from whatever it was trying to break through the wall. She threw the door open and ran straight into the man who had brought her here. Realizing she had caught him off guard and had the advantage, she shot out her arm and repaid the favor by punching him hard in the nose. She smiled at the satisfying crunch as her knuckles ground into face, blood spurting from it, and he stumbled backwards. Not waiting a second longer, drawing on her inner force, she ran at him and punched him again, this time her knuckles connected with his Adam's apple, and he fell to his knees, his eyes streaming with tears as he gasped for breath.

"How do you like that you asshole? That one was for Anya."

There was a loud bang as the door to the apartment was hurled open. Frankie rushed in, shouting, "Maria!"

"He's our guy Frankie! Ryan Fletcher."

Frankie rushed at their perp and pulled him into a tight choke-hold, ready to cuff him.

An almighty crash vibrated the whole floor and as the lights went black, the temperature in the room dropped to sub-zero. Maria, who had forgotten all about the thing in the bedroom, felt every nerve in her body begin to freeze.

"Run! We have to get out of here, now! It's too big."

Frankie dragged the killer to the top of the stairs as he read him his rights and Maria turned to slam the door shut behind them. If it stalled it for just a few moments, it was better than nothing. They needed to escape whilst they could, with their souls intact.

FORTY-NINE

Frankie pushed through the front door, dragging his prisoner behind him. He was closely followed by Maria. Almost barrelling into them, standing on the top step was Miss Green, Ms Carter, the man who'd warned her to keep out, and a priest. Maria shook her head.

"Miss Green, what are you doing here!"

Missy stepped forward. "Maria, what happened to you? You're bruised and bleeding."

The elderly woman reached out her hand, tenderly stroking Marias cheek.

"I'm fine, I'll mend. What are you all doing here?"

Mikey stepped forward. "Sorry to break up this reunion, but we have work to do. As much as I'd like to make small talk with the cops all day, we have a pressing matter to deal with."

"Maria!" Harrison ran down the steps and Maria, blind-sided for the hundredth time that day, exclaimed, "And you too!"

"I'll explain later,' he replied.

"Maria—we're here to do something we should have done a long time ago. We're going in."

"You can't go in there, there's something inside, something terrible."

"I know, it's been there since 1952. Hiding, watching, waiting. Well, not any longer, we're here to send it back to hell."

The priest walked toward the door and began to pray, while Missy and Emilia clasped hands and followed him in. Mikey crossed himself and turned to Maria. "I have no idea how I got roped into this goddamn mess. If I don't make it out, you can put that on my gravestone."

Then they were gone. Maria turned to Frankie who had the suspect in cuffs and was on the phone for backup. "We can't leave them!

Frankie shrugged. "Damned if I know."

"But they're old... Miss Green is a sweet, old lady. How can she fight that?"

She began to run in after them. Frankie yelled. "Don't you dare! Get your ass out here now."

She waved a hand toward him as she disappeared inside, leaving Frankie waiting for a squad car with Harrison Williams by his side and their killer cuffed to his right arm.

Emilia led the way. The house was dark. Much darker than she'd ever known it to be, and the smell was back. It was so pungent it made her eyes water. She turned to Anthony who nodded at her. He began to pray. At each apartment door, he used the holy water to make the sign of the cross. Then, he spoke to Mikey.

"You be the look out. We'll keep on moving up until we come face to face with it or until it decides to come down to see what we're doing."

Emilia gripped Missy's hand even tighter. She whispered, "We'll take the staff stairs, maybe take it by surprise."

Missy nodded, the fear in her eyes reflected back in those of her friends. This was it. There was no going back, and she knew that.

Missy began to recite a prayer in her mind; it was one she'd made up, but it had served her well all these years. They broke away from Mikey and Anthony, hurrying toward the far end of the building and the hidden staircase.

Maria came flying through the front door and ran toward the first floor where she could hear male voices.

Maria felt her heart skip a beat. "Where are the others?"

The priest ignored her, his brow furrowed. There were beads of perspiration on his forehead. Mikey lifted a finger to his lips.

"He's blessing this part of the house so it can't come down—we need to keep it trapped upstairs."

All the bulbs exploded at the same time sending glass flying. Maria and Mikey both ducked, but the priest wasn't so lucky, and a shard of glass embedded itself in his cheek.

He winced at the sharp pain, but he didn't stop what he was doing. "You can try your worst, you won't stop me, demon. By the power invested in me by the Almighty, you will leave this house."

The roar that filled the hallway was so loud that the walls vibrated. Maria felt the air around them turn into a freezing cloud as if they'd stepped into an artic blast. For a second she was frozen to the floor. Then she heard an almighty smash from above and her instincts kicked in. Miss Green and Emilia were up there, alone with it. The monster. The mean son of a bitch. She wasn't going to stand for it.

She ran toward the stairs, only making it halfway up them before an invisible force slammed two huge hands into her chest, sending her flying backwards through the air. Her arms and legs began to windmill as she tried to slow herself down.

She felt herself falling toward the floor and landed with a loud crash at the priest's feet. Stunned, she lay there for a moment trying to catch her breath.

The priest bent down to her, made the sign of the cross on her forehead with the holy water and blessed her. Mikey held his hand out to her and pulled her up. She might have been bruised and winded, but she wasn't going to let it stop her.

Mikey whispered in her ear. "There's a servants' staircase at the far end of this hall. I'll distract it."

Maria moved as fast as she could. She nodded and watched as he climbed onto the first step. "Come on, you asshole, you're big and tough when it comes to hurting women. What about men?"

Maria wondered if the man had a death wish, but she didn't stop to find out. She began to limp towards the second staircase, wondering if she'd make it to the top She could hear the priest shouting and Mikey let out a yell, then the sound of pounding footsteps filled the house. As she reached the attic staircase, in the darkness she could no longer see her hand in front of her face. Gagging, she tried not to inhale. Running up the narrow steps, she pushed her way back into the room she had tried to break free from not long ago.

Missy and Emilia stood staring at Maria, their eyes wide open in fear.

"You're both okay! I have no idea where it is or what it's doing, but it's pissed off. Whatever you need to do, please do it."

"We can't until the house has been blessed and it has nowhere to run," Missy replied. We need it to come back to the safety of this room and then we can seal it in the pentagram and send it back."

A low, growl came from behind Maria, and she turned to face the huge, black shadow that had come in behind her. The two horns on its head so large they seemed to be alive. It was then that she realized the horns were moving of their own accord.

Every single belief Maria had held her entire life was wiped clean from her mind. She heard a small gasp come from behind her and turned to see Missy clutching her heart. Her eyes wide, she was trying to suck in huge gulps of air but couldn't. Maria knew what was happening: it had happened to her at the library. That thing was squeezing the life out of her friend and she was going to die because she was too old and frail to fight it.

Maria screamed in anger at the top of her voice and all hell broke loose. She heard the thundering of footsteps coming up toward them, and Mikey ran into the room, followed by Anthony. Both men stared at the black figure in the corner, then at Missy who was struggling to breathe. Anthony threw holy water over Missy and made the sign of the cross on her forehead. Then he did the same at the door, sealing them into the room with it. Maria nodded at Mikey and they both ran at it. She had no idea how to fight something made from smoke and shadows, but she sure as hell was going to try. She ran toward it, grabbing at it. The smell of rotting flesh repulsed her—she wanted to run the opposite way, but her stubborn heart wouldn't let her. Mikey hit it from the other side and they both began to push it toward the bedroom and the pentagram on the wall, with Emilia and Anthony walking behind them, blocking its exit. The howling wind and roaring noise the monster was making drowned out all other sound. But whatever they were doing was enough for it to release its grip on Missy and she fell to the ground with a thud.

With one final roar they pushed as hard as they could, forcing it back into the wall, its black body becoming one with the bricks and plaster.

Emilia threw the rest of the holy water at it. "Get out of my house. I forbid you from ever coming back. You are not welcome here. Take your twisted values and go back to where you came from. In the name of God, get out of here now!"

She ran at the wall and made the sign of the cross. The pentagram on the wall burst into orange flames, the heat so powerful that Maria dragged Emilia away before she got burned. Anthony ran to the sink and filled up a jug, saying a prayer over the water before launching it at the wall. As the flames were extinguished, smoke and steam began to rise from the bricks, making all of them cough and splutter.

Maria ran to Missy, whose face was pale, her eyes closed. She pressed two fingers against her friends pulse which was faint, but at least it was there.

"You did it, you all did it. You sent it back. Missy, hang on, please hang on! EMS will be here soon." No sooner had she spoken than a flux of footsteps began to hammer up the steps toward them. Maria yelled. "Get me a medic now!"

Frankie ran into the room followed by several armed police. He looked at the smouldering wall, then at Maria.

"I'll tell you about it after..." she replied.

The cops looked around, confused by the unlikely trio who were standing with their hands raised above their heads. Maria shouted. "They're good, they're witnesses, not suspects." Maria only stood up and left Missy's side as two medics arrived. "Take care of her, she's very special," she said, and she left her old friend in their capable hands.

A loud bellow behind them made both Frankie and Maria grimace.

"What in the name of holy fuck has happened here?" Sergeant Addison stepped into the now cramped apartment and his eyes fell onto Anthony.

"I'm sorry, Father. I didn't know you were here."

Anthony smiled. "I think your initial observation was right, Sergeant. I am tempted to ask myself what in the name of holy fuck has happened here."

"Sir, it's a long story," Maria exhaled.

"What happened to you Miller? You look like shit."

"I'd rather speak to you back at the station."

"Yep, you don't want her to talk about this in the public domain."

Addison looked at her wrists. "ER first—you can tell me after you've been checked over."

Maria remembered her bloodied, burnt wrists and immediately the pain hit her. She had to go and let them clean her up—she didn't want them getting infected. Plus, it would buy her a little more time before she had to begin to try and explain all of this to Addison.

Frankie gently took hold of Emilia's arm to lead her out. The older lady looked shocked. Mikey followed, not looking much better.

Anthony held back and whispered in Maria's ear. "The attic still needs cleansing."

She looked at him. "Can it wait until investigators have finished?"

He turned and looked at the burned shape of the pentagram on the wall. "At least let me cleanse this room."

The medics had a line in Missy's arm and an oxygen mask on her face, and were just transferring her into a chair to get her downstairs. With Missy out of the room, this was their chance. She waved Addison over.

"Father Anthony needs to cleanse this room; it's vital that he does."

"Are you kidding me, Miller?"

"No, sir. I'm not. If we don't, then we'll be back at square one before we know it."

He looked at her serious face and then the priests. Waiting for the medics to leave, he turned to the officers still lingering.

"Right, you lot downstairs. This is a crime scene. I need CSI here now and I need to speak to detective Miller and the good Father here."

The cops did as they were told and followed the medics down the stairs leaving the three of them there.

Anthony smiled. "Thank you, Sergeant. If we don't cleanse the room, it might be able to come back through the portal and trust me, it's the last thing you want."

Addison's eyes bored into at Maria's. "He's right, sir. You don't want that demon coming back. It's mean as hell, trust me on this."

"Do what you need to do."

Anthony sprinkled the holy water and salt around the floor in front of the pentagram. He began to pray, making the sign of the cross inside the pentagram with the water. Maria held her breath, imagining it breaking out of the wall again and dragging the priest inside. When he finished praying and stepped away, she exhaled.

"It's done."

"Are you sure?" Even as she asked the question, she knew that it was true. The atmosphere in the room was no longer heavy; it felt much lighter, and the terrible smell had gone.

Addison shook his head. "Right, now you've messed up my crime scene, get out. Father, thank you. I'm not sure what it is that you've done, but I get the impression it was very important. Miller, get down to the medics. *Now*."

As Maria left the room, she felt compelled to turn back, to take one last look. The pentagram had faded significantly. Its marks may one day disappear, but she was going to have nightmares about this house for the rest of her life.

Maria stepped out of the building into the beautiful, bright sunshine. It's warmth on her face made her realise that thankfully there was more good in the world than evil. Harrison ran toward her, pulling her close. Normally she wasn't one for public shows of affection, but now she let him. She needed to be held. She looked over his shoulder at Frankie who smiled at her, and she felt her whole body relax into the safety of Harrison's embrace.

Her eyes met Emilia, Anthony and Mikey. They had shown such bravery that few people even in the force could ever dream to have. She pulled away from Harrison to go and talk to them.

"Now what?"

"Now Emilia can live her life," Anthony said softly. "Mikey can live here without fear—and hopefully Missy will make a full recovery. We'll all live to tell the tale."

"What about you?"

"I can go back and tell Father Morgan that his theory worked. That with a bit of teamwork, we did an excellent job."

Maria laughed. "You can say that again. I don't know how to thank you, I owe you big time."

Frankie caught her arm. "I hate to break up this party, but Addison said we have to get you to the emergency room and get you checked out."

"I'm coming."

Harrison waved them over. He was standing in front of a stretch limousine.

Maria shook her head. "I'm not going to the ER in that, but you can be a hero and take my friends home please. I'll catch a lift with Frankie, I'll call you when I'm done."

He bent and kissed her cheek. "Whatever you say, Maria."

She laughed and Frankie led the way toward a squad car, opening the door for her. Maria gave him the finger.

"What, what's that for? You don't mind Mr Look-at-me-I'm-a-millionaire opening a car door for you. Did you give him the finger?"

"That's different."

"How is it different? Your loyalty should be to me—I'm your partner. If anyone gets to open a car door for you it should be me."

Her heart sank. Frankie did give a shit about her and Harrison's relationship. She paused, finding the words to speak to him, and he began to laugh.

"I'm kidding! Open your own door. You get a couple of friction burns and think you deserve to be treated like royalty? Not on my shift, Miller."

She grinned. "Frankie, you're an asshole."

"I know, but you love me despite my failings?"

"I do, I love you very much."

FIFTY

TWO WEEKS LATER

Maria took one last look around Miss Green's apartment. It would have to do. The air felt much lighter in here than the last time she'd been in. The light from the lamps lit every corner, banishing the shadows that had begun to creep in which made her much happier. She hadn't been inside her own apartment either. Frankie had insisted she either stayed with him or Harrison whilst it was redecorated.

For once, she hadn't felt guilty choosing The Plaza over Frankie's. She didn't want Christy thinking her and Frankie had been carrying on behind her back. Frankie had filed for divorce and it could mean the difference between him getting his fair share or losing everything.

Maria picked up the envelope addressed to her and let herself out. Walking across the hall and standing outside her own front door, she took a deep breath. Frankie had wanted to accompany her, so had Harrison. She'd declined both of their invitations. She needed to do this on her own. Opening the door, the smell of fresh paint filled her nostrils. She'd take that any day over the horror that she'd never forget.

She expected to feel a rush of emotions as she stepped

inside. Instead, she felt nothing. It was just her apartment. Scrubbed free of all the blood; the glass long gone. She stared at the hall closet, her palms a little sticky. Her childhood fear of monsters in the closet had turned into a reality for her. But she'd faced the monster head on and lived to tell the tale.

She opened the closet door, despite the racing of her heart, and pulled the string to bring the light to life. It was empty and the crawl space she hadn't even known existed until Frankie told her about it was now filled with bricks and mortar. Nothing could hide in there, ever. Satisfied she felt her heart rate return to normal, turned off the light and shut the door.

Walking through the rest of her apartment, she felt better. It wasn't much but it was hers. She liked living here and despite Harrison's best offers of penthouses in apartment buildings she could only dream about, she'd declined. She couldn't even detect the motion sensor cameras they were so discreet, or the intruder alarms. Tight security was the only compromise she'd agreed to. She'd lived here ten years and never had a bit of trouble. She expected to carry on living here without any. Maybe if she and Harrison stayed together and they had more than a no-strings-attached relationship, she would on day take him up on his offer of a luxury upgrade. But for now, she was happy. She could come home and that was what she wanted most.

She opened Miss Green's letter and read it through eyes which were so blurred with tears it was hard to read the delicate, handwriting. Miss Green informed Maria that upon her death, Maria was to help herself to the entire contents of her wardrobe of designer clothes, bags and jewellery. Everything she owned was to be given to Maria. The tears continued to fall with love for the warmth and generosity of her friend. After a few minutes she dried her eyes, tucked the letter in her kitchen drawer and went back downstairs to where Frankie was waiting outside in his car for her.

. . .

He parked at the back of the station and looked at Maria. "I'll carry the boxes, but you can deal with her. I can't face that this early in the day."

"You're such a wimp at times Frankie."

He shrugged. "Call me what you want, I'm still not doing it." She ran down the steps and hammered on the basement door. Frankie kept his distance behind her. The door flew open and Layla stood glaring at the pair of them before leaning forward and grabbing Maria in a bear hug.

"Girl, am I glad to see you."

Maria hugged her back. "I'm good."

Frankie cupped a hand over his mouth and coughed. Layla gave him her death stare.

"You Conroy, I'm not so glad to see. Get those boxes signed in. You've had them so long I thought you were keeping them."

Layla followed them in and watched as Frankie sheepishly returned them to the shelving unit.

As Frankie and Maria walked into their department, everyone stopped what they were doing and began to give them a round of applause. Maria's cheeks burned. She'd never been so glad to get the applause it was reserved for near misses and heroes. Even Frankie began to clap his hands, and she burst out laughing. "Enough, thank you! It's great to be back."

Addison's voice boomed across the department and just like that, the clapping stopped and they all went back to work. "Miller, Conroy, my office now."

Just like every other time, Frankie let Maria go in first, and Addison pointed to the chairs.

"Now what are we going to do about this sorry mess, how do I file a report on it?"

They both shrugged.

"Jeez, you two are most helpful. What would I do without you both?" He walked to his door, which he shut, not slammed.

Maria took this to be a good thing. Then, he sat down opposite her.

"I'm glad to have you back Miller, this department would go to shit without you solving most of the homicides."

Frankie coughed. "What about me?"

"Conroy, you know she does most of the work, but I'll admit it. You two make a great team. That's why I have something of a proposition for you."

"Sir, what have you got for us?"

"Well, this is top secret—only a handful of people know about it.

"Know about what?"

"The strange case review team."

Frankie looked at him. "What the hell is the strange case review team? Have you just made it up?"

"Keep your voice down Conroy; it's strictly a need-to-know matter. The commander has decided that you two need to know. He wants you two to run it. You'll get your own office. You can come and go as you please, no one breathing down your neck. What do you say?"

"Okay... But what sort of cases?" How could Maria know if she even wanted to, without knowing what the work really involved?

Addison squirmed. "Well, it's stuff that we don't know how to deal with."

"Like the thing at the house?"

He nodded.

"There are more cases linked to it?"

"No, not to that—at least I don't think they are. But yes, there are other cases not dissimilar in nature. Let's just say they're out there; a bit on the woo-woo side. It's not something the NYPD likes to talk about or admit. Apparently, your handling of the case and the fact that you managed to not die has made them want you to take over and review them."

Frankie stared at Addison as if he'd gone mad, then turned to Maria. "A bit woo-woo. What the hell, did he just say that for real?"

Maria looked over her shoulder out of Addison's window, no more working in this shit hole, their own office, their own hours.

"So we're are own bosses, keep our own hours, keep our pay rate?"

"Yep, oh and a yearly bonus for having to keep it all quiet. You know it won't be something you can talk about down The Cat."

Frankie pushed himself forward. "How much of a bonus?"

"An extra ten thousand a year."

"I'm in, what about you Maria?"

"If you're in, I'm in."

"Let's do this then. I think we both know that someone has to fight the good fight after what we witnessed."

Addison stood up and passed them a file each. "Good, this is your next case. I'll show you where your new office is up on the fourth floor. I'll still be in charge; anything you need you come to me about."

As Addison began to walk toward the door, Frankie whispered. "Ten K."

Maria hoped the money was worth it. Could you put a price on your sanity?

Harrison smiled at Maria; this time she didn't berate him for picking her up in a limousine. She wanted this to be special. It parked outside the entrance to the hospital, and she got out. "I won't be long." She went inside, her mind a whirr. Today had been both surreal and amazing—and this was going to be by far the best part. She walked along the corridor until she reached the private room. Knocking gently, she pushed open the door and smiled.

"Maria, I've never been so happy to see you."

Maria walked over and kissed Miss Green on the cheek. "I'm even happier to see you." She turned to look at the woman sitting on the chair. "How are you, Emilia?"

Emilia laughed. "Much better now I don't have to come to this damn hospital every day."

Maria took hold of the wheelchair Miss Green was sitting in. "Come on then, your carriage awaits. I can't believe you two are going to be sharing Miss Green's apartment. It's amazing, I couldn't have better neighbors."

Emilia grinned. "Well, someone has to look after her, it might as well be me."

"Uhuh, that's true. It will be nice to have some company. And Maria, you really have to start calling me Missy. Miss Green makes me sound far too old."

Maria laughed. "You two better not argue all the time."

Emilia grabbed hold of Missy's hand. "Oh, we won't, at least not all the time. Especially not now we don't have to live under the threat of evil that cast a shadow over the last god knows how many years of our lives."

She smiled, and Maria saw the lightness in the old woman's face. Finally, she was free.

A LETTER FROM THE AUTHOR

First of all, I'd like to thank you, my fabulous readers from the bottom of my heart for buying this book and I hope you enjoyed it. If you want to join other readers in hearing all about my Storm new releases and bonus content, you can sign up for my mailing list!

www.stormpublishing.co/helen-phifer

If you did enjoy it I would really appreciate it if you could leave a review. They make such a difference and are a wonderful way to let other readers know about my books.

If you want to know more about my other books you can find them all on my website at www.helenphifer.com. You can also sign up for my newsletter there to keep up with my bookish news.

Since I was a little girl, I've dreamed about visiting New York City. In 2015 I was lucky enough to be invited to a Black & White Ball at the Waldorf Astoria by my first publisher, Harlequin. I like to think it was fate that it came at a time when I could make this dream come true. What can I say, three weeks later I was in New York and speechless. I've never felt more at home anywhere in the world than I did there, and I fell completely head over heels in love with it.

I knew I wanted to set a book on the streets of New York and as we toured the city and all its attractions, the idea for tough, homicide detective Maria Miller began to take shape. I was lucky enough to visit again in July 2017, this time as a research trip for the story that I knew I had to write. I dragged my poor husband Steve along on a two-hour walking ghost tour of Greenwich Village which I loved—he wasn't so enthusiastic, bless him.

The walk started in Washington Square Park, where I stood and listened to the most amazing pianist who did indeed push his piano home when he finished. I know this because I passed him an hour later, with his piano. He was so good I could have stayed there and listened to him all night. From there we toured the haunted locations of the village. The Fat Black Pussycat is a real bar, so are all the streets and most of the locations used in this book. There is a haunted house on West 10th Street which I'd read about, and this became the inspiration for my story. The house and the haunting are a lot different to how I've portrayed it, but I'm a writer and making stuff up is what I do best.

facebook.com/Helenphifer1

twitter.com/helenphifer1

instagram.com/helenphifer

tiktok.com/@helen.phifer

ACKNOWLEDGMENTS

A huge thank you to my amazing editor Kate Smith at Storm for loving this story and her input into making it so much better. I've loved working with you on this book Kate and I'm very excited about the next books in this series. Writing scary stories is my absolute favourite and I'd like to thank Storm for making this possible.

It goes without saying that a huge thank you goes to Oliver Rhodes for once again believing in my work and giving me another fabulous opportunity. Thank you Ollie, it means the world to me.

Thank you to Natasha Hodgson for the thorough copy edit and the rest of the team for the hard work too. It takes a lot of people to take a story in its draft stage and get it polished enough to turn it into a novel. I am so lucky to have had a fabulous team to work with.

I'd like to thank my fabulous beta readers and very good friends Jo Bartlett, Sharon Booth and Julie Heslington who are all brilliant authors. They have a whole array of bestselling, fabulous books on Amazon so go check them out. They have held my hand through this process and made me believe that I could do it.

I'd like to thank my good friend Deirdre Palmer for helping when I didn't have a clue what I was doing! Deirdre is another bestselling writer whose books are available to buy on Amazon.

I'd also like to say a huge thank you to the rest of the Write Romantics for their unwavering support. Jackie Ladbury, Lynne

Davidson, Helen Rolfe, Alex Weston and Rachael Thomas. All of them successful authors, we got together ten years ago, and it's been one hell of a rollercoaster ride. The pride I have at seeing all my super talented friends filling the Amazon charts is mind blowing.

A very special heartfelt thank you goes to Paul O'Neill for his amazing surveyors report and proofreading. Also, to his late, much missed, gorgeous wife and a very special friend Gail. You were my biggest cheerleader from day one and I can't express how much I miss seeing your lovely face.

Thank you to Joanne Grainger, Donna Trinder, Nikkie Capstick and Kirsty Ann Dawson. You have no idea how much I appreciate all your support.

As always, I'd like to thank Sam Thomas and Tina Sykes for being my go to coffee girls. Good friends are hard to come by and I'm very lucky to have you both.

As always, a very special thank you goes to my gorgeous family, who both drive me mad and fill me with more love than I know what to do with. I'm a truly lucky woman to have such an amazing, supportive tribe around me. One day we'll have a table big enough to sit around for Christmas dinner without having to bring out the emergency chairs.